Natasha Boyd is an author wi⸻ and public relations. She hol⸻ Psychology from Royal Hollow⸻ lives in the coastal Carolina ⸻ complete with Spanish moss, alligators and mosquitoes the size of tiny birds. She has a husband, two sons and a host of internationally scattered and scared relatives who worry the next book will be about them. She is a member of Georgia Romance Writers, Romance Writers of America and Island Writers Network, where she has been a featured speaker. *Forever, Jack* is the sequel to her award-winning and first full-length novel *Eversea*.

Praise for Natasha Boyd:

'Boyd creates magic once again'   *A Bookish Escape*

'If I could give this book 10+ stars I would!'
                                        Luscious Literature

'5 Eversea* glass Loving Stars!'   *Sizzling Pages Reviews*

'Natasha Boyd weaves a fascinating tale of love, loss, heart-ache and redemption'   *Tome Tender Book Blog*

'You will get lost in the characters and their stories. This book is escapism at its very best. A beautiful coming of age story with lots of lovely romance mixed in'
                    Laura, *Bookish Treasures Blog* and Founder,
                    New Adult Book Club on Goodreads

'You are a fool if you don't add this book to your "To Be Read" list. In fact, you should bump it right up to the top'
                                        Madison Says Reviews

'So if you'd like a book that's full of vibrant characters, swoon (fracking hot) males that leave you hot under the collar, and just generally a book that leaves you wanting so much more, then pick this book up!'   *Book Passion for Life Blog*

'A perfect blend of heartbreak, angst, romance, steam and pure love in its rawest and sometimes most painful form'
All Romance Reviews

'A completely captivating read'   *Romfan Reviews*

'Total escapism!'   *Aestas Book Blog*

By Natasha Boyd and published by Headline Eternal

Eversea
Forever, Jack

NATASHA BOYD

forever, jack

headline
ETERNAL

First published in paperback in Great Britain in 2014
by HEADLINE ETERNAL
An imprint of HEADLINE PUBLISHING GROUP

2

Cataloguing in Publication Data is available from the British Library

ISBN 978 1 4722 1966 4

Typeset in Sabon by Palimpsest Book Production Ltd, Falkirk, Stirlingshire

Printed and bound by CPI Group (UK) Ltd, Croydon CR0 4YY

Headline's policy is to use papers that are natural, renewable and recyclable
products and made from wood grown in sustainable forests. The logging and
manufacturing processes are expected to conform to the environmental
regulations of the country of origin.

HEADLINE PUBLISHING GROUP
An Hachette UK Company
338 Euston Road
London NW1 3BH

www.headlineeternal.com
www.headline.co.uk
www.hachette.co.uk

To *my husband*
For asking me to marry him on our first date

And to
Al Chaput and Dave McDonald
I may never have taken writing seriously without you.
I am forever grateful for your
time, patience, encouragement and expertise

Thank you

ACKNOWLEDGEMENTS

Paul Coehlo wrote that "Writing is one of the most solitary activities in the world." And he's right. In a way. When I live in Jack and Keri Ann's world, I'm there whether I'm actually putting the words on the page, or going through the mechanics of the rest of my life. My mind is plotting away, having conversations, and arguing with what my characters seem to want to do versus what I think they should do. They usually win. That sounds dumb, I know. If you'd told me I'd say that a year ago I would have laughed in your face. Seriously. How things change! One year ago from this writing I hadn't finished a book! What you are holding in your hands is my second book!

The reality is, far from a solitary enterprise, writing a book and bringing it to market takes a village. Heck, it takes a whole freaking town. My husband let me work over the weekends and my mother took over on school runs and dinner making (and laundry folding). And my kids were so patient with me. My critique partners, Al and Dave, kept me from clichés and getting too complacent. They also buoyed my spirits when I wasn't feeling it. My *Stormy Nights* girls kept me sane and laughing! And thank you to my sweet friends who don't take offense when I drop off the map for weeks at a time, sometimes months, because I am so consumed.

The terrific font of Jack on the cover of my original e-book edition was hand-drawn by my sister Cassy Poulos. Thank you, Cass. I love you! And the e-book cover was designed by Adrian Repasch. Bow to him! Bow to him! Thank you to Angela McLaurin of Fictional Formats who formatted both e-books of *Eversea* and *Forever, Jack*. She is seriously good at her job!

My editor Judy Roth (she needs her own paragraph) is so much more than an editor. She has become a friend, and makes me laugh with her little comments in the side bar when I'm about to tear my hair out, and she has unbelievable patience. And we've never met in person! I can't wait to meet her and take her out for a boozy lunch! My readers – aaaah, my readers. Do you have any idea how much I love you? How much it means to me to get a message at 2am Australian time (Rommy!) to tell me you couldn't wait until morning to contact me because you were still so giddy over Jack and Keri Ann! And that was just one! There were hundreds! From all over the world! You guys FLOORED me. I literally didn't sleep the whole month of June because my heart was pounding so hard and I wanted to respond to each and every one of you. Thank you for that. Those words seem so inadequate.

Thank you to my agent, Elaine Spencer, who continues to grow our working relationship! I'm excited!

The bloggers who read and reviewed and raved about *Eversea* – thank you! Thank you for spreading the word and being so encouraging.

Thank you to the group of readers and friends of "Let's get Jack-ed!", who took up the mantle of keeping *Eversea* and Jack fresh in everyone's minds. You will probably never understand how much that means to me. I hope I can continue earning your care and enthusiasm. Lisa W., Lisa H. R., Kimmie, Karen, Faith, Shannon, Nasha, Julianne, Bonnie, Denise, Amy, Jess, Nicole D., Nicole B., Drue, Elaine, Rea, Clemmie, Rommy, Heather, Mary-Nancy, Melissa, Caroline, April, Carole, Layla, Dawn, Stephanie, Dawn, Angela and Tugce Nida. And so many more who have supported me.

If you received a birthday card from Jack Eversea (Friend him!) on Facebook, you can thank Julianne Burke! She is phenomenal!

Thank you, Faith Martens (Apocalypso) for creating the turtle necklace I wear almost every day that is also featured on the front of this book! Her store is Hula Tallulah on Etsy if you'd like one.

Okay, the music is playing, I have to get off stage.

Keep in touch! I'd love to hear from you!

https://www.facebook.com/authornatashaboyd
http://www.pinterest.com/lovefrmlowcntry
Twitter @lovefrmlowcntry
Instagram @lovefrmlowcntry
Tumblr eversea.tumblr.com

Thank you.

forever, jack

PROLOGUE

JACK

$\mathcal{T}$he sound of the front door . . . slamming after Andy seems to jar everyone into action. Not me. My heart is pounding, my hand is throbbing, and my stomach is roiling, but I don't move.

"Jesus," says Devon. He strides to stand beside me, the only friend I seem to have right now. "We need to get Sheila on the phone, like, yesterday. We need damage control. I've never trusted that little fucker." He jerks his head after the agent I just fired.

I replay the scene in my head. Andy's smug face as he congratulated himself on keeping me in line by faking my girlfriend's pregnancy. Girlfriend? Audrey may be my contractual girlfriend, but our relationship just had its final death throe.

The mention of Sheila, my publicist, causes me to look up and stare Audrey straight in the eyes. She is standing there unmoving, I guess unsure of what to do since I snapped. Her brown eyes are large and watery. A look I've fallen for before.

"Or does Sheila already know, Audrey? Was she in on this pregnancy hoax? Was this part of your team 'management' of poor fucking clueless Jack Eversea?" My voice is harsh, like I just screamed it hoarse. Something I wish I could do.

She shakes her head vehemently, a tear streaking down her cheek.

I grit my teeth against the instinctual urge to comfort and protect her like I always have. Ever since our contrived romance began years ago, brokered out of a movie franchise to keep the fans engaged in the love story. She was a friend, and at times something more. A partner. Or so I thought.

Devon taps out something on his phone.

After everything, I'm still finding it hard to believe Audrey's lied to me like this. About something like this.

"No, Jack. It wasn't me, it was all Andy," she tries.

"Oh please, Audrey, show me the fucking courtesy of honesty at this point."

"I swear—"

I snort dismissively.

"Wait, Jack," she pleads. "I went along with it, I admit, but it *was* his idea. I confided in him after I was . . . late."

I swallow hard. *Oh my God.* She was late. Of course she was. I'm guilty as charged. It's why I believed her so readily. It's why I left Butler Cove. The knowledge of my part in this cools my anger, leaving crashing guilt in its wake. Followed by equal parts panic. "So . . ." I start, keeping my voice as steady as possible. "So, are you still . . . late?" I can't say pregnant any more. I just assumed after what Andy said that she wasn't, but . . .

Audrey hiccups out a sob, and I take an instinctual step toward her, catching myself just in time. I take a moment to really look at her then and see true grief. Though her face is flushed and swollen from tears, she is still beautiful standing there in her white dress and her long dark, chestnut hair coming in gentle waves over her shoulder. She's banking on this, I know. Banking on the fact that she is beautiful and we have . . . history. But I also see her sadness.

It occurs to me then, that Audrey, far from filling contractual obligations in our friends-with-benefits pairing, might have truly been in love with me.

Snippets of her words come back to me now with new meaning. About how suited we are, how it would be the last laugh if we eventually got married and had a family one day, how we'd be a team of respect and friendship.

The idea that she might actually still be pregnant despite the fact that Andy used the news to their advantage makes my throat seize. No, she's not. It wouldn't have gone down like it did if she was. I feel like I'm drowning in some bizarre dream where the life raft is right there, but just out of reach.

Blowing out a deep breath, I fist my good hand at my side and wince in pain as my injured hand tries to follow suit.

Audrey hangs her head. "I lost it. I lost the baby," she whispers, her voice breaking.

My insides lurch violently. Nausea caused by the sickeningly sweet rush of relief, sandwiched between the hard press of guilt, leaves me swallowing back bile. I suck my lips between my teeth and bite down hard, trying to get my shit together. "When? Are you . . . are you okay?" I get out, finally. I'm vaguely aware that we are the only ones left in the room, the others having thankfully filed out.

Her eyes flick down and she hesitates. "When we were in London."

For a moment, I don't believe her, but I do remember her crying in the bathroom at the Lanesborough Hotel. I was being a complete dick to her and everyone around me that day. I was beating myself up about not calling my mother, even though she lived less than two hours away and knew I was there. It was a media circus outside, and I was a caged tiger. Luckily, we only had to be there for two nights before heading to Paris.

"I'm sorry. I should've realized." I run my good hand through my hair and, dropping my chin to my chest for a moment, see I have a few drops of blood on my white button-down shirt.

Audrey hiccups again and takes two tentative steps toward me.

I don't stop her or move away, and she continues until I open my arms and fold them around her tall, slender body. And even still, after months, and in the midst of all this shit, I am wishing I had my arms wrapped around a smaller girl, a girl who flipped my insides over just looking at her, and who I may never get to hold like this again. I squeeze my eyes closed.

Audrey's shoulders shake from her crying, and she sniffs. "I love you, Jack."

Tensing, I ease away her head from my shoulder to look at her face. I am instantly on alert. She may be hurting right now, but Audrey should always be handled carefully. I've seen how she's dealt with perceived threats to her career before. And I am in the starring role of this perceived threat. I need to be able to do this on friendly terms, but the way she's looking up at me, has me thinking she's not on my page.

"Just give it time, Jack. We'll get back to where we were, where you were in love with me, before I hurt you."

My heart hammers. My God, she doesn't know me at all. "Audrey," I say as gently as possible, knowing there is no good way to say this. "I cared for you, do care for you, and I loved you, true. But I was never *in* love with you."

Her eyes widen.

I know I'm botching this but I can't seem to stop. It's like an exit sprint. "My *ego* was hurt more than anything."

Her slap to my left cheek is fast and painful.

I seem to excel in pulling this reaction from women. I don't move, but she's not done. Her face transforms into a scowl, and before I know it I have seized her flying fist in midair, gripping it inside my good hand, squeezing hard.

"Bastard," she snarls and tries with the other.

I sway back. "Calm the fuck down, Audrey."

"No, I won't *fucking* calm down," she screeches. Her eyes have transformed from her soft doe-eyed expression, designed to elicit sympathy, into hard slits of anger, and she wrenches from my grip. "You are *not* doing this to me!"

"Doing *what*, Audrey? Taking my life back? Ignoring some stupid contract? The movies are *over* now." I grit my teeth and finish this. "*We* are over. We have been for ages. I'm not sure what qualifies for a functional relationship, but I can promise you, we are *not* it."

"No. You are not doing this to me! Not with *her*."

"Don't you fucking dare bring her into this," my voice booms out like thunder, causing her to jump.

Her cheeks are red and splotchy, but crossing her arms over her chest, she recovers quickly. "I can do what the hell I like. But you can't. Do you think Andy will take you firing him lying down? Or think I'll let you walk away from me? We are a *team*, Jack. We are much more powerful together than we are apart. You *need* me. You may not think so, but you do. And do you know why? Because I'll make sure you don't even *have* a career if you walk away. Have you thought about what it'll do to your poor, sweet country girl to have paparazzi hounding her every move? I didn't want to draw attention to her before by tipping them off, but maybe if it's spun the right way . . ." Her voice trails off, as she taps a fingernail thoughtfully on her chin.

I'm listening, speechless, and watching her face morph into ugliness with each word she utters. My jaw clenches tightly to keep myself from exploding back at her. I shake my head.

She turns to an imaginary person next to her. "I was driven to another man's arms because Jack Eversea is so cold and heartless." She affects a whiny, hurt voice. "I felt emotionally bullied, *all the time*." She sniffs for effect and looks away for a moment. When she looks back, her eyes are watery again, and a single tear tips onto her cheek. "And the most horrible thing of all was he got me pregnant, and then, when I *lost* his baby he was so *mean*, and so *relieved*. He *laughed* and told me he had never been in love with me. *Laughed!*"

She heaves out another sob. "All the time I thought we were together, he was sleeping with slutty waitresses he picked up from *anywhere*. There was this one girl—" She stops and looks at me. "Well, you know where I can go from there."

She wipes carefully under her eyes, and then lets out a shrill laugh. "Your face is priceless, Jack."

I take a step back and bump into a chair, sinking down on it gratefully. I need a few moments to clear my head. My hand fucking hurts like hell, but right now this Audrey, like a grenade with the pin out, is scaring the shit out of me.

I'm not sure how she and Andy can ruin my career, what she's threatening is bad enough, but I feel pretty sure Audrey has thought long and hard about it and has a few aces up her sleeve.

I think back to my early days—the stupid partying and

drug taking. If there's even a chance Peak Entertainment thinks I'm still doing that, they'll drop me faster than I could piss in a bottle. Their liability won't cover it, and it was part of the no-uncertain-terms deal of doing the *Erath* movies, as well as the upcoming films they've contracted me for.

If Peak drops me, there's not a chance in hell any smaller boys would pick me up. Gossip is king in this town. But worse is they could sue me to pay back what I've made from them until now, and Audrey knows it.

At this moment, I realize Audrey will say anything and make up any story to make sure I play by her rules. I've known this fall out was always a risk, but I truly never thought Audrey would be the enemy here. I never thought she'd be the one to drive the nail in my coffin. I thought she might want out as much as I did, that we would find a way to do it together.

How could I have been naïve about so many things? And now she's threatening Keri Ann too, and if I know Audrey, it won't be idle and it won't just be damage. Keri Ann will be decimated.

I clutch my head and breathe, trying to calm down. One fist through a wall is enough for tonight. I don't know how to appeal to her not to do this to me. I don't want to make the choice she's forcing on me. But I will. I'll walk away from it all. I almost did it before, but then there was the baby. The baby that doesn't fucking exist.

It would be a while before people got over the scandal enough not to make me a bucket of chum in the Indian Ocean. If ever. And where would I go this time? And for how long until people didn't care? By then I would have lost my career *and* the girl. Of course, I've probably lost her already.

"Please, Audrey—"

"And just what are you begging for, Jack?" Her haughty tone betrays nothing of the hurt emotions she was portraying just minutes ago.

I tilt my head back up and look her straight in the eye. "I'm begging for the rest of my life."

KERI ANN

CHAPTER ONE

Five Months Later . . .

I rolled up the windows in the pickup as I glanced nervously at the heaving pregnant gray bellies of the clouds above me. It was just in time, too. The first fat raindrop splattered over the windshield, followed by a deluge, as the cloud waters broke.

I flicked on the wipers, peering ahead at the bright sunshine that shone up the road and shook my head. Nana always used to call this *A Monkey's Wedding*. I had no idea what that meant, still didn't, but there'd be a heck of a rainbow in a few minutes. I'd have to look out for it. The April showers were incessant this year.

A shrill ring emanated over the loud roar of the heavy drops hitting the truck, and I felt around blindly on the seat next to me trying not to take my eyes off the slick road.

"Hello."

"Hey, sweetheart. You almost here?" Colton's deep voice comforted me.

I tucked the cell under my chin so I could keep two hands

on the wheel as the road got trickier to manage. "Yeah. Almost. I hate driving in the rain. Did you miss it?"

"Just. I wish you'd let me drive you."

"I know, Colt. But surely you have other stuff to do besides take care of your best friend's baby sister 'cos he's too freaking busy to come home. This way you can get on with your day after you help me unload this stuff."

There was a beat of silence on the other end of the phone. "Colt?"

"Yeah." He cleared his throat. "I'm here. I'm parked at the service entrance. When you get to the front of the Westin, drive to the left around the building." The line went dead.

I let the phone slide down to my lap and pursed my lips as I squinted through the water-distorted view. It was dumb to make the baby sister reference again. But it was Joey who was supposed to help me drop these pieces off for the exhibit. He was the one who called Colt when he couldn't make it. Setting me up again.

"Shit," I muttered. I shouldn't have agreed to go out with Colt when my heart wasn't in it. He was such a nice guy. Well actually, several girls in Savannah would probably disagree with me, but he was nice to *me*. Too nice. I was leading him on, and I knew it. Even though I'd told him, repeatedly, I wasn't ready for a serious relationship.

But a month ago, I'd capitulated. Well, I had agreed to go out to dinner with him. Like a date. *One dinner*. That had turned into a couple of other dinner occasions, taking me for lunch after I went to drop something at the admissions office at SCAD, going to a few movies, kayaking trips on Saturday mornings, and heck . . . we were basically dating. Or at least *special-friending* as Mrs. Weaton, my elderly tenant, called it. I snorted and rolled my eyes. I felt bad. It was exactly why I hadn't asked him to help me out today.

The rain finally eased up as I turned off William Hilton Parkway toward Port Royal Plantation and made my way under the canopy of curvy live oaks that lined the main driveway.

"Is that it, then?" Colt asked as I brought the last piece, a base for the sculpture I had made, from the truck. His dark hair was cropped short, making him look a little like a marine.

I nodded. "I just have to do the install on a few pieces. This, for example," I said, heaving my load up slightly. "Thank you so much for helping, I know you probably have to get going."

He rocked back on his heels and stuffed his fingers into the front pockets of his distressed khaki jeans. "I'd like to stay and watch, if that's okay?" He looked at me questioningly.

"Uh, yeah, sure."

"Then afterward I can buy you an early dinner at View 32." He paused, trying to sound innocent. "Since we're here and all."

I shook my head as I laid down the piece I was holding, but I was smiling. He never gave up. "You don't have to buy me dinner, but food would be good."

He smirked with satisfaction and came close, sliding a hand around the back of my neck and depositing a kiss onto my forehead. And I swear, *I swear*, he inhaled just a little.

Pulling away, I elbowed him jovially in the ribs.

I worked fast, and then checked in with the events coordinator, Allison, before heading back to find Colt. I'd met

Allison at my opening at the Picture This Gallery back in December. She'd invited me to be a part of this exhibit. Soon I'd be back here on Hilton Head Island for a black-tie cocktail party, with me as one of the star guests. It seemed totally surreal. And all my sweet friends in Butler Cove were raiding wedding rental companies for formal attire. Who knew what I was going to wear? It sent me into a flat panic every time it crossed my mind, so I tried not to let it. Now the party was just around the corner, and I was still dress-less.

Colt wasn't where I left him, so I headed to the walkway deck then looked over the pool area and followed it toward the restaurant. I found him leaning on his elbows overlooking the beach and the ocean beyond.

"Hey," I said coming up beside him and resting my arms next to his.

"Hey you," he returned softly, bumping my shoulder.

We both fell silent watching the shadowed pool area as the sun lowered somewhere behind us. White ribbons tied to some wooden chairs near the beach flapped haphazardly in the sea air, the remnants of a wedding celebration.

I had yet to attend a wedding in my adult life, although I remembered going to one when I was nine with my parents in West Virginia. My mom's high school best friend was getting married. My parents fought for the entire car trip there about something my young mind didn't think to retain. They were stone cold silent for the entire ride home. I was looking forward to seeing some of my friends tie the knot in the years to come, happier occasions they'd be, I was sure.

Colt breathed in a loaded breath, bringing me back to the present. "This is a huge deal, Keri Ann. I don't want to sound patronizing, but I'm so proud of you and what you've accomplished." He angled his head to me.

I smiled self-consciously. "Thank you. It's pretty cool, huh? I can't quite get over it, really. I mean, I know this is just a hotel and not a New York Gallery, but this island gets over two million visitors a year, and I think they are promoting the heck out of this exhibition all summer long." I shrugged my shoulders and felt the beat of heat in my cheeks.

Colt grinned. "Come on, let's go get you fed."

I watched him turn away to walk toward the restaurant entrance. "Colt?"

He turned back, eyebrows raised above bright blue eyes. "Yeah?"

"Thank you." I clasped my fingers together nervously and looked away as I spoke. "It was good to have a friend here. *You* here," I quickly amended and glanced at him. "Helping. Today was kind of a big day for me."

Colt took an almost step toward me, then halted, like he'd purposely stopped himself. He shook his head and blew out a breath. "You're welcome."

The heavens opened again as soon as we were on the way home, this time with huge gusts of wind. I slowed the truck as the visibility went from bad to worse and checked the rearview mirror.

Colt's dark BMW followed, as well as a smattering of other cars. It seemed he'd decided to follow me. I really appreciated that, but wondered whether I'd have to invite him in, or if he was just seeing me home. Ugh. This whole *special friends* thing was driving me nuts. I didn't know what was expected of me, or scratch that . . . what *he* expected of me. Was I supposed to kiss him and let him think this was something more out of some warped sense of duty? I didn't think so. I wouldn't. But spending time with Colt had given me a whole new understanding of the general dating scene. It was an ocean of unspoken expectation and misunderstanding. And pressure. Some real and some imagined. There was also undoubtedly a lot of frog kissing on the way to the prince. Not that Colt was a frog . . .

No, this was Colton Graves, my brother's best friend and friend of mine. And I had definitely made myself clear, both by explicitly stating I wasn't ready for a serious relationship, and with my endless comments about friendship. Then again, I had agreed to go out with him. Several times.

I glanced nervously in the rearview mirror again just in time to see the blue tarp I'd strapped down to cover all my pieces earlier rip clear off one side and flap wildly over the edge of the truck bed.

Damn!

I slowed and put the blinker on to pull over. I hated to stop on the side of a highway, but I risked a certain accident if the tarp got caught in the wheels. Just as I rolled to a stop, I thought I felt it do just that. A ripping sound emanated from behind me and the truck shuddered.

Wrenching open the door, I climbed out into the warm and driving rain that had me soaked within nanoseconds. I bent to inspect the wheel then heard Colton's door slam and looked up as he approached, holding a dark windbreaker over his head that he extended over me, too.

"It's jammed. Dammit," I yelled over the gusts of wind and passing cars, kicking the tire with my wet sneaker.

"We'll probably have to take the wheel off like we're changing a flat."

I nodded at his yelled words, just what I was thinking. "I have a jack in the truck bed."

Turning to go get it as Colt did what he could to pull the tarp away from the wheel, I saw a silver Jeep Wrangler slowing down and pulling onto the hard shoulder ahead of us. Then it reversed closer. I was glad I wasn't out here alone. No one got out right away. I caught Colt's eye and we both shrugged.

I was soaked and getting more chilled from the wind by the second. Grabbing the iron and the jack, I went back around the truck in time to see the door on the Jeep open. A long denim-clad leg ending in black biker boots, the kind that were etched in my memory, like forever, swung out the door of the Jeep and hit the pavement at about the same time my stomach did. And perhaps given the loud clang, the tire iron, too.

This was not happening.

My eyes traveled upwards over an olive green button-down shirt that was not only rapidly turning dark khaki in the rain but was also plastering to the body beneath. Then I looked up over a familiar roughly stubbled jaw to the shadow of a ball cap, where eyes I couldn't see, but could certainly feel, should be.

"You've got to be fucking kidding me," I heard Colt say harshly next to me.

My eyes tracked back down to the boots, and I watched as they headed toward us. I willed my mind to work. Hadn't I thought of this scenario a thousand times? Okay, maybe not on the side of a highway, but hadn't I rehearsed what I would say, over and over, and pathetically, over again?

But, *nothing*.

Nothing came to mind as the boots approached. The boots I remembered sitting by my fireplace after a rainstorm like this one. And as the water poured, streaming rivulets over me, I couldn't look up. I just stood there.

CHAPTER TWO

*P*art of me wanted to look up and feast my eyes on the face I thought I would never see again in the real world. Of course, the other part of me kept saying, *don't do it.* So I just stood there, in the rain, on the side of the road.

I'd seen him in the last five months, of course, online and on the front of tabloids here and there. And yes, in a fit of self-destructive misery I had given in to the urge to read every damn thing about him, thinking if I knew all his sordid details, it would help me get over what he did, or help me understand. It didn't.

I absorbed story upon story and pictures of him gallivanting around the world, actually London mostly, always with some trashy blonde. I mean, seriously? He was into blondes? Who knew? Certainly not me, nor Audrey, apparently, the woman who was important enough to leave me for, who he was now no longer even seeing. Talk about a splinter under the finger-nail of my self-esteem.

Five months ago Audrey and Jack had had some public break-up which I'd heard about from his friend Devon, the actor-producer friend who was supposedly 'up' with all things

Jack. Devon told me the news with the thought that I actually meant something to Jack, and that he was coming back. To me. Only to have him . . . never . . . show . . . up.

I shuddered at the embarrassing memory and turned away from the person in front of me to face my truck. I needed a moment. Shit, I needed a lifetime of moments. But no, here I was, a drowned-rat version of the small-town girl he'd messed around with. I tilted my face to the rain. The silence was getting awkward.

"Colton."

Aaargh. His voice. Deep, familiar, and resonating, singing over my chilled skin.

"Jack." Colton's voice had an odd inflection.

"I thought I recognized the truck. Is everything ok?"

"You should have kept on driving," said Colt.

There was silence. I refused to tilt my face away from the pouring rain and look at him. Either of them. I could literally *feel* the weight of Jack's eyes on me. The wind breaker came around my shoulders, courtesy of Colt. Whether it was a gesture of protection or the fact I was wearing a white t-shirt in a rainstorm, I didn't know. My fingers accepted it gratefully.

The rain eased up.

"Maybe," Jack responded.

Suddenly there was the sound of a fast footfall, and I turned just in time to see Colt's fist fly out and land squarely on Jack's jaw. "You have some fucking nerve, jackass," Colt shouted. A car horn honked loudly as it passed, spraying water over us.

I gasped and instinctively leapt forward toward Jack, stopping myself just in time as he bent forward cradling his jaw, his face cinched up.

"Shit!" He stamped his foot down hard, as he breathed out sharply. "Shit," he yelled again, straightening up and taking a lunging step forward.

Both Colt and I reared back. As Jack glared at Colt, I saw his eyes for the first time—hard, angry, and breathtaking. Then he stopped, his expression easing slightly. "I guess you were due one of those," Jack said, referring to the last time they had met. He had sucker punched Colt, sending him to the floor of the club in Savannah after he saw us kiss.

After he'd left me for Audrey.

"Get back in your car, asshole."

"Colt!" I said, before I could catch myself.

Colt whipped his head toward me.

So did Jack.

Our eyes clashed together and I felt winded for a moment. His hair was longer, shaggier, coming out from his cap that he'd pulled low over his eyes, shadowing his chiseled face. He looked . . . older. And bleak. And just as devastating to my soul.

"You have *got* to be kidding me." Colt's voice exploded into the moment. I tore my eyes away from Jack's to see Colt looking incredulous. "He uses you, fucks you, and leaves, and I can't defend your honor? *You* won't even defend your honor? What? You want to do that all over again?"

I was silent and standing there soaking wet on the side of a South Carolina highway with a stalled truck and two men at odds. Over me. Words had yet to come to my aid. Finally, I snapped out of it. "Why don't you both step aside. I need to fix this."

I grabbed the jack and the iron, slapping Colt's hand away as he leant down to help.

They both stood, and presumably watched, while I jacked

my truck up, removed the lug nuts, pulled the wheel off, unwrapped the mangled tarp, and replaced everything. I bunched up the tarp and dumped it into the bed of the truck. Then I flung the jack and iron in on top and wiped the black grease down my jeans. *Dang it*, they were my nice jeans, too. The whole process took less than ten minutes.

I didn't even look at either of them as I marched around toward the driver's side. Halfway there, I suddenly remembered the windbreaker Colt covered me with, so I stopped and yanked it off, revealing my wet and clinging white t-shirt. I tossed the jacket toward Colt, not even looking or caring where either of their eyes were focused. I could guess.

Climbing in the pickup, I pulled my door closed and gunned the engine. Luckily, there was a break in traffic to make my exit more effective, and I took it, pulling out onto the highway with a screech of tires.

My heart pounded.

I risked one look in the mirror and saw Colton's scowl and Jack standing with his legs akimbo, his arms folded, and a massive grin on his face. And whoop-de-do, there was a huge freaking rainbow in the sky taking up the width of the view, too. *Ugh.*

"Jazz. It's me. *Again.* Call me back, dammit. This is *truly* an emergency." I hit the 'end' button and flung my cell on the bed behind me.

Jazz was frolicking on the beach down in Florida with "Brandon of the chocolate brown eyes" whom she'd finally decided to go out with since Joey couldn't get his head out of his ass. Now they were a lovey-dovey gooey mess of public affection, which they'd thankfully relocated for their spring break. I was happy for her, really. I just seriously needed her right now.

My phone beeped and I lunged for it, my chest deflating when I saw it was Joey. "Hi."

"Great to speak to you, too. Colt just called and told me Mr. Jack Ass-ersea is back."

I bit out a humorless laugh as my chest seized and flopped back on my covers, my feet dangling off the bed. "I'm not sure if he's 'back.' He just happens to be here in the Lowcountry. We were driving home from Hilton Head, he could have been heading to Savannah for all I know." Wow, I sounded so calm. Of course I'd obsessed about this detail of why he was here and where he was headed incessantly for the last three hours. Ever since I'd left him and Colt standing on the side of the road. But I wouldn't admit that to Joey.

Where the heck was Jazz when I needed her? I took a breath and held it.

"Well, he is. He told Colt he was back." Joey let out a sigh. "Indefinitely."

My belly flipped over, and I brought my free hand up and covered my eyes. This was a nightmare. I thought I'd be over him. But if this and the way I had gone into total shock on the side of the road earlier was any indication, I was not over him. Not entirely. *Damn it*. Not at all. How was it possible to completely delude oneself for months?

Indefinitely. What did that mean? And more importantly, he was here, in Butler Cove, right now. I blew out that breath I'd taken upon Joey's news before I passed out.

"Keri Ann?"

"Yep," I croaked, trying and failing, for a jovial inflection.

"You have a lot going on. You've accomplished so much.

You start SCAD this fall. Please don't let yourself get involved with him again. Please. For me."

"Sure thing, boss man Joey. I can promise you, I have no intention of doing that."

There was a long pause on the end of the line. "I guess that's about as good as I could hope for." He sighed. "Do you promise?"

"Joey. I can solemnly swear I have no intention of getting involved with, or even having a conversation with him. Does that ease your mind?"

"Nope."

"Yeah, me neither."

"Great," Joey responded with a tone that said anything but. "I'll be home in time for the event. Stay out of trouble until then?"

"I'll try. Love you, big brother."

"Love you too, kiddo."

I hung up and stared at my phone then glanced toward my window and the darkness beyond. Jack Eversea was out there. I assumed at Devon's beach house. So . . . less than a mile away. I fought the urge to go and bang down his door and scream obscenities in his face.

He was back.

And he had to know he hurt me.

Hurt? I snorted.

I thought of that smile I'd seen in the rearview mirror. What did that *mean*? He wouldn't have been smiling like that maliciously, right? I mean who *did* that? He was either back to rub salt in my wound, or he was back thinking I'd be a convenient *lay* over again. How nice he had a break in his filming schedule to come and wreak a little more havoc. I knew my strengths, and I'd have a better chance of coping if he was just here to be a prick than if he actually tried for a repeat performance of his last visit.

I remembered telling him, back before we'd even kissed, that I was out of my depth, that I was not cut out for him. Not cut out for him to go back to his Hollywood life when he was done with me. I wished I fought harder and protected myself better. I couldn't be sure why he was back, but if it was because of me, then I *would* fight harder. There was no way I would make the same mistake twice.

And what became of Audrey and Jack, or the baby she'd claimed she was carrying? I was guessing that was a fabrication, since there was no news of a pregnancy. And I would know. To my shame I'd trawled the Internet one particularly frigid and rainy day in winter for seven hours straight, not pausing to even pee or eat. Jazz finally staged an intervention by ripping the cord to the wireless router out of the wall, and I kid you not, *cutting* the plug off the end.

All I'd learned was that he was in England, filming some movie about a coal-miner turned artist, and out with a different girl what seemed like every night. In true British paparazzi style, it was a lurid splash-fest of debauchery, with them lapping up his antics. It was so unlike the Jack I thought I knew. It was like he was deliberately having his picture taken with as many slutty-looking girls as possible.

In one picture he was in some bar or something, maybe a nightclub, and he had one girl in a short pink dress and platform stripper heels draped at his back, and a girl in front who was holding his head and sticking her tongue in his ear. And he was smiling—that devastating smile of his, dimples and all, right at the camera. He had to know people would see it. That *I* would probably see it.

I'd stared at that picture for a good hour out of the seven, with a rock in my chest, and I couldn't decide which was worse—wondering if he was doing it to hurt me on purpose, or if it never *occurred* to him it would hurt me to see him like that. By the time Jazz made her dramatic statement of disabling my Internet access, I was barely able to take much more torture anyway.

Pulling myself back to the present, I brushed my teeth and changed into my sleep shorts and tank. I lay wide-awake watching the shadows of swaying branches on my ceiling and listening to the creaking of my two-hundred-year-old house and praying for sleep.

At some point I may have dozed off, but the chirp of my phone at three in the morning had me jerking upright and fully awake.

CHAPTER THREE

*W*hen my phone beeped, I'd been in a semi-conscious state, so I was unsure if it was in my dream. *But seriously, who could sleep at a time like this?* Realizing it was real, I lunged for it in the dark, aiming for the glow of the incoming text.

Jazz: Hey, K! Hope this doesn't wake u, but had to leave phone on charge, just got back in from amaze-balls beach party. I'll call u in the am. Hope all okay.

Jazz. Perfect. I quickly typed back.

Me: No, nothing is okay. Can you talk?

I got out of bed and went to sit on my little window seat I'd made from an old bench and lots of pillows and stared at the bright screen on my phone. An incoming call sounded less than ten seconds later.

"Thanks for calling," I greeted her.

Jazz's voice was breathy, quiet, and worried. "Word, what's the matter? Are you okay? Is Joey . . .?"

"Fine, he's fine. Sorry to freak you out. I'm fine, I just . . . Oh, God, Jazz. Jack is back in Butler Cove." There was no other way to say it.

"Oh my God. Seriously? Did you see him or you heard? Wait, start at the beginning."

"I saw him." Looking out the window, I could see the silvery dark silhouettes of the massive trees in my front yard as a sliver of a moon made it through the cloud cover. The rain looked like it was finally over. I sighed and told her the whole story.

When I was done, she chuckled. "Damn, girl. Most of us could only wish to have an exit like that. How freakin' awesome."

"It wasn't awesome, Jazz. It was a nightmare. And he just stood there. Smiling," I added disdainfully.

She laughed again, with glee and a few cocktails. "Oh, it's priceless! Just in case he forgot who Keri Ann Butler is, you managed to remind him like a two-by-four to the head. Especially with the wet t-shirt." She giggled, and there was a muffled thump. Then she whispered away from the phone, "Sorry, go back to sleep."

"Is that Brandon? Sorry to make you call me in the middle of the night."

"It's fine. You know that. I would have called you back earlier if I'd had my phone. Yeah, big choco-eyes over here has been hitting the sauce since the pool this afternoon. He is baked and done. I better catch forty winks myself otherwise I'll be unplayable tomorrow. You gonna be able to sleep?"

I sighed and looked out the window again. I could swear someone was leaning against the trunk of the live oak by the driveway. I needed sleep, and the darkness and shadows were beginning to seem weird.

"Yeah, I'll sleep now. I feel better just telling you about it. Like I've made it into a manageable event. Not sure what tomorrow will bring, if anything, but I guess I'll worry about that then."

"Look, you've done enough waiting and wondering," Jazz admonished. "The last thing you need is knowing he's around and waiting for him to show up at any moment. This needs to be on *your* terms, not his. You need to go see him, ask him what his deal is, and then get on with your life."

The thought that I should be the one to seek *him* out surprised me for a moment. But she was absolutely spot on.

I remembered back to the week after Devon showed up on my birthday telling me about Jack, intimating he thought Jack was coming and then the pity on everyone's faces as the days went by and there was still no sign of him. Not that I'd said anything to anyone, but they assumed. As did I, like the stupid, naïve girl I kept proving to be. I assumed he would at least come back and apologize for the way he left. I shuddered at the memory of that time. I needed to face him and get closure as soon as possible, not sit around with his presence like a ticking time bomb.

"Right?" Jazz asked.

"Yes," I said firmly. "Right. So call me back when you wake up, I want to know how it's going with 'choco-eyes.' You're good, right?"

"Yes, Miss Butler, I'm fine. And we'll be back in time for your art opening at the hotel. Or sooner. Have you found a dress yet?"

"Ugh. No." I grimaced. I decided to slide the sash window up and let the night air flow in through the screen. It slid up with a screech. "I'm supposed to go have lunch with Colt tomorrow. Guess I'll deal with finding a cocktail dress tomorrow, too."

Just then another movement caught my eye. There was

definitely someone standing under . . . my stomach dropped, right as my heart lurched up into my mouth. Jack stepped out into the moonlight.

"Uh, Jazz. I gotta go, talk to you tomorrow." I let my hand with the phone slip away from my ear, hopefully hitting 'end' with my thumb, and stared out the window down to the lone figure. He was standing with his hands in his pockets, his face tilted up at me.

I sat uncertainly for a few minutes, my pulse skittering, and tried to get a handle on this new development. The soft night breeze wafted in over my bare arms, bringing with it the scent of newly flowered jasmine.

He wasn't wearing his ball cap, and the breeze ruffled his darker, longer hair.

It seemed laughable now, that I would have waited until tomorrow morning. I cocked my head. "You realize this qualifies as seriously creepy."

I thought I saw his mouth lift slightly on one side.

"I couldn't sleep and thought walking would help. And well, I ended up here." Jack shrugged, his hands still wedged in his jeans. His soft, deep voice that I knew so well, that the world knew so well, was a smooth melody over the jagged rasping of the cicadas. "I didn't know you'd be awake."

You just showed back up in my life, how could I be sleeping? I bit down, holding my teeth together to keep from inviting him in. "Why couldn't you sleep?" I asked eventually.

"Why couldn't you?" he returned.

My skin got warm. "I *was* sleeping." *Barely.* I imagined I saw his eyes narrow. "But Jazz texted and woke me," I added. Not technically a lie.

Jack nodded, pursing his lips and rocked back on his heels. I could see more details now that my eyes were accustomed to the night and the clouds continued clearing the sky. He was wearing dark jeans and a snug dark t-shirt. His eyes hadn't left me. I reached up and smoothed my hair, tucking an errant strand back in the direction of my messy braid, wondering what on earth I looked like after tossing and turning for the last few hours.

"Stop."

I paused.

"You're beautiful."

Wasn't that just great? My blood pressure rose. I clamped my jaw tight again. My upbringing dictated I thank him, but a wave of anger, no . . . make that pure and utter pissed-off-ness, almost choked me. "You can't even see me," I snorted. "Nice try. What do you want anyway?"

"I don't need to see you to know you're beautiful."

Well, didn't that knock an oyster out of its shell? What was he playing at? "Seriously, what do you want, Jack? You need someone to buy your groceries or something?" My acidic tone left no doubt about how I felt.

His shoulders moved almost imperceptibly, and I had the thought he'd either let out a long sigh or he was at a loss as to what to say, and was about to give up and turn around. "Can I come in?" he asked so quietly, I almost didn't hear him. "I'd like to talk to you."

It was on the tip of my tongue to tell him to get lost. But these days I didn't run from uncomfortable situations quite so much. I was fairly certain I wouldn't be sleeping any more tonight, thinking about the coming conversation I needed to have with him. We may as well get it over with. I shrugged, as nonchalantly as possible, and sighed. "Sure." I stood and slid the window shut, hoping he couldn't see the tremor in my hands from where he was.

I pulled on a lightweight cardigan, and swapped my sleep shorts for some khaki cargo ones that were draped over the chair in my room. I pit-stopped in the bathroom and pulled my hair out of its braid, letting it drape over one shoulder. Then I glared at myself with disgust and hastily scraped it back into an ugly, messy bun. What was wrong with me? I stomped downstairs and went to the entry hall. Taking a deep calming breath and flicking the hall light on, I opened the front door.

Jack was leaning against a pillar at the top of the porch stairs watching me. His arms were folded across his chest, one booted denim-clad ankle crossed over the other, and he made no move to come in. Light spilled out from behind me, casting a warm glow. Dammit, why did he have to be so attractive? I caught his green eyes for a second, which felt like about all I could stand, and then I stepped back to the side looking anywhere but back at him. I waved my arm in a single sweeping gesture into the house and tried to sound bored. "Come on then."

Jack pushed off the pillar and started toward me. My pulse increased in tempo with every step he took, and I swallowed hard over my nerves. I could do this. I really could. I just had to hang on to my anger. It was suddenly very clear how damn weak I was. I gritted my teeth.

He paused as he got to the closest possible space in front of me. I made the mistake of glancing at him before resolutely looking at the wall across from me. He was breathtaking. Consequently, I didn't. Breathe. His hair really was darker and longer and curled around his ear. He seemed much less the boyish but intense Jack I knew from before. Now he seemed simply . . . intense.

A few elongated and excruciating seconds ticked by, and then he stepped past me and into the house.

CHAPTER FOUR

Jack Eversea was in my house again. He paused in the hallway and did a slow three-sixty turn, his eyes taking everything in and ending on the *K. A. Butler* original light fixture above him. His face broke into a small grin, and he nodded as I closed the front door.

By his reaction, I expected him to say something, but he continued appraising the freshly painted walls in pale gray, white moldings, and slip-covered furniture I'd sewn from canvas drop cloths. Coupled with the antique pieces that belonged to Nana, it looked amazing, and I'd worked hard to get it there. His eyes dropped to the beautiful warm dark wooden floor beneath our feet. The floor he had tried to pay for me to have refinished. That I still owed him for. Irritation surged through me.

I figured it was safe to look at him since he was staring at the floor. It didn't help. Jack Eversea still flipped my insides over and made me feel like a starstruck fan who desperately wanted to know him, but couldn't. In fact, it seemed he was more of a stranger to me right at that moment than he'd been before I'd actually met him.

It had been seven months since I'd seen him in person. *Seven months.* "Shouldn't you be having a baby any day now?" I asked before I could stop myself. Wow. I needed to engage my mind with my mouth, and quickly.

His head snapped up, green eyes locking with mine.

"I'm sorry, that was a totally insensitive thing to say." I looked away. *Gah*, I'd already put myself at a disadvantage in this conversation, and everyone knows your rational mind takes a vacation between two and four in the morning. This idea to talk now, rather than later, was looking dumber by the second. And I couldn't even hold eye contact with him. The weight of his gaze was just too much for me.

"It's fine. I deserved that."

"No. Nobody deserves a thoughtless comment like that. Especially when I have no idea what . . . happened. I'm sorry." I turned and headed for the entrance to the kitchen. We'd stood in this very hallway the night we almost kissed. The night that started it all, and I realized there was the potential for far more than friendship going on between Jack and me. That night, I'd shocked us both by asking him *not* to kiss me. For all the good it did me.

If we stayed in this foyer any longer we would both be reminded, and I didn't need that. He was here to do the overdue *it's not you, it's me and my pregnant girlfriend* talk that he'd been too cowardly to do properly last time. "Let's get this over with."

Jack followed me into the kitchen. "Let's get what over with?"

Seriously? Hmmm. Where to start? "I get that you're sorry about the way things ended between us, how you handled it or whatever, or that you even got together with me in the first place."

He folded his arms back across his chest again, tilting his head to the side.

I swallowed nervously and busied myself getting us some water. "And I get that you want to spend time here in Butler Cove, and you don't want it to be awkward, having some ex . . ." I paused. Lay? Notch? Groupie? I flipped my hand in the air. "*Conquest*, or whatever, around. But I can promise you I'll stay out of your way. As long as you stay out of mine. We can just agree to be . . . friends, or acquaintances that need never interact ever again."

"Are you done?" he asked.

"Actually? No. While you're listening, you should know *I'm* not pregnant, but thank you for checking on that, by the way." I looked over at him.

Jack went pale, his eyes widening.

It was satisfying.

"What?" There was a protracted silence, and he slumped back against the wall right inside the kitchen door. "But I, we—"

"Used protection? Yeah, I've heard that's always one hundred percent guaranteed." My sarcasm and bitterness was becoming an almost physical thing. I needed to rein that in. It wasn't a comfortable outfit.

Jack unfolded one crossed arm long enough to scrub his hand down his face and blew out a harsh breath. He looked weary. Granted it was the dead of night, but Jack wore a deeper weariness.

To my annoyance, it cracked a tiny piece of the frost I'd encased myself in. I set a glass of water on the counter in front of him and made my way to the kitchen table, creating some more distance. I didn't want to see the vulnerable Jack again. I couldn't, wouldn't put myself through this again. Thankfully he stayed where he was.

"You asked me what I was doing here. Just now, when I was outside."

"Actually, I asked you what you wanted." I started pulling at a loose thread on the cuff of my cardigan.

"Yeah, that—"

"Do you think this is a good idea? I mean, maybe we should talk tomorrow, if there's anything else to say."

"There's a lot to say."

I met his eyes, waiting for him to continue. As much as I didn't want to look at him, I wanted to see him while he said this. I needed to. I wanted to feel every second of it so I would have no more questions when we were done.

"I'm sorry," he said.

Nothing. I felt nothing.

"It doesn't cut it," he went on. "I realize that. But I'm sorry." Jack left the wall, braced his hands on the island, and hung his dark head for a second, before looking back up at me. "You have to understand something, I didn't stay away because I wanted to. I stayed away because I had to." Jack gritted his teeth and winced imperceptibly. "I know that doesn't mean much to you, and I know you are dating someone else now, but I just needed you to know that. That's all. That's all I came to say."

I gripped my glass of water tighter at his mention of me dating someone else. I'd been about to lift it and take a sip and his words stopped me cold. I guess he and Colt really did have a big old pow-wow on the side of the highway. Nice.

"I guess you spoke to Colt?" I was neither confirming, nor denying. But as I watched Jack carefully, and took in his tension and the way his hands gripped the counter, I realized I was admitting it. At least as far as he was concerned.

Jack nodded and cleared his throat. "He's a good guy. Cares for you. A lot. That's good."

"I know," I said simply and watched Jack's throat bob as he swallowed. This was fascinating.

"It's a pity for him," he said with an even voice, "that I won't be walking away anytime soon."

My skin went cool, as the blood drained from my head. I think my jaw may have dropped open. I consciously closed my mouth firmly, and pulled my lips in, lest I do something as dumb as gasp. I counted to five in my head and blew a slow breath out. "You already did walk away, Jack."

"Not from *you*. I never walked away from you. Not willingly."

Okay, so technically Jack Eversea hadn't walked away from me. If we were talking the pure ambulatory mechanism of a person moving from one place to another, and physically removing herself from a room full of tension, then yes, *I* walked out of Devon's beach house the day Audrey showed up with her pregnancy news. *I* walked out on him again the night we were all in Savannah, right after he punched Colt in the face. But what else was I supposed to do?

I didn't like the challenge he was throwing down like a threat. His words smacked of the assumption that if he stayed around it would automatically push Colt out of the running. "Nice to see you're as *confident* as ever. I'm not some kind of trophy," I said with disgust.

Jack's lip twitched. "God. The things that come out of your mouth . . ." He shook his head, then broke into a tense chuckle. "You're perfect."

Jack Eversea was divinely beautiful, but Jack Eversea

laughing and resting his vivid green eyes on me at the same time was a cosmic event. His smile was so sad and beautiful, it pulsed like a solar flare and shattered my crudely mended heart into a million tiny pieces.

"Jack." I recovered then hesitated, unsure of what I wanted to say. "This is pointless. Let's start over. Let's . . . be friends who haven't seen each other for a while, and just . . . catch up."

I gripped my water and took a sip. Deciding maybe we needed some coffee, I headed back to the kitchen cupboards and glanced over to where he stood, his dimple etched into his cheek and into my heart.

"Okay, I can do that." He nodded, slowly. "I'd like to do that."

I wanted to get it all out tonight and move on, but we could start slow and just talk. A small awkward silence followed. Jeez. Where did one begin? *So how are all the sluts in London?* I pulled down two cups and measured out the coffee, freezing in mid-action as I heard and felt Jack move around behind me. The smell of the fresh ground coffee that I normally loved so much was suddenly secondary to the warm spicy scent of the man behind me. He smelled different. Like sandalwood. Decadent.

And the heat . . . not for the first time since I met him did I wonder what it was about *us* that could make him standing this close to me, but not touching, feel so *physical*, so *warm*, so . . . *charged.*

His forearms, hard and sinewy with a light dusting of hair, appeared on each side of me. Strong hands with long-fingers braced the counter.

"Please. Don't," I managed. "We're just going to try and be friends, remember?"

"I do. It's just really hard to stand here with you and not touch you." Jack breathed in, and then let out a deep sigh that stirred the hair at my nape.

I faltered with the scoop, dusting coffee over the counter, and closed my eyes a moment.

Then he pushed away and went back around the counter.

Shit, this was awkward. I relaxed my shoulders and casted about for a topic of conversation. We needed to get onto neutral ground. "So, what was the movie you just made? I heard it was about an artist. Were you the artist?" I asked, trying to sound normal as I turned our coffee on to brew.

"Yeah, I was. I, uh, it was kind of a favor. The actor they'd cast pulled out for personal reasons, and they were stuck without a lead."

I glanced at him over my shoulder then focused on the coffee, willing it to percolate faster. "So you stepped in?"

"I was young for the part, but I kind of . . . owed them. The same group that did the *Erath* movies put money behind it. They had a limited budget, but it's a great story, and I got to work on the script some too, as well as the directing. I'd been looking for a way to do that, prove to them I could."

There was a silence where it seemed Jack wanted to say more. Perhaps about being in England, but that was surely a can of worms. I poured the coffee a few minutes later and handed a cup to Jack, black, the way he liked it, before heading back to the safety of the kitchen table.

"Thanks." Jack blew on his. "Colt told me you got into SCAD, and you're starting in the fall. Congratulations."

Still somewhat safe territory. I nodded. "Yeah, it's amazing. I'm excited and nervous. You and Colt had quite a long talk today, huh?" *Why did I do that?*

Jack chuckled. "Actually, his exact words were: *she's going to SCAD this fall and she doesn't need you distracting her or fucking up her life again.*" The smile fell off his face toward the end of his words. "Did I?"

"Did you what?"

"Fuck up your life?"

"Don't give yourself too much credit, Jack. I got off my butt and applied to school, got some scholarship money, and was featured at a well-known art gallery. In fact, I'm going to be in another exhibit all summer. So yeah, when you left I was sad that I'd fallen for your *Lost Boy* routine, but no . . . you didn't fuck up my life. If anything, you galvanized me into doing something. A lot has changed since you left. A lot is better."

Jack's face remained impassive. "*Lost Boy* routine," he murmured. "The boy who never grew up. Clever."

I shrugged.

Jack looked up at me and gnawed on his bottom lip. I didn't like having my attention drawn there so I glanced away to the window. The darkness outside bounced this awkward situation back at me like a mirror. I looked down at my sleeve instead.

In my periphery, Jack shifted nervously. "I saw your exhibit in December at the gallery on Hilton Head. Congratulations, it was beautiful."

What? "What do you mean?" I looked up. "You were here? I mean, in the area?" My stomach lurched, the water I'd sipped a few minutes ago burned like acid. He'd been here, back then, when Devon said he was coming, and he hadn't . . .? And I hated the way my voice had just gone all high and breathy. "I don't . . . I don't understand."

CHAPTER FIVE

Jack put his cup down and closed his eyes tight, running both hands through his hair, and then gripping the back of his head. His neck and shoulders looked strained with tension before he let go and exhaled a long breath. "Yeah. I came back. I flew into Hilton Head Island and rented a car. I was coming back here. I . . . can I sit down?" He pointed to the chair opposite me.

I nodded dumbly and watched his tall frame as he walked over and pulled out a chair, and then hid the lower half of himself beneath the chinked wooden table.

Every nerve and muscle in my body was frozen, waiting. I almost didn't want to hear this. Almost.

He rested his elbows on the table and leaned forward, his shoulders hunching up. The heel of his foot bounced a rhythm on the floor. A lick of dark hair fell down across his forehead, finally tired of staying where his fingers had raked it back. "I . . . Audrey lied to me about the baby. She and Andy concocted the plan to get me to leave here. I found out she'd lied about the pregnancy after our tour wrapped up and . . . I went ballistic. But then she said the pregnancy *was* real and that she'd *lost* the baby. God, I didn't know what to believe. I'm assuming she said she lost the baby to make me feel guilty for breaking up with her. But I'm not sure I'll ever know the truth, and with her, it may never matter. She'll get people to believe anything if it paints her in a better light. I didn't know whether to be relieved, to grieve, or to hit something." He laughed, humorlessly. "I went with all three."

There was so much to process. My stomach continued churning. I folded my arms tightly across my midsection. "How were you so sure the baby was yours? Hadn't she just cheated on you? And didn't you tell me you guys had been over for a while? I . . ." I swallowed thickly. So much for us keeping the conversation in the friend-zone. "That was the hardest part, Jack."

I hadn't meant to stop him telling his story, and I still wanted to get back to it, but I couldn't help myself now that we were on this topic. I looked down as I spoke. "I couldn't believe you just trusted the words that came out of her mouth that day and let me walk out the door. You basically told me without words right then that you lied to me, that it wasn't over with her. That I was the chump. I felt so stupid."

He didn't answer right away, so I finally looked up and met his eyes. A muscle ticked away in his cheek, and I knew he was struggling with how to respond. After a few moments, his shoulders slumped and he leaned down and rested his elbows on his knees, inspecting his feet. "Our relationship was over, we hadn't . . . in forever . . . but . . . yes, there was a chance it was mine."

I squeezed my eyes shut for a moment and steeled myself for the torrent of boy crap that was about to come. Jazz and I had always shaken our heads in bewilderment and snickered as we watched TV shows where the wife or girlfriend, or boyfriend for that matter, believed excuse after excuse from their no good partner. How could people not see it coming, I'd wondered? And now I knew, of course. You *want* to believe. That *want* being stronger than any fact that could be slapped in your face.

"Go on," I said. I could actually *be* in a TV show right now. Here I was looking at Jack Eversea, a face the world knew so well. That *I* knew so well. A collection of features that were so familiar, yet buzzed in and out of focus from my personal recognition and that of tabloid pictures and movie parts.

"I—" He swallowed, loudly. "I don't think you hate me right now, but you may hate me when I get done telling you." He looked up.

His eyes were deep, mossy green pools of emotion and it walloped me straight in the chest.

I held my breath.

"I feel like I just climbed out of a river of shit. I can't . . . I won't risk you hating me right now."

"Just freaking tell me, Jack." My voice was hard and bitter. "Tell me the truth, tell me all of it. Do me the courtesy of *not* deciding which parts you think I should hear."

"That's not—"

"Otherwise what's the point of this? Why are you here? If I end up hating you, it would be easier for us all. Please. *Please* make me hate you. Why don't you just finish the job so I can get on with my life!"

Oh my God.

My heart pounded and my breathing was choppy. Shame and humiliation poured through every fiber of my being as my words reverberated in the silence. Me admitting that I couldn't get on with my life, that I wasn't over him.

Way. To. Go.

Seven long months to get over him, and I threw away my pride in seven seconds. My skin flashed hot.

Jack stared.

I couldn't look away.

And then he moved, his body lunging out of the chair, the sound scraping across the floor in a loud screech as he came at me. His arm was around my body lifting me against his chest, crushing the air out of me.

I gasped to get my air back, and breathed *Jack* in, just as his mouth crashed onto mine.

His lips were hard and demanding, and then they parted, his tongue licking into my mouth.

I felt wounded, open, and . . . consumed. The feel of his mouth on mine was a shock of sensation. I'd been reliving his kiss every day since the moment I'd first felt it. I craved it. I craved him.

His taste was exotic, extravagant, like something I shouldn't have. The silky slide of his tongue. I parried against it, even though I could barely move with the way his hand held my head just so and the hard press of his chest that rumbled with a suppressed groan. I was madly clutching his soft hair, fisting long tufts of it, trying to hold him, to taste him. Inhaling him. *When did my hands get up there?*

The tornado of long denied emotions and latent sexual frustration spun and tumbled and then touched down throughout my body. I was dizzy, like we were simply sensation and emotion and had lost our bodies.

Jack's arm tightened, his chest heaving, his desperation intoxicating me. Then his hands were holding my face, his lips gentling and molding to mine. As his tongue slowed and stroked, the pace became agonizingly sweet and infinitely more dangerous.

I suddenly let out a half-sob that slapped me in the face. *No! Oh my God, no!* I couldn't do this.

With everything I had, I pulled away, pulled my lips from his, struggling not to sink back into him.

His arms gave a little as he felt my resistance.

I tilted my face up as I shook my head and saw his eyes flicker open to meet mine. His breath sawed in and out, fanning across my skin.

Confusion morphed into something indiscernible as his fathomless green eyes focused on me. And then he was cupping my face.

I tried to turn my face away.

Jack closed his eyes tight once more, his brow creasing up, his mouth grim, like he was in pain.

I dropped my arms.

"No," he said harshly, through gritted teeth. Pulling me in, his hands wrapping around my body, gathering me close, and holding me tight against him. "Don't let go."

But I didn't hold him back. My arms fell limply to my sides, and I willed the beat of desire to slowly ebb from my body. It wasn't difficult now that the shame was winning out. Inhaling deeply, taking a last hit of Jack's scent as my cheek pressed against his soft t-shirt, I steeled myself to push him away. I didn't want to be held like some baby who needed comfort. I couldn't stand his pity a moment longer.

And then everything shifted. His shoulders sagged, and his back curved out as his head slid down to my shoulder. He turned his face into my neck and . . . clung to me.

CHAPTER SIX

*J*ack clung to me like he'd never let me go. He inhaled the scent from my neck and held me tighter, his fingers curling in to my back like a drowning man.

Unsure of what to do, I hesitated, then gave in to my instinct and brought my arms up and tentatively slid them around him, trying to ignore the terrain of his well-muscled back.

He tensed for a moment then relaxed into our embrace, breathing in deeply.

We stayed like that for several long minutes. They were too long and not long enough.

"I don't know how to go back," he whispered, shifting slightly, his hand running up to my hair and his mouth moving to my ear.

My skin chilled at the feeling, a rush of a tingle across my nerve endings as his breath fanned out with his words.

"I don't know how to go back to where we were, to what we had," he breathed softly, "to what we were supposed to be." He paused again. "What we are *meant* to be."

"Jack—"

"Shhh. Please," he whispered, hoarsely. "Please, just listen."

I closed my eyes and focused on his voice as it danced over my skin and my fears as if they were nothing. Melodious, but rough. Whispered but heavy with emotion.

"I know I'm probably too late, and I know you are probably better off with him, and I know you probably don't want me to fight for you. I have no right to. But I want to. I *want* to. I *have* been fighting for you. It's taken me seven months to get back to you, to try and do it the only way I knew how, to protect you."

I stiffened, my stomach rolling. *What did that mean?* I shook my head. "No, Jack, don't—"

"Listen," he said harshly, keeping my head still so I couldn't look at him. "Listen. Not by looking at me, not by remembering who I am and why you don't believe me. Don't look at me and see the guy in the media. The guy you think I am after what I did. *Listen* to me."

I stilled and after a few moments nodded. I'd told myself I wanted to get through all of this tonight, so I would listen even if it killed me. I may not believe it, but I'd listen. He could tell me any excuse or reason under the sun, and it wouldn't change the fact that I had neither the temperament nor the inclination to be the casual girlfriend of a Hollywood superstar like Jack Eversea. I wasn't going to pick this up where we left off like nothing ever happened.

He breathed out in my ear.

I shivered. This was torture. Pure and simple.

"I can tell you everything that happened whenever you want or need to hear it, but none of it matters. I can't change it. I can't go back and do anything differently. But there are *some* things you don't know that you *need* to know." Jack's hand on my hair burrowed in, loosening the bun that was already coming unbound, and massaged my scalp. His other roamed up and down my spine.

I took a calming breath, trying to keep my head while I rode this out. *I could so do this.*

Jack moved his lips closer to my ear lobe, and my pulse hiked up another level. He swallowed, audibly. "Let's start with something I never told you before. I, Jack Eversea, am . . . utterly in . . . love . . . with you, Keri Ann Butler."

I froze, my breath ceasing to function normally. *No.* He was not doing this, throwing around the 'L' word like I was young enough and dumb enough for it to be a cure-all. A magic bullet to defuse a situation. I ground my teeth. Oh my God, if I survived this encounter, it would be a miracle.

Hysteria swirled in me, making me nauseous and light-headed. I could laugh in his face. That would throw him. I wrenched my head away from his, grabbing his upper arms and held him at bay, needing to see his face as disjointed feelings and reactions boiled inside me.

His piercing green eyes held nothing but sincerity in them.

"You knew me for ten damn days," I spewed. "And you haven't seen me for *months*. When did you decide *that*, Jack? Was it when you were thinking with your dick before you fucked me? Or did you just suddenly decide it, since you've seen me again? How romantic."

He flinched at my words. Shocked?

Damn, *I* was shocked. Shocked at my words and angry as hell. Angry that he thought he could use me again.

"It was never a *decision*, Keri Ann," Jack said harshly and shook his head.

Moments ticked by and his expression cycled through confusion and emotions I couldn't read. Didn't want to read.

His mouth became a grim line. "You don't . . . *decide* . . .

to stand in front of someone one day and have them splinter you apart by just looking at you."

My throat felt thick.

He swallowed. "And I didn't *fuck* you. Believe me, I've done enough *fucking* . . ."

I flinched.

". . . to know the difference."

I licked my lips, trying to find moisture.

His eyes dropped down.

My back was against the counter, I had nowhere to step back to. My mind failed to remember what I wanted to say to him. "You'll forgive me if I have trouble believing you. Did you manage to remember that you '*loved*' me," I made air quotes, "while you were cavorting around England with every girl who crossed your path? Did you think I wouldn't see that, or didn't you care if I did?"

"That's not what it—"

"I mean, who *are* you right now, Jack?" I didn't want to hear his excuses. "Are you the actor who's playing the part of the good guy? Are you trying to do the right thing *now*? Because I don't need it. I don't need you." I took a deep breath and tilted my chin up, staring him in the eyes, ignoring how upset he looked, with his jaw tight, his shoulders rigid, and his bottom lip white as he worked it repeatedly with his teeth. "I may want you," I said, emphasizing the word and pausing. It was a word he'd used with me, a word that had ultimately led me to kiss him. But a word that should simply mean an attraction and nothing else, that shouldn't have led to anything else. "I may *want* you and be attracted to you, but I don't *need* you—"

"Let's work with that. You 'want' me. That's a good start. We can't go back, so let's start again. Just give us a place to start. Give me a place to start."

I held onto his upper arms, feeling their heat, their strength, rock hard under my fingers, and I drew on that strength to do what needed to be done. "It's not a start, Jack. It's what got this all so messed up in the first place. I'm attracted to you, sure. So is probably everyone you've ever met. It's how you're made. But that's neither here nor there."

"That's not all you think of me. I know it isn't."

"It doesn't matter if I have real feelings or not—"

"It does. It means everything."

"No. It. Doesn't." I cast my eyes away from his and his arms tensed under my hands. I couldn't look at him while I said this. "Since it turns out I didn't really know you at all, I'm going to assume I was just like every other girl who's ever fallen into your bed. Maybe it was the *idea* of you. The part you played with me. The Jack I knew then wouldn't have deliberately hurt me . . . maybe I never felt real things for *you*. How could I when I'm not sure who you are?"

I looked back up at him and faltered a moment at his expression. Even the flush on his cheekbones had leached away. Complete and utter devastation. I'd thought for a second that he wouldn't believe me. *I* barely believed me. That was a seriously low blow and not like me.

Oh God.

"You do know me," Jack said, his voice rough. "You know me better than anyone on this planet. And I pegged you for more honesty than that. I *know* you felt something real, not based on the illusion of Jack Eversea. I can see it. I can feel it. It is real. The only real fucking thing *I've* felt in forever."

"Stop it, Jack." I winced, resisting his words as best I could. "It doesn't matter. How I feel about you isn't even up for discussion. It's irrelevant because I already know where this ends. I've been there."

I knew I couldn't have Jack in moderation. I wasn't capable of it. I'd opened my whole heart to him already, and it had ended in a nightmare. All I could do now was put the dead-bolt on, close the shades, and pray for daylight.

"I understand why you're saying this, but you're wrong," he implored. "Shit. I did this all wrong. I'm pushing you. I went too fast. I'm sorry. I just needed to see you again, tell you what happened, not freak you out."

"Jack. I'm not an idiot. Whether you push me or not still leads to the same place. Fast or slow, I'm not going there. And I thought it would matter to me to know what happened, but I don't think it will make any difference."

"I should have told you before how I felt."

"God, Jack. What you should have done *if* you really felt the way you say you do, was not leave the way you did and not contact me for over half a year. What? Did you expect me to wait around pining after you? Well, I did. Does that make you happy? Make you feel more appreciated? Do you not get enough love from your adoring fans? I *was* devastated. But I'm moving on now. Or trying to. And I will as soon as you leave."

I breathed through the crushing pressure that suddenly sprang up in my chest and gripped his arms tighter to stop the shaking in my hands. I needed to finish this, give him no way out. I couldn't go back now. I'd only be here again the next time. "If there's any truth to what you are saying about being in love with me—"

"No," Jack said desperately, his green eyes flaring. "Don't say it, Keri Ann. I know what you're going to ask of me. Please . . . don't do it."

"If you truly love me, then you'll respect my request . . . and *walk away* from this. Leave. Me. Alone."

JACK

CHAPTER SEVEN

When I was nine, Alex O'Rourke hit a six in cricket that nailed me right in the chest. It was a hell of a shot, and he made the Second Eleven's team for it, even though he was only on the Under-Nine's up until then. I was out for the count and flat on my back. There was no air, no oxygen, and no capacity to get some. I lay on the field presumably turning blue before the umpire made it over to me.

The evidence of the hit was a smear on my Aran v-neck from the red leather cricket ball right above my solar plexus.

The bright blue and cloudless British sky above me darkened around the edges and narrowed to a pinprick as my starved lungs communicated frantically, and in vain, with my brain. That tiny spot of light was the last thing I remembered until I woke up in hospital while they were x-raying my chest.

Standing in front of Keri Ann, as she closes the door on our relationship feels like that day. I know I need to keep breathing in and out. And I know I should say something, anything, to stop her, but my brain doesn't know how.

I've said too much, anyway. And I haven't told her enough. I've fucked up.

I need to keep it together. I don't want to beg and plead, but I'm already dangerously close to doing that.

Seconds drag by as I watch Keri Ann's face deliver those words to me. Words that strike me where my deepest fears and insecurities lie.

I'm winded. My lungs, my mind, my tongue won't co-operate. My entire body has betrayed me. If my mind was fully functional right now, and not in catatonic shock, if it was able to bark out an order for me to walk, walk to her and wrap my arms around her small frame, or even to walk out, I'm not sure my legs would get the message.

The only thing I *can* feel is a clawing, dark nothingness moving like sludge through my veins—taking over. It's seeping dead emptiness through every inch of me, shutting me down in increments, until I can't even see in front of me.

Finally, a synapse must make a last-ditch attempt to fire and rescue me because I find myself turning away. Able to move.

I don't even remember getting back to Devon's, which is a miracle in and of itself because it's so fucking dark here. *Because of the sea turtles.*

I enter the house and sag against the wall. The memories of Keri Ann hit me like an avalanche. All the feelings that have been quiet and dead for the last twenty minutes switch back on at full volume.

I put my hand out on the same wall that I had her pressed up against right before I'd carried her upstairs seven months ago. A swift kick in the libido comes along with the memory I seriously don't need right now. *Damn, this is bad.*

I remember looking in her eyes and seeing the emotion there, feeling it in return so strong the reality was. She was holding *me* up as much as I was her.

I know she's lying.

Please let her be lying.

I swallow over a throat that feels like it will never close.

The thing about pain, whether physical or emotional, is there's no running away. You can't escape it and you can't hide from it. Not by ignoring it, not by drugging it, not by doing a swan dive into a bottle. Sooner or later you'll have to take a breath, let the pain rush in and get to the other side like your life depends on it. Because it does.

I know this, I've been through versions of pain many times. And yet, it doesn't stop me from trying all three remedies in quick succession.

I grit my teeth and will my mind to shut down as I push off the wall and stalk into the kitchen, heading for the cabinet that houses the liquor. I can compartmentalize well, but this time it's like trying to shove the Michelin man into a tiny ring box.

Sloshing several fingers of Blue Label into a glass—damn—Devon's getting fancy in his old age, I head straight for the stairs. In my room, I grab an Ambien and knock it back with the Scotch. Dumb, I know, but I would like to be in complete oblivion just for a little while. And I haven't slept well for weeks.

I stare at the bed in Devon's guest room.

Visions of the last time I slept here with Keri Ann, naked, and spread out beneath me, and so Goddamn sweet and beautiful, clang down in rapid fire one after the other, and I back out.

Making it back downstairs, I top up my drink and head to the couch.

I want to make the selfish choice and just go all out to get her back. It's a physical struggle to not turn around and go back and grab her and kiss her and love her and keep talking until she understands. Like I can force her to hear me or force her to love me.

What was I thinking? I've made so many mistakes, but it seems I just keep making them. Why did I tell her how I felt? Of course she wouldn't believe me. Just hearing her reaction made me realize how dumb it was. And she was right. Part of me did think I could use that to my advantage.

My arrogance.

She'd called me on my arrogance once, and I'd denied it and claimed confidence instead. But she was right. It was my arrogant streak that believed telling her I loved her would buy me some time.

Without working too hard, I'd gotten what I wanted from women all my adult life. I traded on my looks and my celebrity and got laid when I felt like it. Even with Audrey, if I was honest. That was the normal course of events. But of course, there's nothing *normal* about Keri Ann Butler.

I've been convincing myself I did the right thing, handled Audrey the right way by throwing the world off the trail and staying away from here until the dust settled after *Erath*.

Why didn't I tell Keri Ann five months ago what was going on, back when I almost came back? I know the truth of it. I was a coward. I'd already seen her disappointment in me, and I didn't want to own up to what I'd done to Audrey and . . . I didn't want to hear that Keri Ann didn't want me.

As I stare up at the white ceiling and wait for the sleeping pill to work its magic, I think about how I got to this moment. I knew after I left here five months ago I was dragging my feet. The longer I stayed away, the harder it was to come back because at the very heart of it, I *knew* this would happen.

Why wouldn't it? The exact reason most women run toward me is the exact reason Keri Ann always stepped away.

I take one more deep sip of Scotch, feeling the heat unfurl in my throat and spread through my chest, warming the cold, deep ache of emptiness and soothing the serrated aftermath of Keri Ann's massacre of my heart. Then I close my eyes.

I'm running down the hallways at boarding school. We're not supposed to run, but it's dark, and I don't know where any of the other kids are. It must be after *lights out*, and I have no idea *why* I'm running. My breath is wheezing in and out of my chest, my legs burning as I round the corner by the school kitchens. But . . . I just turned this corner, how did I get back to the beginning? Who am I running from?

Then I hear him breathing right behind me. "William."

I lurch up into a sitting position and snap my eyes open only to be blinded by whiteness all around me. "Shit," I mumble, squeezing my eyes closed to blue negatives dancing on my lids. My brain unpeels from the inside of my skull and settles with a deep thud.

Ow.

"Jack, Jesus. Jumpy much?" Devon's voice is over to my left.

I carefully slit one eye open and look to my left. It *is* Devon, and I'm at his place. Butler Cove. Shit. I close my eyes again and acknowledge the hollow ache in my chest. I can't tell if my head or my chest hurts more. "What time is it?" I croak.

"After six in the evening. You've been asleep all day, and by the looks of it, could sleep another twelve. I was just making sure you weren't actually in a coma. Everything all right?" He hands me a glass of ice water. "Here."

"Thanks." I close my eyes and take a sip, the iciness splashing in my empty insides. "Why did you call me William?"

"What?"

"I thought . . . never mind. I must have been dreaming." I haven't had that dream for years. "Where've you been?"

Devon takes a seat opposite me, a beer bottle dangling from his hand.

"Savannah. It's all a go for *Roberts*. We got all the permits for the Riverfront and as long as SCAD still wants in, we should begin set design by next week and hopefully begin shooting by September."

I wince and pinch the bridge of my nose. My whole push to set the movie in Savannah seems so fucking stupid now. "Great," I muster.

Devon tips his beer back, taking a long sip. "Again, is everything all right?"

"No." I let out a long breath and lie back down, flinging my arm over my forehead. "No. Nothing is all right. I fucked up. I went to see Keri Ann last night, and I fucked up."

"How so?"

"I may have told her I was in love with her."

"You're a sick sadistic bastard, you know that?"

"To her or to myself?" I manage.

Devon lowers his beer. "I was going to say to her, actually, but this is an interesting turn of events for someone who didn't seem to give a shit about her before."

I look over to where he's sitting, wearing ripped jeans and a black t-shirt, the tips of his hair bleached yellow.

His brow is furrowed as he looks at me. "You sure had

me fooled. First I thought it was the real deal, then you disappeared off to England and we *all* got to see how you spent your time there. So forgive me if I'm not following."

"It's complicated."

"It always is. You want to give it a shot?"

CHAPTER EIGHT

I eye Devon, one of my best friends in the plastic, ego-filled circus I live my life in. He deserves to know what was and is going on with me. And frankly, I need the help. I am tired of the isolation. Exhausted actually.

Sorting through the happenings of the last five months since Audrey showed me the depths of her emotional depravity, I decide to start at the beginning. Devon wants my story, and I need to give voice to it, if only to diminish whatever is devouring my insides.

Five Months Ago . . .

A skinny, red-faced and hyperventilating guy, who doesn't look old enough to work, has just given me the keys to the Hertz rental I ordered delivered to the General Aviation Terminal on Hilton Head Island. He obviously had no idea he was going to be delivering a car to a celebrity when he woke up this morning. Now he keeps saying "I can't believe it! I can't believe it!" over and over again while I try to get around him to the car. I've already given him a personalized autograph "to give to his girlfriend." It would be amusing if I were in a better mood.

I don't remember being this nervous about anything for a long time. Not since those first couple of screen tests where it's down to you and that other guy who's been all over *Variety* and you're wondering how you're gonna pay your rent that's two weeks late. Where *everything*, your whole future, is riding on the outcome of how you play the next few hours.

"Do you have a map of the area?" I ask him patiently. I'd flung my bag into the back seat of the rental with my good hand and tugged my cap down, sliding my shades back on. I pull my wallet out of the pocket of my worn jeans and balance it on my bandaged right hand to remove a twenty. "Here. Thanks. Do you have a map?" I repeat.

The guy, still blocking the driver's side door, takes the money and looks at my hand. "Wow, like, thanks. Dude . . . what did you do to your hand?"

"I punched a wall. Map?"

"Oh, yeah. Sorry. There's a complimentary map on the passenger seat. Why'dya punch a wall?"

"It was better than punching a person."

The guy nods emphatically like he "*like, totally, gets it.*"

"Thanks for delivering the car."

My hand was fucked from punching the wall so I went over to Nick's. Being a tattoo artist, I knew he had bandages and antiseptic. Thank God he also persuaded me to get it x-rayed. He knew a guy who played for the Lakers who had his own doc on call, so I got it taken care of fast and, more importantly, privately. Hairline fracture to the third meta-carpal. Great. So I'm in a cast.

The kid still doesn't move, so I reach out for the door with my left hand and open it, slowly nudging him backward until I can safely get in. He steps away finally, and I nod and close the door.

I take a deep breath and start the car.

This is the kind of fear that sits heavy on your chest—a fundamental, incessant anxiety like you're stuck in a dark alley—it's life or death, and your feet have forgotten how to run. You've glimpsed your salvation like a glittering empire in the distance, but you can't fucking remember how to get there. Every moment you spend pondering, is a moment your goal drifts further away, the road becoming more and more complicated and hazardous until it's gone.

My phone buzzes again. It hasn't stopped with messages in the twenty minutes it took to get from the plane to the car. I grab it and scroll down, starting at the bottom.

Duane/Peak Ent: CALL ME RIGHT THIS MINUTE OR WE'RE PULLING OUT OF ROBERTS

Devon: Dude, seriously. I expected you a week ago. I need to talk to you about scheduling filming too.

Devon: you realize there's a high school sweetheart trying to help her get over you, right?

I hate that one.

Sheila PR: Why do you keep doing this to me? You don't pay me enough for this. Peak is breathing down my neck about damage control. I need a statement!!!!!!!

*Duane/Peak Ent: Okay look. This is serious. Just call me back
we can work this out—if it's really over, we just need to schedule
some photo ops, outings, we can cover. JUST CALL ME.*

I stop reading and pull out onto the road following signs for
the mainland. "*Cover*" my ass. Duane, from Peak Entertainment
is looking to persuade, threaten, and cajole me back in line.
Everyone is getting hysterical, but there's a reason why I don't
call them back. Yet. Either Duane or my publicist, Sheila.
They want me to put out a statement saying Audrey and I
are fine, but I don't want Keri Ann to see it. Not until I speak
to her and tell her what's going on.

But how can I find the courage to explain that even though
I'd told her Audrey and I were over, I *believed* I had gotten
her pregnant. With one hundred percent certainty.

The morning the news broke about Audrey cheating on
me.

The day the pictures came out.

I knew about the cheating before Audrey knew that I knew,
of course. She came to find me in my home gym where I was
pounding up a ten percent incline with bricks in my backpack
because I was just *that* pissed off. I'd thought we had a deal.
I'd passed up a *lot* of women to stick to it, to respect Audrey
privately and publicly and to not make her look a fool. For
the most part, I'd managed to keep my dick in my pants,
even though Audrey and my occasional sexual relationship
had mostly fizzled out around the second installment of *Erath*.
That was a long time with only sporadic sex.

Audrey was all hysterical and sorry and kissing me and
undressing me. And call me a bastard, but my ego needed,
no *demanded*, I show her what she was missing.

I was pumped up, sweating, and pissed off, in the middle

of a workout, and I just did it. I fucked her. And I didn't use any protection, something I had *never* done. I'd taken some kind of perverse pleasure from that fact. I was like a stupid animal staking his claim. For nothing. Wounded pride. That was *it*. And I was so disgusted with myself afterwards. I still am.

How did I explain *that* to a girl like Keri Ann? It would never even occur to her to use someone for her own gain. In *any* way. And I had used a woman in the worst and basest way possible. And then moved on to Keri Ann, and like the animal I was, decided to rid her of her virginity before abandoning her.

As I turn off the airport road, I let myself think about Savannah, what seems like a lifetime ago, in a secluded corner of that dark club. I'd been sitting, numbing myself with a bottle of Bushmills, while I figured out what I would say to Keri Ann, how I would explain. And there she was. I couldn't believe my lying eyes. It was wishful thinking, surely. I mean, the way she was dressed—those legs coming out from the tight, short black dress, long, tanned, toned and ending in the sexiest shoes I had ever seen. Probably just because they were on *her*. Keri Ann didn't dress like that, or even wear makeup. I seriously thought I was in a drunken stupor.

She'd looked so different. But God, she'd looked breathtaking. And I acted like an animal. Again. It was a primal response, pure and simple. I was on top of the guy before I could even process that I wanted to rip his throat out for touching her. Kissing her.

He *kissed* her.

I never wanted him to breathe again.

I knew, *I knew*, that it was because of me she was doing this. I had turned that amazing, pure, unaffected and *untouched* girl into the haunting siren who was bewitching every guy in the room and unknowingly asking to be touched. I could see it on their faces.

Now as I drive toward Butler Cove, I don't know what to say, how to say it, or if she'll care. I mean, it's been two months since I last saw her. Since I stood in the back office in that club in Savannah, half drunk, and let her walk out of the door, and out of my life. Again.

Her eyes. Fuck, her eyes—the look in them just about kills me every time I let it creep into my mind. Watery, with the unshed tears she was failing to hold back. Blue. Blue like rough denim, and they always said exactly what she was thinking. And right then it was disappointment. In me.

That thought shudders through me, and I pull over. I need to check my directions anyway. I lay my forehead on the steering wheel for a second and take a deep breath, then reach for the map. It's attached to a magazine. *Hilton Head Monthly.* I pull the stapled map off and fling the magazine back to the passenger seat where it lands face down.

Holy shit!

I grab the magazine again and stare at the back cover. Then I check the map again and drive not to Butler Cove, but to a gallery.

CHAPTER NINE

The elegant, female curator at the Picture This Gallery reminds me of my eleventh grade Lit teacher and she is madly trying to place me. Southern politeness, perhaps, precludes her from asking. I guess. I don't really care. I can tell she's taking in my rumpled attire and trying to work out if I can afford anything. Not in a mean way. Just in an efficient way. Or maybe she's wondering if I'm trouble, what with my bandaged hand and perma-scowl.

What I *am* interested in is what I am staring at, transfixed. In the center of the room . . . and perhaps there are other things around it, but I don't see them . . . is a wave. Seriously. A wave. If I deconstruct it, if I take what I see down to its elements, I don't see it. And if I step around to one side, I don't see it. But right now, where I'm standing, I have the perfect view. A swell, no, a forming barrel of a wave, made up of a huge piece of ashy driftwood, carved back to its pale beige core in parts, and rising up to spill its breakwater in a cacophony of beach. Beach stones and sticks and broken shells and a single piece of red sea glass that glares so bright it's like a wound.

I'm unable to tear my eyes away.

"Spectacular, isn't it?" The curator's voice jars me back to my surroundings.

Clearing my throat, I manage to nod. "Yeah. Is it for sale?"

"Unfortunately, no. The artist just dropped it off this morning, a few hours ago in fact. Her exhibition doesn't technically open for another two weeks. And frankly even if it was for sale, I wouldn't be able to let you have it until her show is over. It is the star piece, I'm sure you'll agree."

Keri Ann was here, *in this room*, mere hours ago. I breathe in, as if I can still smell her. Which, of course, I can't. I step closer to inspect the piece of red sea glass. "So once the exhibition starts, it will be for sale?" It seems odd that the curator won't take a presale on an item. She is a business owner after all.

"I'm afraid that is the one piece that won't be for sale. I wish the artist would change her mind." Her voice is filled with disappointment. I'm disappointed too, and of course, satisfied she's not selling it. The idea that someone else could potentially own this doesn't sit right. I wonder . . .

I turn to look at her. "Just out of interest, would you mind calling the artist and asking *if* there was a hypothetical price tag on it, what it would be?"

I can tell my question surprises her, but she also looks intrigued. Not greedy, but she is a businesswoman, and it looks like she just realized I am the real deal despite my wrinkled shirt, unshaven jaw, and probably blood-shot eyes. Oh, and . . . there it is, she just realized who she's talking to. Her eyes widen fractionally, and she flushes a deep crimson, her breath coming out in a small gasp.

"Oh, um. Y-Yes, sure." She's flustered. I wish I could put her at ease, but it's always this way. I just have to keep talking and wait it out.

"I mean, everyone has a price, right?" I say quietly, weighing the words. "So you'll call her?"

She nods.

"Now?" I raise my eyebrows expectantly, and she snaps into focus.

"Y-Yes, of course. I'm sure if the artist knew who—"

"No!" Christ, I didn't think of that. Shit. "Sorry, but, and this is important, you can't reveal to anyone who I am or that I'm here. Not even the artist. Are you able to do the purchase anonymously if she'll sell?"

She furrows her brow. She's disappointed. I can tell she thinks that my name would be good publicity for her gallery, not to mention going a long way toward making Keri Ann amenable to selling. Little does she know it would probably do the exact opposite.

"Yes, it can be anonymous. It happens quite a lot in the art world. Although I can safely say that if it happens here at my little gallery, it will be the first time in my history." She seems to have recovered. Her tone is amused.

"Well, let's just see if there's a price, shall we? And make sure you have her agree if that price is met, you can go ahead and make the sale. And just so you know, if the issue comes up, it can stay in the exhibition."

"Well, yes, it would have to be contingent on that."

"And also any future exhibitions, until the artist is ready to let it go." I'm skating on dangerous ground here, risking more questions.

Her eyes are appraising.

I fumble for an answer. "I'm going to be traveling a lot for the next six to twelve months, and well, I have nowhere to put it. Yet." It's true. I put my house in California back on the market yesterday. Even though I'd designed its renovation myself, I am beyond relieved to be getting rid of it. The soul has been gone from it for a while, since long before all the shit went down with Audrey. In fact, ever since I became disillusioned with the entire business I'm in. But I'm not a fool, I know I can't walk away from what I know, my job. I just need to find a way to not have it define me. A way to live it, without it living *me*.

Things seemed to clear out and smooth out in my head the last time I was in Butler Cove. Being around someone so anchored to her own soul could do that to you, I guess. Obstacles just didn't seem so big. Or at least she made me want to hurdle them like they were anthills, and not mountainous threats to everything I'd worked so hard for and all the compromises I'd made clawing myself up. A climb where the void dogged me at every step, ready to suck me back to the wastrel I'd been at seventeen. Let's face it, with the amount of times I've been tempted to dull my insecurities and sacrifice my integrity, I could just as easily be dead right now.

It's kind of fitting that the wave is spitting the red sea glass up and out of its belly with all the other detritus of the shoreline.

"I'm not sure the artist will go for keeping it if she agrees to sell," the curator says as she goes around her desk toward the phone. "It'll cost her money to move it properly each time and keep it undamaged. You'll probably want to insure it."

"Well, I'll pay for that, too, if she sells. You can make that sound like your idea, as part of the deal you negotiated for her."

She narrows her eyes at me. "Do you know the artist?"

"No," I say easily, the lie tripping off my tongue, as I slide my eyes back to the sculpture. She is dialing the number, Keri

Ann's number, and I am as nervous as if I'm the one about to hear her voice.

Will she sell it? She obviously doesn't want to. Maybe the curator put a recommended price on it that was too low for her to want to part with it. I want the answer to be no, she won't sell. Or the price to be so high I'll laugh. I'll pay it, of course. Although it will invite way too many questions.

I close my eyes and listen.

"Hi, Keri Ann?"

My pulse hammers.

"Hi, this is Mira. Yes, I'm fine . . . thank you. No, No, it's fine. It looks great. Listen, I know you said it wasn't for sale . . . What? . . . Yes, I know. But I was just thinking it would be good for me to know perhaps a ballpark, like a reserve, perhaps, not that I would share it with anyone, just for me to know, in case . . . I mean, if someone were to offer something you thought fitting, I'd like to be able to know whether to even call you. Uh huh . . . yes, yes, of course." She pauses. A long time.

I glance over to the curator, Mira, to see her pursing her lips and drumming her pencil. Then her eyes widen fractionally, and she gets a bemused look on her face. She scratches out something with her pencil on the paper next to the phone. My heart thuds heavily. Did Keri Ann give a price?

Mira turns and winks, then nods at me.

Dammit, I want to hurt something. Disappointment that Keri Ann will sell it makes my stomach curdle, perhaps something to do with my slight hangover, too. I'm also relieved I can own it so no one else can.

She still hasn't hung up. "Wait so, yes, I should just add the gallery commission and tax on there, add it to that amount, and that will be the specific price? Like specifically that?"

Mira's brow cinches up, seemingly confused by the conversation she's having. "Okay, hang on." She fumbles around, grabs a calculator, and punches in numbers. "Okay. Yes, I understand. Specifically. Yes, I promise."

I feel worse as the reality of the situation sets in.

This is bad. It was one thing driving here, nervous as shit about seeing Keri Ann again and not knowing her reaction. But now that it's being laid out to me that she will excise me fully from her life for a high enough price, I am gutted. I blow a harsh breath out and glance around for a place to sit. My legs feel weak. I listen to them wrap up their conversation, and then Mira approaches.

"So good news and bad news—although slightly odd."

I look bleakly up at her. If she notices that I suddenly appear like I might vomit, she doesn't say anything. Definitely a hangover. That's all. I really need to stop drinking so much. I tell myself that every day. But honestly, I want to get this done and go drown myself again as quickly as possible.

"She will sell." Mira cocks her head. "But only for a specific amount. And when I say specific, I mean . . . *specific*. Then eight percent South Carolina sales tax and twenty percent gallery commission will be added on *top* of that price, rather than from it. Her idea, not mine."

"Okaaaay. So what is the artist asking for?"

She shifts slightly. "I can only confirm or deny the amount. And when I say specific, I really mean down to the penny. No more. No less." She hunches her shoulders up and shakes her head in bewilderment that mirrors my own. "So unless you're a mind reader, we're both shit outta luck."

Her phrase startles me. She doesn't seem like a curser, but then again, she is having a bizarre day. I am absolutely confounded. And relieved. Thank God. At least no one else will be buying it either. She's not selling it, not really. But why the cryptic pricing? Why not just say no? It's weird as hell. "And I don't suppose you would betray her confidence by telling me anyway?" I ask.

"No, I'm sorry. She has some other pieces—"

I shake my head. I'd glanced around at her other stuff. They were beautiful, and I'd buy them all if I wouldn't be casting Keri Ann in a strange light by doing so.

"No, I didn't think so."

She walks over to her desk and grabs two business cards. "Here, write who I can contact if anything changes, and here's my card in case you need anything else or . . ." She cocks an eyebrow. "Suddenly, magically, you know the secret number." She snorts with disbelief.

I concur. I can tell she's disappointed, but I'm quite impressed she'll keep it to herself. Although it must be such a bizarre amount that it would only be traced back to Mira herself.

I take the cards and her offered pen and scrawl Katie's number on the back. "That's my assistant in California, she always knows how to get me. And seriously, call me if anything changes," I say, shaking my head. "Please don't tell the artist who was asking."

I take one last look at the extraordinary piece of artwork before heading to the door. There's something so raw and primal and . . . painful about it.

"What is it called?" I ask before I leave. I don't even know where I'm going. I wanted to go and see Keri Ann and face up to all my shit, but now I'm not so sure.

Mira walks around the other side of it and looks down at the card. "Just want to make sure I get the words in the right order. Oh! Oh, how funny." She looks up, and then the quizzical smile on her face flattens out, and she looks nonplussed as she glances back down.

Oh shit. What?

"It's called *Ever Broken Sea*."

Jesus H. Christ.

CHAPTER TEN

$\mathcal{O}$utside the gallery containing the bold evidence of my badly handled relationship with Keri Ann, I fold my body back into the compact rental car and drum my fingers on the steering wheel. What the hell was I thinking coming here? I'm the last person Keri Ann wants to see, but I start the car anyway, and before long, I am almost at Butler Cove.

I haven't even told Devon I'm finally coming. He's at his beach house taking some time off before hitting the road to get investments for the Dread Pirate Roberts project. Peak Entertainment, the people who fashioned the leash I'm attached to, are going to be a part of it. Of course, that is as long as I keep playing by their rules.

My phone buzzes again. Expecting it to be Duane from Peak, I grab it, thinking I may as well get it over with. It's not Duane. It's Sheila, my publicist. Well, she's on my callback list, too.

"Yeah?"

There's a long silence on the other end of the phone.

"Sheila?"

"Yeah, I'm here. Sorry, I'm scraping my jaw off the industrial carpet with the heel of my Leboutin." Her voice carries the husk of late nights and too many cigarettes. "You answered the fucking phone. Are you kidding me? You don't call me back *all week*, and you answer "yeah?" I was getting ready to leave you a speech dumping your ass. I have it written out, typed up, *beta'd* and everything. I've been rehearsing. You've got some kind of luck, boy. One more trip to voicemail and I was *done*."

The great thing about Sheila is she can talk the hind leg off a donkey, so I usually only have to nod, smile, or on the phone, grunt in the affirmative. It's a good relationship. I do my part.

She goes on. "Imagine? No agent *and* no publicist. What a world, how would you cope? Now, seriously, the shit is hitting the fan. How did I never know what a fuck-face Audrey is? Shit, that bitch is *eee-ville-town*. How did you manage to tap that so long? To think *I* even wanted to schtupp her once. *Oi vey!* So have you seen the picture?"

"What picture?"

"The one of you and that waitress chick all Romeo and Juliet-style on a balcony."

My blood freezes in my veins. "What? What the hell are you talking about?"

"Well, if you'd answered your fucking phone or listened to any of my seventeen thousand and two messages, you would know Audrey gave you until *today* to get in a room with her and Peak to, as *she* said, 'save her reputation,' or she'd take yours down. When she found you before, she had a P.I. track you down at Devon's. The P.I. hung out having a nice beach holiday and taking lots of gooey pictures. How the hell she got him to not sell the pictures himself is beyond me. That broad is one capable c—"

"All right, already." My hand is trembling with barely

controlled shock and rage. I feel like I . . . "Hang on." I've managed to drive almost to Devon's so I pull into a small parking area near a beach access path. I get the door open and gulp a breath of cool Carolina air.

On a balcony?

Son of a bitch.

I know exactly when that was, the morning after we . . . the day Audrey showed up. Keri Ann had been standing at the open French doors of the bedroom, looking out to the ocean. I remember coming out of the bathroom and seeing her there, re-clothed in the sexy little dress I'd pulled off her body the night before. The morning sun spilled around her, and the ocean breeze was sifting through her hair.

She'd spotted a sea turtle nest and was pointing it out and all I could think about was wrapping her back up in my arms and working out ways to persuade her to spend the whole day in bed with me. I loved the surprise and wonder in her eyes, mingled with her knowing smile that told me she knew what she could do to me, even while she looked unsure. And I loved her gasps and moans and how she suddenly became an expert at taking me from zero to sixty so I had to perform mental gymnastics just to keep from exploding into a hurricane of frantic want.

Instead, I'd wrapped my arms around her and tucked her small body against my bare chest, settling for asking her to come to California. Planting a seed for a future. I could get through the next phase of my life knowing Keri Ann would be at the end of it.

And some asshole had taken that private moment and turned it ugly. And Audrey had seen it, too.

"Anyway, Sunshine," Sheila rasps from the phone I've pulled away from my ear. "You better get your ass over to my office so we can get a statement together before she presses the button on this. She's going to say she lost the baby from grief over you having an affair, and *that's* why she sought comfort from her director. She has a tag on your toe, buddy. The timing of it all is irrelevant, she'll say those pictures were taken whenever it suits her story, although I'm assuming they were taken the last time you went off the grid and drove me mental."

Sheila never pauses for breath.

I head down to the beach so *I* can think and breathe.

She goes on, "She also has footage of you assaulting some guy in a nightclub. Says she's afraid of you. I've told Duane it's bullshit, it's not even you in the video, but as you know that's also kind of irrelevant at this point. Where are you, anyway?"

I make it out onto the sand, it's almost high tide. I close my eyes for a second. "It *is* me in that video. And I'm in South Carolina."

"Fuck me sideways. Can you make my day any worse?"

I snort. "Probably, just give me time."

"How about after I navigate this mess with the least amount of dings to your persona, we re-negotiate our contract?"

"Fine."

"I'll take that as written in blood. Now, how soon can you get back here?"

I think about everything Audrey is threatening. It's bad. It doesn't take a genius to figure that out. The public loves a good scandal. The more convoluted the better. And in the end she is threatening Keri Ann, too. Her privacy. Her reputation. Everything.

I conjure the image of what I've just seen at the gallery in my mind's eye. This is the first of many great things to come for Keri Ann Butler. As long as I don't ruin it. If I do, she'll no longer be Keri Ann Butler, Artist . . . she'll be my latest conquest and tabloid fodder. The saying *there's no such thing as bad publicity* is a crock. For her, there would be. For evermore, people would assume she became well-known due to her association with *me*. She'd be stuck in whatever seedy story Audrey spun for eternity. I can't honestly think of anything worse. For anyone.

"Give me a second." I waffle between heading back immediately and doing an amended version of what I came here for. Seeing her. But, I can't go and face Keri Ann's disappointment in me, and at the same time risk blowing up her entire life. I can't be that selfish. It's one thing if *I'm* going down in flames, but how can I take someone else with me? How can I take *her* with me? Who knows what story would be spun, what lies would be seeded? I wouldn't put anything past Audrey. It still stuns me how little I know her.

I take a deep lungful of cool ocean air and open my eyes to the beach. It's midafternoon and warm for December. I'd love to just run right now and clear my head. Feel the rough sand and surf on the soles of my feet. Then when I was done, I'd head to Keri Ann's, like that first day when I jogged to her house and she opened the door all sleepy, irritated, and dressed in the tiniest but most innocent-looking pajamas I'd ever seen. I'd lost my balance trying to get the door closed and fallen practically on top of her, getting a mainline hit of strawberry shampoo and warm bedroom skin.

I turn and look the other way—down the beach—and my chest thuds. Someone, a girl, is jogging. It's her. I know it, although she's way too far away to see clearly. I back up a few steps.

This is her world, her life, and I just keep crashing it.

I understand what I need to do. It might mean I lose her in the end, but it's the only way to go forward. The only way I even have a shot at making this work. It also occurs to me I'm being a coward, but I swallow that thought quickly.

"Sheila, I'm headed back right now. Can you stall Audrey, or do you need me to call her?"

I turn around and head back along the beach path, and I don't look back. I start the damn car, turn around, and head back the way I came.

Sheila barks out a hacking cough that has me wincing. "You should probably be the one to call Audrey. Just tell her to wait. Tell her you'll hear what she has to say. Try not to say anything else *like where you are*." She punctuates each word, in case I don't get it. I do. "Audrey is seriously unhinged right now."

"Fine," I tell her. "It'll be late when I get back . . . call you first thing."

"I'll be on the edge of my seat."

"I'm sure." In my mind's eye I see Sheila rolling her eyes. "Thank you, Sheila. Thank you for helping with this."

"Yeah, well. I know it doesn't always seem like it, but I'm on your side. As long as you do me the courtesy of taking my calls, I'll earn my wage and make you look as good as possible."

"Will do."

She grunts and hangs up.

Of course, I still plan to come back and see Keri Ann. At some point. Explain. Something. I just don't know how long it will be. I pause at a stop sign and punch in Katie's number. "Katie, it's Jack. I just got to Hilton Head, but I need to head back to L.A. Can you make sure the jet doesn't leave again? I'll be back at the airfield in thirty minutes."

I'd smile, but I feel too damn grim. I'm standing at the window on the twenty-second floor of an office building in Century City, looking out over the smoggy haze of downtown L.A.

Sitting around the table behind me is Sheila, Audrey, her agent and her publicist, Duane and two other guys from Peak Entertainment as well as a member of Peak's legal counsel, a reasonable-looking guy named Andrew. The cavalry. Their cavalry.

Audrey has finally shown up and the way she is acting should be laughable. But everyone is lapping it up. I left the table because I couldn't sit still with all the bullshit flying around.

"These are some serious allegations, Mr. Eversea. Would you like to comment?" Reasonable Andrew asks.

What I'd like is to shower, shave, sleep for forty-eight hours, and wake up in a parallel universe. A universe where I was supposed to wake up and see Keri Ann Butler lying next to me and Spanish moss swaying outside the window.

"Well, obviously, none of it's true." Sheila jumps in. "Ms. Lane is a little confused by the sequence of events. Those pictures were taken after Ms. Lane's affair. But, as we all know, that's probably neither here nor there as far as the public is concerned. As for the assault, Mr. Eversea did, in fact, hit someone in Savannah, Georgia. But he is not, nor would he ever be, a physical threat to Ms. Lane."

It's a good thing the California coast is beautiful because there is nothing redeeming about the ugliness of the city I'm existing in right now. I turn around and put my back to the window.

"Mr. Eversea, your statement says you punched someone two months ago, and yet you have a bandaged hand. We will need a release from that individual in Savannah stating he waives the right to press future charges. But Ms. Lane's state-ment says that during a disagreement eight days ago, you expressed rage and punched a wall so hard that you, obvi-ously, required medical attention." He looks meaningfully at my hand. "This doesn't sound like Ms. Lane can be assured you pose no physical threat to her, and frankly, this is worri-some for your future dealings with Peak Entertainment in general."

My shoulders are so tense, I'm in danger of going into a spasm. "Well, Andrew . . ." I face the window again and address the group behind me whose reflection is super-imposed on the gray city haze. "In the ten minutes preceding the point where I punched *my* wall in *my* house, I'd been informed that Ms. Lane, with guidance from my *ex*-agent, had fabri-cated a pregnancy. I'd just spent two months believing I was going to be a father."

"I appreciate the surprise of that, Mr. Eversea, if it was indeed the case, but Ms. Lane claims it was not a fabrication and that she *lost* the baby."

"I know what she's claiming. We all do. You all have both our statements written out in front of you. And you're clearly of the impression that she's telling the truth and I'm lying. And frankly? I don't give a shit. What I would like to know is what you'd like me to do to get past this point. How do we get to a point where I don't have to interact with Ms. Lane in any further capacity, personally or professionally? Ever." I hear a shocked gasp from Audrey's direction but refuse to look at her.

"Well, obviously, we have a duty to protect the brand we have created with the *Warriors of Erath* franchise. As per your contract and our normal procedure, the relationships created as part of the brand should continue at least six months beyond the last project. As it stands, the brand took a rather large hit with the actions of Ms. Lane. In order to overcome that, we either need you all to continue being seen together—"

"No." It's out my mouth before I notice.

"Unacceptable," Sheila says at the same time.

"Let me finish," Reasonable Andrew says calmly. "The alternative is, since that seems likely to cause more harm than good at this point," he looks pointedly at Audrey and then at me. God, I feel like I'm eleven. "We let the relationship end *naturally*, but to protect the public perception of both parties, neither can be seen to have a relationship for a period of time."

For a moment, I regret not having my agent, a legal representative, in the room with me. But Sheila has danced enough of these proms to steer me right. I see her thinking hard.

"No. That still leaves everyone remembering what *I* did. That's not fair!" Audrey pouts.

"Well, the fact remains, Ms. Lane, you did violate the contract first." Reasonable Andrew is not such a bad guy after all. He obviously doesn't believe Audrey's claim that my relationship with 'the girl in the picture' drove Audrey to do the same.

I fold my arms and look over at Audrey in detail for the first time since she walked in. I honestly feel like the last three years have been a dream. A different Audrey. This Audrey's a stranger.

Dropping her eyes from me, nervously, she confers quietly with her agent and her publicist by means of some scribbled notes back and forth. Then she vehemently shakes her head. "I'm scared of him!" she bursts out, and her agent almost rolls his eyes before he catches himself.

Now I really do feel like smiling. I don't, of course. There's nothing funny about what's going on here.

"Okay," says Andrew. "I understand if you have a legitimate safety concern, we can address that issue in a moment. But first, the contract between you two is easily amended. As of today your relationship, as encouraged and endorsed by Peak Entertainment, is done. We had an earlier meeting to address some of our available options. Moving forward, as long as you both are under the time line from the original contract, we *can* amend the relationship portion, and Peak will adopt the position that we *have* no position on whether you are romantically involved or not."

A small drop of tension slowly seeps from my shoulders.

Audrey looks spitting mad.

Andrew looks to Duane, who nods. "So given that we'd like to protect both of your reputations, and by extension the brand of the *Warriors of Erath* franchise, Ms. Lane will not make *any* accusations of infidelity toward Mr. Eversea. And in return, Mr. Eversea will not enter into any other relationship for the remainder of the contract term."

Shit.

CHAPTER ELEVEN

My mind is churning. No relationships for the rest of the contract. That's at least four or five months.

Fuck.

Unreasonable Andrew looks at both of us, in turn, for a reaction to his proclamation that neither of us can date. At all.

I can see Audrey is bristling, but she's also quietly smug at winning that round.

No relationships means no relationships. It means, really and truly, any idea of going back to Butler Cove and figuring things out with Keri Ann may be impossible in the near-term. But surely I can at least go there. Briefly. It doesn't need to be common knowledge. I'll have to do a better job at hiding it.

Audrey is clearly on my wavelength. "Wait," she says, her eyes glinting. I tense further. "If Jack is photographed with *any* girl on more than one occasion, then I will consider, and Peak should too, that he hasn't held up his end of this deal."

And I'm sure she'll make sure there are photographs.

"That sounds tricky. That could easily occur incidentally, too much room for error for us to add that into a contract."

Thank you, Andrew.

"Fine." Audrey sticks her chin up. "Then he has to stay away from Keri Ann Butler, specifically."

God, she's a bitch. I try to stop my jaw dropping. "Wow, Audrey, I never knew you to be so threatened." I pause and swallow. "Don't worry, she's more of a person than you or I put together. You should congratulate yourself, I'm not sure she'd have me anyway after the stunt you engineered." My chest tightens with rage, and I'm curling and uncurling my fingers under the table.

"That shouldn't be a problem," Sheila interjects, shooting me a warning look and then looking at Andrew. "But Mr. Eversea would like any and all copies of the photographs that Ms. Lane ordered taken without Mr. Eversea's permission that include both himself and Keri Ann Butler. I'm sure you'll agree that in accordance with this *amended* contract and to *protect the brand*, the new terms should specify that they should be removed from potential circulation?"

Andrew is nodding, I think, but I barely notice. It's sinking in that Keri Ann and I are probably done. Done before we got a second chance. Wow. There's nothing like being told you can't have something, to really bring the loss home. I release a long breath from my crushed chest, and I'm almost surprised when I don't hear it whistling through the cracks. Getting to my feet again, I pace back to the window. This room is as suffocating as the dense smog outside.

"I think that would be fair," Andrew says.

"How is that fair?" Audrey gasps. "That's my leverage. What about . . . my safety?" she corrects herself, quickly.

I glance back at her with narrowed eyes. She really is a piece of work.

Seriously? No one in the room believes her, but she's still beating this horse.

"Audrey—" Her agent admonishes her.

"Yes," Andrew cuts back in, "we can address your *safety* issue. We'd like to offer to move Mr. Eversea out of the country for the remainder of the time on the contract. We have a project we could use his help on, in England actually, which we will discuss with him offline after the close of this meeting."

I turn my head to look at him, gritting my teeth, trying hard to remain impassive. Every damn time someone opens his or her mouth, the hole I'm in gets deeper. I vow to myself then and there that I will *never* get into a situation where someone can control me like this ever again. It's a promise that burns through my gut like a red-hot cattle poker. *Never*.

Audrey casts her eyes about. I guess she's trying to work out if I'm being given an advantage. Another project. If she's being passed over? God knows.

"Do we have an agreement?" Andrew asks.

I turn around and see Sheila give me an almost imperceptible nod. "Yes, fine with me," I say to Andrew, and then nod at Duane and look at everyone. "Whatever we need to do to move past this quickly and efficiently is fine by me."

"Well, it's not fine with me!" Audrey bursts out, childishly. She's gotten what she wanted, me not to have anything to do with Keri Ann for as long as it'll probably take Keri Ann to never want anything to do with me anyway. What more can Audrey possibly want?

"Why do I have to look like the evil one in all of this? If we break up now, people will still remember that terrible *mistake* I made. If Jack is all goodie-two-shoes for the next few months, I'll still look bad. How can that be good for the *Erath* brand?" She points at me then. "And does no one care that I lost a baby because of him?"

My mind churns. *What the hell?* "Audrey."

She looks at me, stonily.

I lock eyes with her and will myself to be able to see what's going on in that messed-up head of hers. "If you truly lost the baby, I am sorry. Believe me. I'm grieving right along with you. It was my baby, too. But I don't even know if I have anything real to mourn. And that kills me. I'm sure making me suffer on this topic satisfies you for some God-forsaken reason. I've already asked you, no, *pleaded* with you not to control the rest of my life, too, but you seem to have accomplished that as well. Congratulations," I spit out. "But Jesus, Audrey. You can't have it both ways. You either don't want me seen with anyone else, or you do—which is it?"

I have a vague idea based on Keri Ann's sculpture that she is pretty fucking pissed at me the way I left. The last thing I plan on doing is rubbing her face in it by being seen with anyone else.

Audrey narrows her eyes and the cunning I see there makes me realize she has probably planned her final act as the scorned woman. And that is to hurt Keri Ann, too. Because clearly she wasn't hurt enough.

"Actually." It's Audrey's publicist who speaks, who looks like it's her time to shine. "I know we said no relationships, but I think it would be better to level the balance here and have Mr. Eversea seen with one or two other *potential* love interests. That way," she looks around the table with gravity, "people can feel a small modicum of sympathy for *my* client as well." She pauses for effect, and I see the net that was cleverly cast, closing around me. "The only *other* way to garner public sympathy for Ms. Lane at this point is to talk about the failed pregnancy."

"Fuck, no!" I explode, causing everyone in the room to

jump. Anger and panic at this idea washes through me in physical waves. It's painful. Or maybe I'm not breathing. Either way, I feel light-headed. I have a mental image of me suddenly, bone-crackingly, transforming into a massive tiger and eating my way out of this cage of assholes. Not Sheila, she can live. Shit, I need to calm down. Keep my head together.

Sheila nods and says, "We have an agreement. Let's not make it any more complicated. No pregnancy mentioned *at all* in return for a few staged paparazzi photo ops. No perceived long-term relationships for the remainder of the contract term for either party. And *we* get the existing pictures. Let's wrap this up. Mr. Eversea has another appointment with his new representation who was unable to make this meeting, but whom I will inform of all the decisions made today. We'll be back by to sign the amendment and hear about your plans for the project in England."

I'm unaware of the meeting she's referring to, but I need an agent, like yesterday. Especially, if I'm about to sign on to another project with Peak. Thank God Sheila is looking out for me. I pull my chair up to the table and lay my head down on my arms. I am beyond exhausted, mentally, emotionally, and because I haven't slept more than three hours in the last thirty. The sounds of everyone filing out washes over me.

I am so relieved this meeting is over, even though I'm left for dead on the battlefield. All I won was getting Audrey removed from my life.

I lost everything else.

CHAPTER TWELVE

"Jesus, Jack. Why didn't you tell me?" Devon is staring at me hard when I open my eyes. I'd been lying there on his couch like I was in a damn therapist's office, letting the last five months of my life pour out.

"Tell you what?" I ask. "That I was a coward, and I should have fought harder? That I was too tired and depressed to really fight? That I was so relieved to get Audrey out of my life, that I let the person I really wanted to be with slip through my fingers?" I sit up. "Because I didn't want to face the rejection? Because I've gotten what I want for most of my life, but I chose *not* to fight for Keri Ann because deep down I thought I would lose?" The truth hits me hard.

Devon is quiet a few moments. "Is that truly what you think?"

I pick up the water, wishing it were whisky and down it. "I don't know. The reality is that Keri Ann is as far from the kind of lives we lead as one could possibly get. This bullshit *is* my life. I can't see it changing in the foreseeable future. Maybe I don't want it to. I enjoy acting. I don't enjoy the BS that comes with it, but it's the price, right? Is there really a place for her in that? A place she would want? Deep down inside me I think that if she had the choice, she would choose *not* to be in that place."

"You think she'd choose not to be a famous guy's arm-candy over being her own person?"

"Yeah."

"I think you're right. It's going to be damn hard to avoid that."

"Aren't you supposed to be helping me?"

"I am. That part is impossible and will take time. But it sounds like what she said was she doesn't trust you and doesn't want to risk you flaking out again. Based on what she knows and what the whole world got to see you get up to in England, I don't blame her."

"Did I?"

"Did you what?

"Flake out on her. Before? Could I have found a way around the contract?"

"Honestly, England aside, you probably could have handled it better, and told Keri Ann what was going on, but I know Peak, and they don't mess around. What with the Internet and social media, their movies are mini-universes with interactive experiences, and that means the cast is part of that world too for however long they deem necessary. Gone are the days when people see a movie in a vacuum and go home from the theater to their movie-free lives." He shakes his shaggy blond head. "Peak does it so well, their marketing machine is one of the best. And they meant it when they threatened you. I would have done the same thing you did—ride it out. I'd say the fact they even amended your contract with Audrey says a lot about the belief they have in you. Although, they did give you a failing project as punishment. They'd almost written it off . . ." He looks at me gravely. "But you brought it back from the crapper. I've seen the early cuts, and Jack? It's pretty 'effing' awesome, despite your drunk ass. They're talking awards season. You certainly showed them."

"Seriously?"

"How is this a surprise to you?"

"It's not. I heard from people. I guess I didn't really believe it. I was so pissed about being set up and controlled, I may have gone off the deep end a bit."

"A bit? Dude, I'd say getting drunk and publicly hooking up every night was a *lot* off the deep end, especially when you claim to be in love with someone."

"C'mon, Dev. I told you what happened with Audrey, that stuff was engineered. Staged. None of it was real."

"I thought you all agreed to a couple of photo opportunities. What we've seen over the last few months seems like a lot more than that." He sounds incredulous.

"It looked that way, I guess. I wasn't trying to hurt Keri Ann. I think a part of me must have thought Keri Ann probably didn't even care any more. I mean it had been *months*. Childish, I know. Being there, in England, is tough for me. I don't handle it well."

"You don't talk much about growing up."

I glance at him. Devon has been a good friend. I don't know why I haven't told him until now how things ended with Audrey. But I'm definitely not ready to talk about England.

Getting up, I prowl to the glass wall overlooking the ocean. The low sun has cast an amber filter over the view. A few people are letting their dogs frolic in the surf. It doesn't look like there are any *photogs* with high-powered lenses anywhere, but I didn't notice one when I was here last time either.

"I thought . . . I thought that it would be a big 'eff you' to Audrey. And that it would help Keri Ann get over me—better that she hates me, right? But mostly I wasn't *thinking* at all. I avoided thinking at all costs. I just threw myself into being on that set and getting involved in the movie and drowning my sorrows when the cameras stopped rolling." I drop my forehead against the glass. "Being back in England does that to me."

"Did you explain to Keri Ann the stuff about Peak, about why you didn't come back here in December?"

"I tried, I wanted to."

"But you didn't because . . .?"

"Shit. Because I saw her . . . and because she makes me feel like I don't deserve her, which I don't, even though I crave her with every single fucking ounce of me. And I should have handled the situation last night better, but she floors me. I wish I had a script for how to be with her, but I don't. And I'd basically be saying I chose a movie contract over her. That I let myself be manipulated rather than fighting for her."

"Well, I can't say I expect her to look past the last five months, but maybe if you can tell her the *whys* she can decide whether to trust you again. And Jack, you weren't choosing a movie contract over her, you were *protecting* her from what Audrey had planned. And maybe she should know that. I would've done the same thing."

"It won't make a difference. Anyway, she's with someone else now."

"At least you'll have tried. And you know what? You can't change who you are. If you guys are going to have any kind of future, then she will need to get used to the reality of your life. It's not like you can hide from it. So why don't you use it to get her back? *Show* her what life you could have together. Accept who you are and win her back."

God, I'm losing sleep trying *not* to have thoughts about what we could have together. It's a full time job keeping them out of my head lest they make me fucking crazy.

"I promised her I'd stay away."

Devon shakes his head. "Why the hell would you promise something like that?"

"She said if I meant what I said about being in love with her, I would respect her wishes and stay away."

"So you didn't actually promise her."

"No, but I did mean it when I said I was in love with her."

In. Love.

What a nightmare.

I flash back to her fixing her tire yesterday on the side of the road, giving off sparks with her attitude. I wanted this girl. Like air. All the fucking way.

"Jack, if you really want her, you're going to have to fight dirty. You're Jack Eversea, talented actor and now I hear *screenwriter* and producer. For Christ's sake, you have a face and body that make girls swoon—"

"Ah, Dev," I say turning back to him, uncomfortable with his assessment, and trying to make light of it. "I'm flattered."

"Shut up, *Jack*-ass."

I smirk.

"You just have to make yourself attractive to *her*. We'll start with her basic needs, and you'll more than satisfy every one of them so she can't turn you down. Did I ever tell you I was a psychology major for a while?"

"God, no wonder I just poured my heart out lying on your couch."

"Yeah, well, it comes in handy, I can tell you. Especially

when my pathetic friends become too miserable to help themselves. But right now *I'm* experiencing one of the first basic needs—I'm starving. What say we go get something to eat and start operation *Make Jack Happy Again* right away? Let's hope she's working tonight."

That alone was going to piss her off, since she'd asked me to leave her be. But I'm going to have to trust Devon because I have no idea what else to do. I get up to head to the shower. "I hope you know what you're doing. What's the other basic need?"

Devon smiles and drains the rest of his beer, placing the bottle carefully down on the glass table. "Sex."

"That won't work on her."

"Dude, you don't think reminding her of the chemistry you two so clearly have will at least make it easier to get past her defenses and actually try and fix this?"

I pause at the foot of the stairs, running a hand through my hair. "Shit, I have no idea. She's as likely to hate me more for trying."

And that was the truth.

KERI ANN

CHAPTER THIRTEEN

In all of my imaginings about what would happen if Jack Eversea ever lowered himself to set foot back into my life, telling me he was in love with me had never featured. Okay, wait. Imaginings, yes. *Realistic* scenarios, no freaking way.

And using his feelings against him? Telling him to walk away from me if he meant them? No again.

His eyes had flickered as I delivered my final words, like he wanted to close them against me but willed them open. His breath rushed out of him before he clenched his jaw. Like I'd hit him.

I knew it was a low blow. I was making sure he had no recourse. To *not* walk away would be saying he hadn't meant it. And that was what I wanted, wasn't it?

After Jack had looked at me in stunned silence and walked out of the house without another word, I marched upstairs and flung myself on my bed. I lay there waiting for dawn. Glancing at the clock now and again, it seemed to take like four hours for the clock to inch forward thirty-two minutes.

Of course, I'd had fantasies that Jack Eversea loved me, couldn't live without me, yada, yada, yada. I think at one point it involved him admitting it to forty million television viewers during an acceptance speech at the Oscars. *Seriously.* I was only human. I mean, the entire time he was here in Butler Cove felt like a dream. A fantasy. Let's face it, a delusion.

But never when I considered the *reality* of him coming back, if he ever would, did I expect him to tell me he was in love with me. *Me.* I huffed into the small pocket of heated space that was under the pillow then flung myself onto my back to get some more air.

I replayed every moment back in my head. Jack wanting to talk to me, looking so tense and . . . nervous as he spoke of me dating Colt. A notion I'd taken a perverse delight in not denying. I guess he *was* nervous, although I'd never seen him that way before. He almost seemed . . . jealous. Then the way he'd suddenly launched himself at me when I mistakenly admitted I wasn't over him . . . like I'd given him the permission he'd been waiting for.

Damn, and I was just like some pilot light that had been left on for seven months, just waiting to be dialed up to full flame. Even now a dull ache thudded low in my belly. Why did he have to be the only one who could do that to me? It wasn't fair.

None of it made sense. If he really felt that strongly about me, why hadn't he contacted me for so long? I hadn't even given him a chance to explain that. I was too busy being shocked at his declaration and telling him to leave me alone. And besides, what could he say that would justify his actions? I would stand by my decision. I had to. I couldn't keep going through this. I had my own life to lead, and I wasn't going to get dragged off course.

Trying to park my unwieldy pickup on Broughton Street in downtown Savannah was a nerve-wracking experience, both for me and the homeless guy sitting under the eaves of the vacant storefront next to me. I normally considered myself pretty adept at handling my truck, but my mind was scattered and tired today.

I finally got the truck situated snugly alongside the curve without incident and climbed out, not bothering to lock up behind me. If someone needed something out of my truck that badly, I'd just as soon not have to pay to get a window fixed.

Heading up the street past the Trustees Theatre with its large old school marquise, I did a double take.

The Princess Bride, One Night Only.

I seriously did not need to start seeing signs pointing to Jack everywhere I went, but there it was in black and white. Shaking my head to dislodge memories of the ridiculous flirting we'd done when we first met, one-upping each other with lines from the movie, I crossed the street.

I'd deliberately parked far away from Colt's office on Bull Street where he worked with a team handling the private banking needs of the high net worth families of Savannah and surrounding areas. I needed time to walk, clear my head and get my game face on. I could also hit Blick, the art supply store, before heading back and not have to lug stuff around town. After lunch with Colt, I also needed to shop for a dress.

The sun shone valiantly through the canopy of live oaks in historic Johnson Square outside Colt's office, creating a crisscross of shadows. I passed the fountain, putting flight to a kit of scrounging pigeons, and found a bench dappled in sunlight where I could text and wait for Colt.

Now that I'd resolutely put the idea of any kind of future

with Jack out of commission, an idea that made my chest ache, I needed to address the situation with Colt one way or another. He'd intimated he wanted to be my date for my art opening at the Westin, and I'd been putting him off. I wished there were more time before the event so I could mourn and come to grips with everything that had just happened with Jack. Then at least, I could give Colt a fair chance. But to be honest, I wanted to go back to being on my own.

I looked up in time to see the tall, well-defined frame of Colt striding across the street in a dark suit, accompanied by an elegant and exotic creature trotting as fast as possible next to him in impossibly high red heels and a gray pencil-skirt and fitted jacket. Her dark hair was swept into an elegant chignon. *Yikes.* I couldn't remove my eyes from her, and I felt instantly dowdy, plain, and unkempt. And really, *really* short.

"Hi, sweetheart." Colt leaned down, and wafting expensive cologne onto me, kissed my cheek. "This is Karina Knowles, she works with me. Karina, this . . . is Keri Ann Butler."

Karina's exotic face with its flawless skin and almond-shaped eyes immediately broke into a smile of beautiful teeth as she stretched out a soft hand to shake mine.

"Wow, you're really stunning," I said, *out loud*, and immediately felt my face flush warm.

Karina tilted her head and laughed delightedly. "Colton. You were right, she's delightful." Her British accent took me by surprise. "Nice to meet you, Keri Ann, I've heard lots of great things about you. And thank you."

"You're British?" I blurted.

"Mmmm, well I was born *here*, grew up there, British father, Indonesian mother, time in London, time in Kuala Lumpur, and now Savannah, Georgia. The quick history."

Wow.

"Karina overheard me talking to you about your big event and offered her input on places to shop, get your hair done, et cetera."

I instinctively brought a hand up to my hair. I hadn't even thought about getting my hair done. Or makeup. I blinked.

"Yes, here," said Karina, handing me a thick business card. "I called and set up your appointments, I hope you don't mind. It's just that I had to pull some strings, they're normally pretty booked up. One for today and also the day of the event to do the styling."

I nodded, like I totally understood. "Uh, thanks. Thank you." Spa appointments were a bit alien to me, Jazz's attempts to keep me groomed notwithstanding. I had a feeling the place Karina was talking about was altogether different than the Korean girls who painted stars on my toes for Fourth of July.

She smiled and reeled off the boutiques I should visit after lunch. When I'd said she was stunning, it was an understatement. Why wasn't Colt dating *her*?

I glanced at Colt, who winked at me. Then we said goodbye to Karina.

As we strolled down the street, I became aware Colt hadn't taken my hand. He'd been holding my hand a lot recently, and the fact that he didn't was unnerving to say the least, even though part of me was relieved. I slid my eyes over to him as we walked. He seemed lost in thought. We reached the small gastro pub, and he held the door open for me as we entered.

Colt removed his suit jacket and rolled up his crisp white sleeves as we sat down. "So, have you seen him again?" he asked over the menu.

"Yes. He told me you guys had quite the chat." I quirked my eyebrow at him, trying to keep the situation light.

Colt rolled his eyes. "Yeah, you could say that. After you left, I apologized for punching him, and he did the same. Look, I know we've only just started dating, so to speak, but I'm not under any illusions that I don't quite . . . do it for you . . . the way he obviously does."

I swallowed, guiltily. "Colt—"

He put a hand up. "It's fine, Keri Ann."

We placed our order with the server.

"It's not like you didn't try," Colt continued after we'd made our choices. "But I care about you, you know that, and if you'd asked me two days ago whether I would stand in his way if he came back, I wouldn't have hesitated. I mean, we all got to see how little he obviously thought about you since he was here last."

I flinched, my chest collapsing into the pit of my stomach.

Colt grabbed my hand that was sliding off the table. "That was before, Keri Ann. Before I spoke to him. Before I saw him look at you. I don't know why the hell he spent the last half a year acting like a douche, but as soon as you were gone, it was like he was different."

"What do you mean?"

"I don't know what I mean. The guy you see out there in the world is not the same guy I spoke to yesterday." He exhaled roughly. "I just know that standing between you two, physically and metaphorically, doesn't feel comfortable at all. I realized no matter what I feel for you, you'll never have those same feelings for me. And to be honest, as much as I care about you, because I seriously do, I can't compete with that."

I sat quietly, listening, letting him hold my hand. Colt was such a good guy. A good-looking, successful, thoughtful guy. Any girl would be lucky to have him. But apparently not me.

He sighed and went on, "I know you're not taken in by what he does for a living. I think, in fact, that's probably the least attractive thing about him for you. That's part of what makes you so different than all the asset-driven women I know."

"Is that the gentleman's way of saying gold-digger?" I laughed. "Don't put me on a pedestal, Colt. I like money and security as much as the next girl."

He smiled, ruefully. "It's not about just money. It's the props they get from gossiping with their friends about how hot their boyfriend is, how successful he is, the latest designer purse *he* bought for them. That's why I call it asset-driven. It's all about collecting trophies that make them look good and feel good."

I frowned at him with a bemused smile. "Feeling sorry for yourself, Mr. Bigshot? You realize this is how men have been since the beginning of time? Have to have the hottest girl-friend, flashiest car, best job, blah, blah, blah. The eternal pissing contest, if you will."

Colt smirked. "You're totally right. As always. Anyway, I'm not feeling sorry for myself. I do have the flashiest car and best job out of all our peers as far as I know. I'm just irritated that I have to give up the hottest girl."

My cheeks flushed warm, and I kicked his shin under the table.

"Ow! Jeez! I just gave you a compliment, and that's the thanks I get."

Our server arrived with our food so I leaned back and folded my arms.

"Sorry," I said with contrition. "And I'm not the hottest girl—"

"Whatever."

"I'm not, and you know it."

"And that right there, Keri Ann, is what makes you completely fucking breathtaking. No wonder you had Jack Eversea falling for you."

I paused with a fry halfway to my lips and winked to cover my reaction. "Damn, with that mouth, you should be dropping panties all over Savannah."

"Well, I was. And I plan to get back to it, now that you won't have me."

"I have no doubt." I laughed. I was beyond relieved Colt and I managed to move out of the date zone with minimal damage to pride and ego. "Are you going to eat those fries?"

"You've already stolen five, what's a few more? Go ahead." He leaned back and patted his flat waist through his shirt. "Gotta keep trim now that I'm on the scene again."

"I doubt you'll have to wait long. So about the party at the Westin. Do you still want to go, or would you prefer to bring a date? I can have Joey take me."

"What? You mean Mr. Eversea won't be escorting you? Can you imagine how much more publicity your exhibit will get if he shows up?"

"Frankly, I can't think of anything worse." I shuddered, imagining the circus it could become. "But he won't be going, he doesn't know about it. And anyway, I told him to stay away from me."

"First of all, he does know about it, because I told him. And secondly, what on earth makes you think he'll stay away from you?"

"Colt, I can't believe you told him. What the hell else did you guys talk about?"

"Hmm . . . let me think . . . we covered me threatening

him, him threatening me, your event obviously, the fact that I thought he'd been staring too hard at your wet t-shirt. He accused me of the same, whereupon I couldn't resist joking that it was 'headlight weather' and he literally flinched. I could tell I was getting to him, so, of course, I told him I was dating you now and that you made little kitten sounds when you were in bed with me, just to piss him off further, which worked because he went white as a sheet. That's when I knew I should probably bow out. Not that I told *him* that. A bit of healthy competition works wonders, don't you think?"

CHAPTER FOURTEEN

Three and a half hours later, I was late for work, stressed, and shell-shocked. I jabbed at my phone as I drove past the billboard reminding me that texting and driving was illegal in Georgia. I made it across the state line, marked not just by the Savannah River but also a strip club and a farm stand selling overpriced peaches to lost tourists, and pressed 'send.'

Me: Jazz, call me! I'm traumatized.

She didn't call me, of course. I was defeated in the dress department even after three stores and seven dresses. And the beauty appointment was way out of my comfort zone. I felt like a fluffed poodle.

I made it back to Butler Cove in record time and went straight to the Grill, peeling into the parking lot with a spray of bleached oyster shells. I slunk through the back door of the kitchen.

Hector, eyes wide, was already shaking his head and tutting at me. "Hees here." He jerked a thumb over his shoulder, looking hectic.

Dammit! Paulie, the owner, was notoriously absent off-season. Of course he would show up the one day I was late.

And I was wearing the light pink maxi dress I'd put on to have lunch with Colt instead of what I was supposed to wear, which was shorts and running shoes.

Hector cocked a bemused eyebrow as he took in my appearance.

"Don't you dare say a word," I warned him.

Jazz chose that moment to call me.

I regretfully silenced the phone and let it roll to voicemail as I stuffed my bag onto the top shelf of the storeroom. I glanced at my reflection and saw the trial makeup job I was wearing. At least it covered how tired I was. They'd done me over like I was getting married. I had highlights and soft waves in my normally unruly hair. I guessed it was pretty, but I pulled it all into a pony.

I was about to head past Hector and go apologize to Paulie for being late, when he took my shoulders. He set me at arm's length, gave me a long look with his dark brown eyes, and then sighed.

"It's okay, Hector."

His eyes crinkled up. "*Bueno*," was all he said, and he pulled me into a big hug then pushed me toward the swing door, shaking his head, and making the sign of the cross over his chest.

Okay, weird. I frowned but headed out. Some days I felt like his daughter.

Oh. I stopped dead upon exiting the kitchen.

Oh.

He's here.

The place was electrified. Paulie, his back to me at the bar, his gray hair tied back on his neck, was roaring with laughter at something Devon Brown or Jack Eversea said to him from where they sat across the polished wood.

My blood pooled at my feet.

There were no ball caps and hoodies tonight. Jack was in a dark gray t-shirt snug across his muscled chest, his hair flopped down over his brow. His green eyes, set into the angular planes of his face, were creased with laughter. Why, oh why, did he have to get sexier every time I saw him?

The room was abuzz around them.

The mom of a family of four, holding a pen, tapped Jack on his shoulder.

He turned toward her, his smile warm and open, and signed her paper with his beautiful long fingered hands. Then he hopped off his stool as she shoved her smartphone at her nonplussed husband and practically climbed into Jack's arms for a picture.

I clenched my jaw.

Jack shook hands with the husband, grinning, clapping him on the shoulder. *No hard feelings.*

Trying to reconcile the shattered looking Jack from my kitchen in the early hours of this morning with the smiling, carefree, *well-rested*, made-for-movies looking one in front of me, I stood staring like an idiot. Jack turned to sit back down, and his emerald eyes found mine and locked onto them like he knew I'd been there all along.

My pulse seemed to take one wild beat, and then stop in my throat.

His gaze glided down my dress and back up to my face. Then his lids flickered down half-mast, and he slid his eyes lazily away from me, dragging my heart along for the ride.

"There she is! Keri Ann." Paulie's voice shocked me into

action like a defibrillator. "Look who we've got in tonight. These boys have got this place jumpin'."

Paulie slapped his hand on the bar. "Glad you could make it. *Finally*." He raised his bushy white eyebrows as I headed toward him. "What are you wearing?"

"Sorry, Paulie. I was at an appointment in Savannah that . . . ran long." I deliberately didn't answer his embarrassing question.

Out of the corner of my eye, I saw Jack's hand tense imperceptibly around his drink. *Good.* I hoped he thought I was in Savannah with Colt. And I hoped I was glowing. How dare he come in to the Snapper Grill when I'd asked him to leave me alone? And what was that look he just gave me? That wasn't playing fair.

"No matter, sweetheart, you're here now. Brenda's been doin' a great job, but if it keeps up like this with word gettin' out about these two being here, it'll be a flat-out sprint within the hour."

"Sorry, Paulie," Devon shrugged. "We can always pitch in, if you need it. I mix a mean drink."

"Ha!" Paulie hooted loudly. "I may hold you to it, boy! But I've got two more guys coming in to help in the kitchen so we should be good."

"I'll go check in with Brenda and help her with tables tonight, if that's okay, so you can entertain our esteemed guests at the bar," I offered Paulie, willingly giving up bar duty. I then turned to Devon, pointedly ignoring Jack. "Good to see you again, Devon."

He raised two fingers to his brow, saluting me. "You too, Keri Ann. You're looking beautiful this evening. Did you have a date today or something?" he asked in a tone I just knew jabbed Jack on purpose.

My skin flushed warm. "Or something," I managed, but joined his game by cocking my eyebrow and adding a world of innuendo to my simple answer.

"Fuck you, Devon," I heard Jack hiss at his friend, though his lips barely moved.

Devon smiled and winked at me.

I found Brenda and took over half of her tables. As predicted, the evening was long and busy as word got out about our celebrity guests. It was probably the most exciting thing to happen to Butler Cove residents since they built a new bridge onto the island.

But I found it increasingly confusing.

I thought Jack didn't like people knowing where he was. If he felt like Butler Cove was a place he could escape to, why was he letting the whole world know where he was?

Unless he wasn't planning on staying very long.

My chest felt lined with lead. He'd told Colt he was staying *indefinitely*, but that was before I told him to leave me alone. I wanted that, right?

I waffled between being upset he'd blatantly ignored my request, and by extension, admitting he didn't mean what he'd told me, and being steeped in disappointment that this clearly meant he was leaving Butler Cove and *leaving me alone*.

Over the course of the evening, he must have had his picture taken with at least thirty people. Women.

I tried not to pay attention, but the weight of Jack's presence in the room was hard to ignore. The tension needled across my skin and deep into my belly, getting stronger by the second. I was running on adrenaline, counting the seconds until I could escape.

Clearly having heard the buzz, a group of female students

from *USC Beaufort* came in half an hour before closing in a gaggle of long tanned limbs, lip gloss, and short skirts. I recognized one of them as a friend of Jazz's. We exchanged a few pleasantries as I pointed out where they could sit and tried not to roll my eyes at Brenda.

There may have even been glitter. *Seriously.*

As they passed the bar, they invited Jack and Devon to join them in their booth.

Which the guys did.

What the hell?

I let out a long breath and asked Brenda to handle their drink orders. Heading to the kitchen, I smacked the door open with my palm.

The girls were giggly and ridiculous as they fawned all over Jack and Devon for the next interminably long time. Jazz's friend, her name was Ashley, I remembered now, had gorgeous long blonde hair, and she slung her arm around Jack's shoulder as she snuggled up to him.

"Quite a spectacle, isn't it?" Brenda said next to me sometime later.

I realized I was staring and quickly looked away. "Yep, unreal."

"Rumor has it you two had a thing," Brenda said curiously. "I didn't even know he'd been to Butler Cove before, but I guess it makes sense with his friend having a place here. Is it true?"

I sighed. What did it hurt to tell anyone now? "Yeah. Had."

"Wow." Brenda looked impressed. "Not that I didn't think you could attract a hottie like that . . . but I didn't expect you to be attracted to someone with that kind of career."

I let out a half chuckle with none of the amusement one

would expect. "Me neither, but . . ." I looked over at Jack who moved his mouth over to Ashley's ear. *What the hell?* I couldn't handle this. Watching him was making my insides churn. I knew what she was probably feeling right now—a little shivery with hormones racing up and down her body. "I thought for a while he was a different person. Anyway," I tried brightly, "looks like he's moving on though, huh?"

To see him tête-a-tête like that was an eerily familiar sight from the tabloids over the last few months. My skin heated. What was it with him and blondes?

"Honey, if you only knew the way his eyes track you all over this restaurant . . ." Brenda sighed. "You may have moved on, but this boy, this famous, gorgeous man who can have anyone, anywhere with a crook of his finger, is all about *you.*"

Swallowing, I involuntarily flicked my eyes back to Jack, whose eyes were indeed on me. Yes, I'd felt them all night long. I wished there was some way to translate what was going on in his head. Why were his eyes saying one thing, and his actions another? It was dizzying, and I hated it. Thank goodness the night was almost done.

Soon, the rest of the restaurant had cleared out, and it was just Jack's table left. Sheriff Graves had stopped by to make sure people weren't loitering outside the entrance and, as it was well past closing, to nudge Paulie to close up.

Blonde Ashley picked up her phone and did a selfie of her and Jack, unaware he wasn't looking at her camera, but at me. *Still.* I was beginning to feel a little like prey on the forest floor at night.

"Case in point," said Brenda as we passed by each other again. "Do you think you could leave some available men around for the rest of us?"

I nodded but was unable to look away from Jack. His eyes looked black from here. If he'd been pretending *not* to track my every move earlier, he wasn't hiding it any more.

"Colton Graves *is* available," I answered Brenda. "We broke up today. If we were even technically dating."

Jack's eyes flicked to my mouth as I spoke. There was no way he could lip read from there. And frankly it felt like he was touching my lips not reading them. I licked them without thinking, and his gaze narrowed.

"Good to know, good to know," murmured Brenda next to me. "I'll . . . um . . . leave you to molest each other with your eyes then."

Her words registered. Pulling my gaze from Jack's was like trying to break a piece of saltwater taffy. I shook my head and headed to the bar. "Paulie, how soon do you think we can get these folks out of here so we can lock up?"

"I don't think the guys are gonna make a clean getaway. If they want to ditch these girls, I'll need you to take 'em out the back and give 'em a ride home, okay?"

"What? No, Brenda can do that," I said, panicking.

Brenda passed by again, her hands full of plates. "Sorry, hon, I could kick myself, but I walked. No-can-do."

"Paulie," I pleaded, grasping at straws. "If they walked here, they can walk home. Can't they? Or *you* take them, I'll lock up. And maybe they don't want to ditch those girls."

"I really 'preciate that, Keri Ann, and you know I trust you with locking up, but I want to make sure those girls go on home and safely. I don't want none of them hanging around here and causing trouble when they realize them boys've gone. 'Sides, the guys already asked me for help in leavin'. We need to give 'em a quick getaway, not send 'em home on foot so they can be followed."

A loud cackle stood out from the round of laughter at the table.

Paulie lifted a hand and signaled to Devon, who nodded at Jack, and they both excused themselves from the table.

I tensed.

"Aw!" said the girl on Ashley's other side. "You guys gotta go to the restroom in pairs? I thought only us gals did that?"

Devon just laughed. "Nah, Jack's gotta go, I'm just going to see Paulie about us maybe staying here with you ladies a little longer." Clearly, he was a practiced hand at extracting himself from these situations.

I exhaled a resigned breath and headed to the kitchen before Jack could catch my eye again. I was about to be alone in a confined space with him, I didn't need to get any more psyched out. I knew I was beaten. The sooner we got this over with, the better.

I grabbed my bag, and saying a quick goodbye to Hector and the other guys in the kitchen, jogged out the back door into the cool spring night to get my truck. It roared to life, and I did a quick turn around and brought it to idle with the passenger side lined up to the door I'd just exited. One row, three people. Someone was going to be extremely close to me.

I rolled down my window and breathed the sea air, tainted with restaurant refuse, deep into my lungs. Then I closed my eyes and counted slowly, trying to bring my pulse back to some sort of resting rate, and waited.

CHAPTER FIFTEEN

$\mathcal{D}$evon came out the back door of the restaurant first and ducked to take a quick look inside the truck. Making sure it was me, I guess. He winked, like he was in on some huge secret, then opened the door, stepping aside so Jack could enter first. He hesitated for a split-second before climbing in.

I turned my face and looked stoically out the dark windshield in front of me, as if every cell of my body and senses weren't attuned to Jack settling his tall frame inches away from where my thigh rested on the seat. My knuckles turned paler on the steering wheel. My skin actually felt hotter on that side of my body.

"Thanks, Keri Ann," Devon said as he got in and slammed the door closed, causing a breeze, laced with Jack, to wash over me.

God.

I threw the truck in gear and pulled out of the parking lot onto the dark street, the headlights sweeping over the palmettos lining the sidewalk.

Closer To The Edge by Thirty Seconds to Mars came on the truck radio.

"No problem," I croaked. I was weak at the moment. I was tired, and emotionally spent, and totally on edge. And worse? I was aroused. I had been all evening. For some reason, my body hadn't gotten the memo that Jack was not to be involved with me in any way. I'd managed to find the strength that morning to push him away, even as my body had been responding. Responding to the memory of how it felt to be with him, which was far more potent now that it was a real memory, than when it had been just a concept so many months ago. God, I wanted to shut my mind down, but I needed it to keep my wits about me.

Shifting in my seat, I turned down the road to Devon's house.

Jack took a deep breath beside me and leaned his head back against the seat. His hands dropped together between his jean-clad thighs, causing them to spread slightly and bump against my knee.

I jerked and ground my teeth.

"Sorry," Jack murmured and pulled his leg away again.

I flicked my eyes over to his closed ones and didn't miss the small quirk of his dimple.

Devon was looking at me from across Jack, all innocence, with his brows cinched up and arms folded.

"So, how long are you in town, Devon?" I asked, my voice steady and conversational.

He smiled. "For a while, actually. I'm producing a movie in Savannah that Jack will be starring in, so this should be home for a while."

My heart thudded. I glanced at Jack then back at the road. "That's great. Good for you. Both." So he came back for a movie, not for me. *Of-freaking-course, Keri Ann.* Seriously, I could be a dumbass sometimes.

And why should that bother me, when I didn't want anything to do with Jack? I glanced back at Devon, ignoring Jack's eyes on me. "Gosh, well, if that means scenes like tonight are going to become the norm, you better find some groupies to take your drunk asses home. 'Cos I'm not doing it."

Devon snorted with laughter. "Monica would have my hide."

"We're not drunk," was all Jack said quietly.

I pulled into Devon's driveway, shifting the gearstick into park, and turning down the music. Jared Leto was singing about a moment he would never forget. Instantly, I was hit with a wave of longing. Longing to go back to the beginning with Jack.

Devon thanked me and opened the door. He climbed out, and after a nod at his cohort, closed it behind him.

I whipped my eyes to face Jack. "What the . . ." My words trailed off as Jack leaned in toward me, his scent, his Jack scent that I remembered so well . . . pine . . . soapy . . . clean, surrounded me.

My pulse raced.

The truck's headlights reflected off the white house in front of us, slicing across his eyes, making them glow. A deep green forest floor, sucking me in.

"Jack—"

Our air mingled. Mine were quick shallow breaths un-synched with my starving need for oxygen and reality.

"You think I'm only back because of the movie in Savannah, don't you?"

I licked my lips nervously, and nodded.

Jack's eyes followed the movement.

"I begged," he whispered. "I pleaded, and I sold a little

more of my soul to make it happen." His mouth tilted up into a grimace.

"I don't understand why you'd do that, Jack."

"Yes, you do." He leaned closer, and his arm came up to brace on the driver's side door. "Seeing me whisper in that girl's ear tonight bothered you, didn't it?"

"No," I managed.

"Liar. Do you want to know what I was telling her?"

I shook my head. "No, definitely not."

The truck suddenly went still and silent as he turned the ignition off, then he shifted his body closer, sharing my air and not leaving enough for me. His hand went around the steering column and flicked the headlights off.

We were plunged into darkness.

I swallowed. It was a deafening sound. Every other sense went into high alert. Closing my eyes, there was no point in keeping them open, I felt his rough fingers skate up the column of my neck, setting my nerve endings ablaze. His lips were close, close enough to taste again, if I just leaned forward a little. I resisted.

My mouth watered.

Fingers danced over my cheekbone then slid behind my head. I felt the gentle tug of my ponytail being pulled free, and my hair tumbled down around my ears.

Jack inhaled, breathing me in. "God," he murmured.

I knew I should stop him, stop this, but for a moment I just wanted to . . . *feel* again.

A thumb pad brushed down over the pulse beating wildly in my neck, and I let out a breath that hitched without my consent. I was thirsty for Jack's mouth, but I refused to close the minuscule distance.

"How can you tell me this isn't real?" Jack whispered, his

words caressing my mouth. Then his tongue flicked gently across my lower lip.

Oh God.

A small sound escaped me. I should have stopped him sooner.

"This is as real as it gets, Keri Ann. This is Technicolor, when everything else is black and white. This . . ." His hand trailed down over the exposed skin of my chest then brushed over my dress and the tip of my breast, sending shock waves through me. I arched into his hand without meaning to.

Damn my traitorous self.

His hand didn't stop, but floated down my belly to my thigh, and I tensed, my mouth pressed tight to keep my reactions in, trembling on the edge of a place where my pride would cease to exist.

"This . . ." he continued and began bunching up my dress in his fist and drawing it up my thigh, "what we have . . . is extra-sensory overload . . . where everything else is a silent fucking movie."

I panted out a breath then jammed my jaw shut.

My dress glided up. Heat pooled low in my belly. It was intoxicating. Would anything in my whole life ever feel this way? I'd been numb before he'd touched me and numb since he'd been gone. I wanted to sob with the injustice of it.

How could I not want to be with him and want to be consumed by him at the same time? I wanted to be back on that bed underneath him, the way he'd looked at me as if I was his salvation. His benediction. His release.

But I knew why I didn't want it. I'd lose *myself* in him.

"This," I managed just as his hand released my bunched-up dress and landed hot on my bare upper thigh, sending waves of sensation cascading over my skin, "is just lust."

Grabbing his face between my hands in the pitch dark, I closed the distance and slanted my mouth over his, sliding my tongue into his delicious mouth.

Jack groaned deeply, and his fingers on my thigh dug in.

He tasted so good. So . . . Jack. His face was hard and rough beneath my fingers, his mouth soft as he let me in, kissing me back gently, not responding to my aggression. So I kissed him harder, wanting to punish him for doing this to me. Wanting him to take over for me, make it so it wasn't my fault we were here again. Make it so it was him kissing *me,* and I wasn't *willingly* doing this.

This was so messed up.

His gentleness and his refusal to respond to my fierce need did me in. And made me crazy. I pulled my mouth from his, our erratic breathing reverberating around the interior of the vehicle. I struggled to shut down my body.

He was heavy as I pushed at him in the pitch black, moving him away from me.

Turning in my seat, I flicked the truck lights back on, and the light sloshed over the heated moment like ice water.

"Get out of my truck, Jack."

"What?" His voice was ragged, but I refused to look at him.

"You heard me. Get. Out. I can't do this with you. I won't. How can you even expect me to? How can I even want to?"

Jack blew out a harsh breath and adjusted in his seat. Silence and unspoken words stretched out, wending their way around the truck, sliding into all the available space between us and pressing me back into my seat with their weight.

And then, I heard him move to open the truck door. He paused as the interior light flicked on, and the pressure between us released into the night.

"Tonight, that girl, like all of the girls, the interchangeable, available girls, that girl—"

"Her name is Ashley."

"Whatever. *Ashley* . . . offered to blow me."

I flinched and my stomach dropped. "I don't have time for this, Jack."

"But I told her, very nicely and quietly, so as not to embarrass her in front of her friends, that I had no intention of taking her up on her offer."

"Poor Ashley," I muttered sarcastically. He climbed out, and then leaned back into the cab of the truck, his shoulders hunched and broad, filling the doorway.

His eyes were fierce, bitter, and vulnerable at the same time. "I'm telling you about Ashley to illustrate a point. I'm not just trying to get laid. I can get laid anytime I want. I'm a potential trophy fuck to pretty much every woman I meet." There wasn't even a hint of arrogance in his expression, despite his words.

"Well done, Jack. Very restrained. But seriously, while I appreciate you not rubbing my face in it because I was actually present in the room, what the heck does it matter when the whole world and I have had to see you with the rest of the available women all over the media?" I shrugged my shoulders. "What the hell is *one more*?"

His body left the truck and the sound of gravel sprayed as he kicked at it, his back to me. "Fuck!" he ground out, and clutched both hands to his hair, grabbing fistfuls, his shoulder blades flexing under his t-shirt. He exhaled loudly then turned back to me, his expression pained. "Unlike you," he cleared his throat, "I haven't slept with anyone in seven months."

"What?" My mind reeled. He thought that I . . .? Wait. He hadn't . . .?

"Not since you."

My forehead creased in surprise and confusion.

"Feel free to believe me or not, but you should at least know. And . . ." The muscle in his jaw ticked. "I know what it looked like. For better or worse, I made it look like that on purpose. And I'm sorry. It was fucking dumb. But what you think you saw and what actually happened, or in this case *didn't* happen, are two very different things."

My mind couldn't process the words it heard fast enough to feel either relief or disbelief. I picked one.

"Just like you didn't sleep with Audrey, and yet she was possibly carrying your child?" I looked away. How could I possibly believe him at face value?

"Dammit. Will you let me explain? Or are you scared that when you know the truth, no matter how brutal, you'll have no reasons to hide behind any more?"

My eyes cut to his and his implored me to hear him. And I saw he was surprised by his own question. And nervous of my answer.

"Yes," I admitted in a whisper.

His eyes widened fractionally.

"Please, Jack. Maybe I will believe you and maybe I will forgive you, but . . ."

"But what?"

I swallowed and faced my truth. "What if I *still* don't want to be a part of your life? I have plans and direction and . . . and . . . for the first time I can see a future. *My* future." I paused, struggling to find the right words. "I'm scared you'll swallow me whole."

My admission sliced into the air between us like a guillotine.

"Well." His brow creased and his throat bobbed. His eyes looked desolate. "That's a different story, isn't it?"

CHAPTER SIXTEEN

𝒥 was physically and emotionally drained from my day and from kicking Jack out of my truck . . . and my life . . . *again*. As soon as I got to my bed, I went down like a sack of cement.

I came to with bright sunlight filtering through my window. Casting a fumbling hand out, I grasped my phone off the nightstand to see it was about ten. I was due at the Grill within an hour. I'd also missed another call from Jazz.

Images and emotions from the night before filtered into my mind, wreaking havoc with the sense of peace I should have had after sleeping nine hours straight. Jack's revelation that he hadn't been with any of those girls floored me. But I wasn't sure whether to believe him or if it truly made a difference.

I trudged downstairs to put the coffee on, then came back upstairs to shower. My hair was looking surprisingly pretty with the highlights the salon had put in yesterday. I tied it up out of the way and showered and changed for work. Trying to keep my thoughts from straying to Jack was almost impossible. I felt weird and down about the way things were between us. I'd asked him to stay away, and he hadn't. I wasn't necessarily mad at him for it. It was disquieting to discover I was actually relieved to know he'd ignored my request. But now I'd shut him out *again*. Part of me felt justified. I knew all my reasons for doing so. Then the other part of me, a deep down in my heart part of me, felt heavy and conflicted.

There was a mad lunch rush at the Grill. Residents wouldn't admit it, but I knew they were hoping to catch their own sighting of Devon and Jack. It left me on edge and harassed. I knew they probably wouldn't saunter back in, but the mere possibility they could, brought my anxiety level to defcon five.

At three o'clock, when Jazz walked in all tanned, her blonde hair tousled in messy air-dried waves, I was so relieved to see her, I didn't even question that she was still supposed to be in Florida. I launched myself at her and hugged her hard.

"Dang, give a lobster a break." She laughed and winced.

"Oh, man, sorry," I said as I noticed the skin on her back was flaming hot under my fingers.

"Fell asleep by the pool yesterday, and stupid Brandon just let me burn." She turned around and showed me her back.

"Ow." I flinched in sympathy at the crimson sight. "So he's stupid Brandon now? And what are you doing here?" It suddenly occurred to me to ask.

She turned back around and sighed as I led her to a seat at the bar. "Yeah, well. I needed a break. And Florida's even hotter than here. Brandon's so sweet most of the time, and he's got the prettiest face, but seriously, he just doesn't think sometimes, ya know? And don't get me started on his decision-making. I'm all modern woman, but I'm craving me some alpha-male right now." She rolled her eyes. "Being with him is like taking care of a child!"

I poured her an Arnold Palmer with sweet and laughed. "And yet, you're the one with the sunburn?"

Jazz stuck out her tongue at me. "Why's it so busy in here? Don't tell me our *celebrity* has been parading around town?"

"How did you guess? He and Devon were here last night causing an uproar, handing out autographs, becoming slap-you-on-the-back best friends with Paulie. It was weird and nauseating."

Jazz choked on her tea, her eyes wide. "Wow, he seriously came out in public?" Then her brow furrowed. "While you were working? How was he toward you? My God, were you okay?"

And that's why I loved Jazz. She just knew me the way only a best friend could. She knew my comfort levels and exactly what to ask.

"Is that why you sent me that text saying you were trau-matized? I tried to call you back, by the way."

"I know. And no, I sent that before I even got here to face that. I was traumatized from failed dress shopping and weird beauty appointment experiences in Savannah after a lunch with Colt where he basically ended our non-relationship."

Jazz's eyes widened again, and her mouth wrapped around her straw.

I snorted. "If I'd known how *actually* traumatizing the rest of the evening was going to be, I wouldn't have blown through that word so flippantly. Oh and your friend Ashley was here, promising sexual favors to Jack as she practically licked his ear." She probably did actually lick it. *God*. I shuddered.

"Holy shit," Jazz hissed. "That girl's an STD waiting to happen, if it hasn't already. Trust me. Tell me nothing happened there." Jazz grabbed my hand and squeezed.

"No, thank God."

"But, he was obviously behaving like an ass right in front of you. I need to hear everything from the beginning."

Jazz waited with me until the end of my shift, and then we made our way to my house. I scrounged out a tin of Mrs. Weaton's leftover pecan pie and warmed it on two plates in the microwave.

"God, boys can be so dumb sometimes," Jazz offered as I described everything that had taken place since our middle of the night phone call where I'd told her Jack was back. "If he wasn't doing anything with those girls in England, why did he re-create that whole scene by hanging out with Ashley and her friends?"

"I know, right?" I shook my head and added more ice cream to my pie. "Do you think he really didn't sleep with anyone since he last saw me?" I asked Jazz.

"Damn, maybe."

"But there's tons he could have done without having to do the . . . actual deed," I muttered morosely, thinking of Ashley's offer to him last night.

"True," said Jazz, and then her eyes went round, her mouth stretching wide and downturned in a parody of worry. "My God, maybe you have a magic *vajayjay*, and you've . . . *ruined* him," she whispered the last part in mock horror.

I choked on my mouthful.

Jazz went on dramatically, "Like, *forever*. Goodness, the poor guy must be desperate. Can you imagine?"

Jazz could hardly make it through the last word of her sentence because we both got a fit of giggles.

"Or maybe he just developed erectile dysfunction."

"In which case you probably don't want him anyway."

The back screen door banged, interrupting our mirth. "It's nothing to laugh at, girls." Joey's voice came from behind us, making us jump. "It's a real medical condition. And it sure is good to know that you all don't grow up much while I'm away."

"Joey!" I leapt up to hug him. "What are you doing home?"

"Thought I'd surprise my best girl," he said, putting his duffle bag down and catching me. He looked handsome in jeans and a blue button down. Brown leather cowboy boots peeked out at his ankles. His blond hair was longer and shaggier than usual.

"And make sure I wasn't jumping into Jack's arms?"

"And that." He hugged me back. "Jazz," he acknowledged her over my head. "Anyway, I just have studying to do for the next few days, but I can do it here as well as there."

"Jazz just got back from Florida with Brandon," I added for her sake.

"Hey, Joey," Jazz chirped breezily and cleared her throat. "Well, we were just discussing Jack, so since he has that 'medical condition,' Keri Ann is probably safe."

"And how might you all *know* that he has this condition?" Joey asked.

"We're *surmising*. Despite all evidence to the contrary, apparently he's been celibate since the last time he saw your sister."

Joey snorted with disbelief. "Yeah, right."

"Well, it's either that or you may have to face that Jack's

going after Keri Ann for real." Jazz's proclamation sobered us all. "Sometimes, people just know what they want," she added, and I knew she just couldn't help herself around Joey.

I swallowed.

"Or he's *lying*," said Joey. "You girls are way too trusting of men. Guys often just want one thing and will say anything to get it."

"Us girls are too trusting? Or girls in general?" Jazz snapped at Joey. "And guys in general say anything to get it, or guys like you?"

Whoa.

Jazz slumped back against her kitchen chair then hissed a breath through her teeth as her burned back made contact. "Ow."

Joey stepped forward and caught himself. "What's the matter?"

I smirked.

"I got burned, it's nothing." Jazz winced.

Joey went around behind her. "Shit, that's not good. When did this happen?"

"Yesterday afternoon. I fell asleep in the sun," Jazz muttered. "It's fine really. The Lidocaine I sprayed on earlier before the drive up must be wearing off."

"What the hell? Wasn't your . . . wasn't Bradford, or whatever, supposed to be with you?" I knew full well he knew the name of Jazz's boyfriend.

"Brandon!" Jazz and I yelled. And looked at each other. "Of the chocolate-brown eyes!" we chorused and busted out laughing again.

"Have you all been drinking?" Joey asked.

Still chuckling, I went to the pantry cupboard and pulled the first-aid basket down. I rummaged around and found more Lidocaine and some Soothing Aloe. "Catch," I called to Joey and tossed the items at him.

Joey caught them, flawlessly, one after the other. "I'm not—"

"He's not—"

"Yep, you are. I'm going to shower the Grill off me. Then let's order pizza and watch a movie."

I headed for the stairs and heard Jazz murmur as if bored, "Fine, let's see what you've got, *Doctor* Butler."

"You did always make me want to *play* Doctor, Miss Fraser," Joey returned, and I almost tripped on the stairs in surprise. It was usually Jazz teasing and trying to goad him, and I'd never heard him playing along. I'd have given anything to see Jazz's face right then. Perhaps Colt was right, a bit of healthy competition did work wonders.

CHAPTER SEVENTEEN

The first thing that struck me upon waking the next morning was that I'd made a mistake with Jack. I knew it down to the depths of my Carolina girl soul. The same way I knew it was time to look for sea turtle nests without checking the calendar.

Struggling to pull myself from the arms of slumber, as it seduced me with the promise of going back to emotion-less oblivion, sounds and smells from downstairs penetrated my consciousness. Coffee, bacon, and something sweet promised me a reward for facing these complicated emotions.

How could I possibly feel guilt at hurting Jack after what he put me through? But there it was clear as day. I felt guilt when I thought back to his expression, his beautiful eyes that looked so shattered. Twice since he'd come back only days ago, I'd taken his declarations and carelessly thrown them back in his face. God, but I was right to do it. Right to protect myself. What if I gave him a chance and ended up back where I'd been months ago?

And seriously, that whole stunt with Devon and him hanging out at the Grill signing autographs . . . was that what my future looked like? Being in the spotlight was hard enough with my art, imagine being photographed as Jack Eversea's girlfriend? Being judged as to whether I was good enough for him, what I had that others didn't? I shuddered. No, thank you.

And then when we fell apart again, I'd get pitying looks from the whole world, not just those who knew the first time. Of course it wouldn't last, they'd say. *She wasn't cut out for his life. What did he see in her anyway?*

Abruptly, I sat up. *Dammit.*

Breakfast smelled really good. I quickly dressed in cargo pants and a lightweight black tee and trotted downstairs.

Mrs. Weaton, my elderly tenant, who I might add had her own kitchen in her own cottage, was bustling about *my* kitchen clucking and muttering under her breath. She caught sight of me, and her lined face creased up in a smile. "Hi, love!" she crowed and gave me a quick one-armed squeeze as she held the spatula in the other.

I looked over and saw Joey at the kitchen table bent over a laptop and papers, deep in concentration.

"Uh, hi." I hugged her back, her lavender scent comforting me, and smiled at her eccentric makeup. "Not that I don't love being woken with the smell of coffee and bacon, but what are you doing here?"

"Aw, sugar, you just sit your cute bee-hind down on that there seat, and I'll tell you all about it. First grab yourself a coffee." She motioned to the pot.

"Morning, Joey," I greeted.

"Morning," he mumbled but didn't look up. The movie last night had been awkwardly tense between my brother and Jazz. Eventually, Jazz had begged tiredness from her drive and said goodnight. Joey watched her leaving, a brooding expression on his face, his thumb brushing his bottom lip over and over.

I'd refrained from saying a word.

I headed to the coffee. There was a large white envelope with Keri Ann scrawled on the front of it propped up against the sugar bowl. "What's this?" I asked Mrs. Weaton, picking it up.

"Oh, it's just a letter from Jack."

"What?" The smile slid off my face.

"What?" asked Joey, his head snapping up.

I frowned at him.

"I know," Mrs. Weaton crowed. "Had to give the boy an envelope! You young people should all have your own stationery. How can you possibly correspond when you don't own even an envelope?"

"How . . . when . . .?" I didn't know what to ask first.

"Yesterday evening. I was back a bit late from my Wednesday afternoon Canasta. So I told him to leave it on the porch. He saw Joey and Jazzy's car there so didn't want to disturb you. Then when I woke up this morning and saw you hadn't taken it inside, I thought I'd bring it in for you."

She transferred the bacon out onto an old newspaper, then she sighed and opened the oven, bathing the kitchen in a hot waft of cinnamon and treacle. "That boy."

My stomach growled, drowning out the thumping of my heart, as I fingered the envelope nervously. I finished making my coffee then carried it over to the table. "What about him?"

"Well, dear. It's obvious how he feels about you. I could tell right from the beginning. And I'm just over here to make sure you read his letter and hear what he has to say for himself."

"Please," snorted Joey. "I'd say he's had his chance to tell Keri Ann how he feels, and I think we all got the message loud and clear last time."

My throat closed.

"Sorry," Joey said quickly. "But you're not seriously going to read it, are you?"

Mrs. Weaton carried a plate of bacon and *Heart Attack Cake,* which was like a pound cake that was twice baked with butter, syrup, local pecans, and cinnamon, and plopped everything on the table in front of Joey and me. The breakfast of champions.

I slid the letter to the side and helped myself to the offerings. "Since when were you on *his* side?" I asked Mrs. Weaton, deciding to pretend Joey wasn't there. "You do remember how miserable I was, right?" I thought I may as well throw Joey a bone.

"Sweetie. At my age you gather a wisdom about life and about love. You get to see your mistakes and regrets in all their *nekkid* glory. And it ain't pretty." She huffed. "I can promise you this—you'll wish you gave him a second chance. That boy is in love. He may not even realize it yet, but when he does, I don't believe there is anything he wouldn't do for you. You don't just toss that away when it comes around. It may not ever come again."

Joey had nothing to offer, for once. He got up and left the kitchen.

I bit into the delicious cake, but at Mrs. Weaton's words, its decadence got lost on me.

"Well, he told me he is. In love with me," I said, softly, lest Joey still be in earshot. "But I told him if he meant it, he would leave me alone. And he sure didn't do that. He showed up at work night before last." I shook my head. "How can he possibly be in love with me? He hardly knows me!" I dropped the fork back on my plate with a clang and pushed it away. *How dare he just come back here and tip my life upside down again?*

I lunged for the letter, intent on ripping it to shreds in my irritation. And fear. I *was* scared it would change my mind.

Mrs. Weaton surprised me by whipping it off the table with her bony and liver-spotted hand before my fingers had landed. "No, you don't!"

"Damn. You're fast!" I said, shocked, as we looked at each other wide-eyed. Then I snorted, and we both erupted into laughter.

"Well, that was some welcome comic relief, it was beginning to get rather maudlin around here." Mrs. Weaton sniffed in mock disapproval.

"Sorry," I offered. "I wouldn't really have ripped it up. I guess I'm still so mad at him. How could he be gone for so long without a word if he really feels the way he says he does? And truly? What the hell sorry kind of a relationship am *I* going to have with a movie-star?"

"Well, have you asked him?"

"No," I said, shaking my head. "I mean, I meant to, or at least, we've tried to talk, but . . . I wouldn't listen."

I tried to piece together all the snippets of his explanations I remembered. "He said . . ." I paused, wondering how much to share. "He said he had to stay away to protect me, and he said he hasn't . . . ahem . . . you know." My cheeks heated as I cleared my throat. "Since me."

"I should hope not!" she said, looking incensed. "But I know how you young ones are these days. I suppose that *is* something. Well," she continued, "I'm not saying you forgive him right away, or even believe everything he says, but, honey, you at least need to get all the facts." She slid the letter over to me. "You don't want any regrets over this. Trust me, I know. Now, eat. Then, go read."

I took a big gulp of coffee and chewed my way through

four pieces of bacon and half the cake slice. It really was deliciously vile. When I was done, I hugged Mrs. Weaton and went up to the attic.

I sought out my little reading nook I'd created as a young girl. Ripping open the large envelope, I expected to find a letter. Albeit a long one based on the thickness of the envelope. Instead, I pulled out a folded sheaf of white pages tied with an aged and faded red string. The pages had clearly been torn from a lined book and were filled with Jack's scrawl that I recognized from the grocery lists he used to leave.

As I sank down onto the old mattress and pillows, my heart thudded heavily. The pages were dated. It really was a journal or diary of sorts. Why on earth would he share his private thoughts with me? I sifted through the pages dating from January through to last month. I began seeing snatches of my name, and I quickly folded the pages back up and held them against my chest, exhaling a long breath. Did I really want to do this?

Despite saying I didn't need to know, I was desperate to understand what had happened when Jack left and why he hadn't come back. It was obvious now too, after two failed attempts at speaking in person, that it was impossible to be around him long enough to hear him out before the fight or flight response I was so damn good at kicked in. And he'd obviously realized it before I had and known this might be the only way to reach me. And the only way I might believe he wasn't just spinning me a line.

God. It was real.

He was real.

This was real.

I unfolded the pages and started reading.

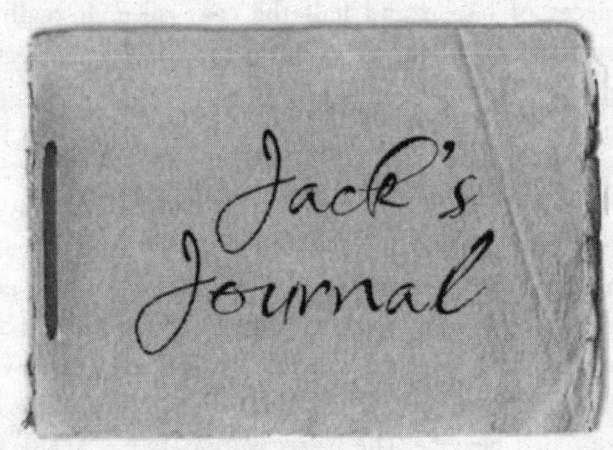

Iver Heath, Buckinghamshire, England
January 10th

I can't believe I'm back here. In England. I'm fucking freezing. The air is white, and wet, and thick with tiny, icy droplets. The green everywhere I look is so deep and dark, I feel like no other colors exist.

"The better part of valor is discretion"
~William Shakespeare

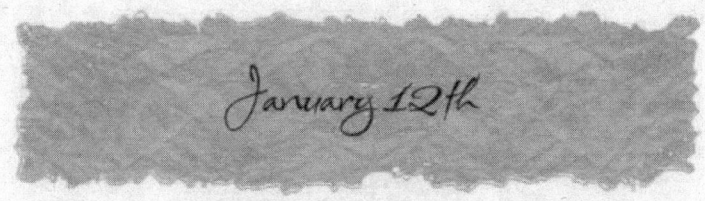

January 12th

My mum used to give me blank journals when I was younger to help me "sort things through" she'd say. "Put it on paper if you can't talk, and get it out of your head so it doesn't fester." That was how she'd found out about the drugs when I was sixteen. Getting me to write everything down was a smart move on her part.

Of course, I went to see Mum as soon as I arrived. I needed to apologize for not coming home when I'd been in London with Audrey. Of course she forgave me. She always does. I went to bed in her and Jeff's guestroom and slept for two days. When I woke up, she gave me a cup of tea and this bloody journal. There's nothing like being with a parent to regress you straight back to childhood. "I don't need it," I told her. But here I am already, baring my soul to the pages of a book instead of to the one person who has ever even tempted me to open up.

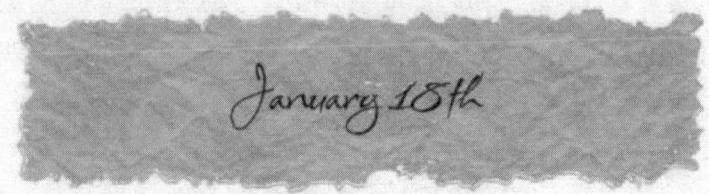

January 18th

Keri Ann.

Just writing her name causes a weird current inside me. Like I shouldn't be writing it.

It's an echo of what I experienced when I was with her. Like she was too good for me to drag into the bullshit that comprises my life. I should have listened to myself.

January 19th

I'm on set. I just met all the crew and the screen-writer today (Alistair) and he's a total prick. I hate to say that about people I hardly know, but he was drunk at the meeting at seven this morning and proceeded to stick his hand up the skirt of this poor runner girl who was delivering coffee to us. He laughed it off and told her she shouldn't wear a skirt to work. Like I said, a prick. If I hadn't promised Peak I'd get this project back on its feet in return for them keeping Audrey quiet and stop her from bringing her scorned woman act down on Keri Ann, I'd walk.

"You cannot find peace by avoiding life."
~Virginia Woolf

January 19th

We're all going into London tomorrow night, the cast and crew. Luckily we're only twenty miles out. It will be my first opportunity to have some pap pictures taken. Duane texted me to say Audrey's been rocking the boat again, complaining the fans still hate her, and I needed to get on with my part of the deal. Maybe I'll ask that runner girl, Suzy, if she'd mind having pictures taken with me. We can ham it up. I'd rather it be someone I can sort of trust, rather than a potential stalker nutcase. Give Audrey what she wants as quickly as possible and hope to God Keri Ann doesn't see it and think I truly don't give a shit.

January 30th

I've been playing the part of the happy go lucky, flirty movie star for so long I've begun to believe it. At least I had started to believe it before I met Keri Ann. I wore the cockiness, the surety, the knowledge that I could, if I wanted to, have anything, and do anything I wanted. Wearing that skin had become easier. I'd buried my true self so deep inside, I'd forgotten him. Or I didn't think he was ever worth digging out. I'm still not sure.

January 30th – Later

The problem is, I love what I do. Today really reminded me of that. I hate the shit, the fakeness, the shallowness, the games you have to play. The little dances you do to stroke egos and keep people happy and show the precise amount of gratitude and humility. But today, we were shooting a particularly emotional scene where my character leaves the love of his life and hurts her . . . crudely and deliberately. It was, or could have been, a brilliant scene, but we've been taking swings at it for days and still haven't nailed it. I've been giving it everything. The scene . . . it was just . . . written wrong. I could see it so clearly. I finally got the balls to say something to the director, Dan, and he let me do it my own way while Alistair, the tool, was doing whatever the fuck it is he does when he disappears off for hours. Why is he even on the set? His consulting period is not supposed to be ongoing.

Okay, rant over.

"There is no exquisite beauty without some strangeness in the proportion."

~Edgar Allan Poe

February 1st

I miss her. How can you miss someone you haven't really spent much time with? I think it must be my soul that misses her then. It's the only explanation.

I'm really getting into the head of my character, this

artist, and I keep wondering what she would say about this. What advice she'd give.

February 13th

Now that we've mostly gotten 'Alistair Molester' removed from the set, things are going brilliantly. I'm really involved, it's been a pretty awesome experience. Dan, the director, is talking about giving me a writing and directing credit. Word's been getting out and we've had some press asking to get past our closed set policy. I've pushed back. I need to keep my contrived off-camera persona separate from what I'm doing here. I've had a few more photo ops with Suzy and some friends of hers. They're cool girls and good for a laugh. And mostly blonde, thank God. It's bad enough when I'm feeling bloody lonely and half a bottle in, that sometimes I think if I met someone with her exact hair color, like burned caramel, it would be easy to just pretend. For a moment. I'm not sure why I don't, actually. I mean at this stage she's got to have moved on. Maybe it didn't even take her this long. Or maybe she's seen the pictures and assumed the worst.

Maybe I should move on, too. I just . . . can't.

Maybe what we had wasn't 'all that.' Maybe I imagined

it all. Maybe she never gave a fucking shit, and I'm the only one who read more into it. I wanted her to see past that ridiculous coat of confidence I wear, but what if she never did? Or what if she did see me, and I wasn't enough for her?

February 20th

Conference call about Dread Pirate Roberts' movie today. It was good to hear Devon's voice on the phone. Some guys from Peak were on the call too, and a money guy from right down the road here in London. I've been pushing for them to set the movie in Savannah. I knew Devon would be on board since he has a place near there that he doesn't get to enjoy enough. I went on about the history of the city and the riverfront docks, etc. We'll see. I just need a way to spend a LOT of time there. No guesses as to why. I called Duane back again after everyone else hung up and practically begged. We'll see what the price is down the line if he goes for it.

February 25th

Fuck, I'm depressed. It's good for my role. The part I'm playing is as morose as they come.

It doesn't even fucking rain here, it's just wet. Like a constant bone-deep chill with the incessant gray drizzle. I keep remembering the rainstorm I trudged through to get to her house, before I . . . shit, I can't write about that right now.

Now that's what you call a raindrop. Just one of those things'll drench you all by itself. They don't mess around with rain there. This shit is just taking the piss.

I found a tiny old copper sea turtle on a leather cord while I was on Portobello Road last week. I seem to be carrying it around in my pocket all the time. Apparently a tattoo on my foot isn't enough. Who knew I was this sentimental? Not me . . .

Oh and it's my birthday. I was given a case of Bushmills. I wonder how long it will take me to get through it? Perhaps I should give it away rather than take a bet on that.

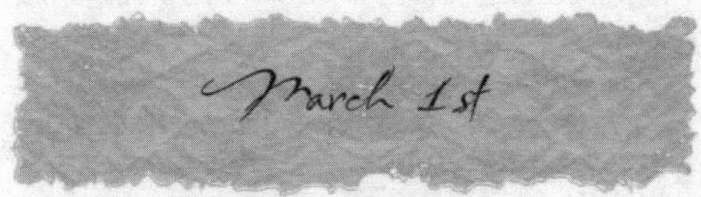

February 28th

Great news. Turns out Savannah has a new studio being built, and a huge film grant ever since Midnight in the Garden of Good and Evil increased tourism to the city by over forty percent. Also, the money guy in London is obsessed with the 'deep south' and was all over the idea. And . . . I'm getting a writing and directing credit on this! Alistair is pissed (pissed off and pissed drunk). Still.

I want to tell her. I want to call her and tell her. I even pulled up her number on my phone and stared at it between takes today.

March 1st

I told my mother about Keri Ann today. It was time we had a really good talk. I've been working on dealing with some of the shit about my father, too. Asking her stuff I just never wanted to know before. She was happy I was talking, said I always bottled stuff up and found it hard to express my own emotions. "You're really good *at it when you are being someone else," she said. "Why can't you just do it for yourself?"*

She called me a man-sized 'message in a bottle.' A love story waiting to happen if the right person found me, and if I would only open up and embrace who I am.

She always was a bit cliché.

March 21st

The movie's wrapping soon. It's been an amazing experience professionally. Personally, not so much. I'm trying not to think of what's next. I've been drinking a lot, more than usual. When we all go out, I just want to get hammered. My few photo opportunities may have led to a bit of a 'party guy' image. In a way, I don't care because it's probably pissing Audrey off, and that satisfies me in a small way. Although why anyone would want to poke at a snake, I have no idea. And of course underneath it all, I'm worried I've probably really killed the last chance I had with Keri Ann because of it. The end of the contract is coming up which means I have no reasons not to go back to Butler Cove. And then there's the movie in Savannah. I'm definitely headed back there either way. And I've done everything I can to ensure she'll never want to see me again.

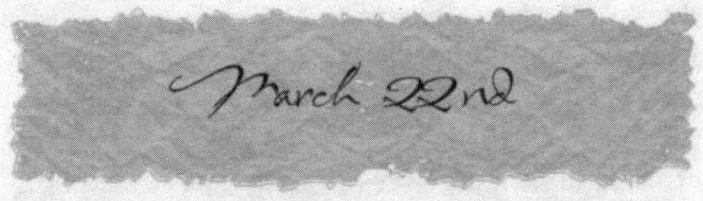

March 22nd

Something almost happened last night with one of Suzy's friends. It didn't get too far. But it was bad. Picture taking bad. And then after . . . well, I thought she knew the deal, but she started kissing me and before I knew it we were in the back of a town car. She smelled really good, like strawberries, and she was soft, and damn but I was drunk. Like really. But all of a sudden her hand was in my pants and she was telling me it was okay, that she knew I was in love with someone else and that she was too, and we should just have fun and no one would know . . . I'd think at that stage I'd be too far gone, but there I was grabbing her hand, squeezing it as I pulled it from me, telling her she couldn't possibly really be in love with someone if she was doing this with me.

I almost want to laugh at myself writing this. The old Jack wouldn't have thought twice, I almost couldn't believe the words coming out of my mouth. It was an out of body experience. That's when I remembered why I liked her smell so much, Keri Ann's hair always smelled like that. Strawberries.

I feel like I may have built this all up in my mind. The chance she ever wants to even see me again is so fucking remote. I realize this makes me sound pathetic. But I really don't give a shit.

March 29th

I'm hung over, and I lost the copper sea turtle, which really pisses me off.

And I'm giving it up. Getting wasted, I mean. I really don't want to end up in another situation in the back of a car. I'm also getting a reputation as a drunk. Not good. I don't want to be lumped in with the Alistairs of the industry. At least I don't molest the crew. We have about a week left of production then I need to figure out what's next. How soon I go back. If I do.

Should I?

March 31st

I can't change what I do. But I can show her who I am. That I'm more than the Jack Eversea the world thinks they know. I'm also going to use whatever assets I have at my disposal to win her back. Even if I have to fight dirty.

CHAPTER EIGHTEEN

$\mathcal{M}$y fingers trembled as I turned the last page. My other hand was pressed to my mouth. I'd just seen real Jack, with all his insecurities and weaknesses. His fragility. It was hard to imagine the man I saw out in the world, in the media, even the one who boldly whispered hot words to me in an effort to seduce me in my truck, was the same person who'd written these words.

I'd spent the last five months thinking I'd been an interesting diversion for him. *He'd* spent the last five months struggling to do the right thing by everyone in his life. *And missing me.*

My skin throbbed and my heart pounded out heavy beats. Reactions cascaded over one another in my head.

I started again at the beginning. Each entry was on a separate page. For all I knew there were horror stories written between, but somehow, I didn't think so.

After reading them through a second time, and having his words still hit every raw nerve I had like I was reading it for the first time, I ran to my room and shoved my feet into my running shoes. Swinging past the bathroom, I wiped my eyes and brushed my teeth, and then took the stairs two at a time, tripping on the last one. "Shit!"

"You okay, love?" called Mrs. Weaton.

"I'm fine," I called and entered the kitchen.

"Well?" She was doing a crossword puzzle at my kitchen table. She'd put on a set of readers and after appraising me a few moments went back to her puzzle.

I pulled up a chair opposite her. "I'm stunned. In a good way."

"Good."

"You don't seem surprised."

"Yes, well, I could see he was upset, and," she peered up at me through her eyeglass rims, "as crazy as it seems, just yesterday before he came by, I had my score book with me that I'd taken to Canasta, and blow me down if a letter didn't fall out of it while I was standing in my own kitchen. And not just any letter, neither." She raised her penciled-in brows.

"Not . . ." I was going the say *the* letter, one of Grandpa's letters, the one Nana says changed her mind about marrying him. I glanced over to the campaign desk. I could just see the edge of it in the parlor from where I sat in the kitchen.

Mrs. Weaton scowled. "I know. I know exactly where you keep the letters, where this one was. But I'm telling you it ended up in my scorebook."

"*The* letter?" My skin chilled. "Really? You're not messing with me?"

"Honey, I would've thought it a coincidence or whatnot, if that boy hadn't but five minutes later been on my doorstep with pages of a letter asking to make sure you got them."

"They were pages from his journal."

"Oh. Well."

"It was better than a letter. It was his diary from when he

was away all this time." God, it was so much more than some letter or email or text he may have conjured up in a fit of rejection and depression.

I still wasn't totally sure about him and Audrey and the pregnancy, but whatever had happened before, I could tell from his journal that they were definitely over now. And that he'd struck some kind of deal for me.

The thought of sharing my diary, my innermost thoughts and insecurities with anyone, made me shudder. The fact that Jack, a guy who people sold out on a daily basis, whether for a picture, an autograph, or a sordid exclusive, gave me these pages was shocking. The fact he trusted me not to share them, or Mrs. Weaton, for that matter, was . . .

"What are you waiting for?" Mrs. Weaton asked, tapping her pencil.

"Thank you!" I yelled out over my shoulder as I jogged outside into the bright sunshine and jumped into the truck. To Mrs. Weaton or Nana, I wasn't sure. Joey's car was gone, and I was relieved.

I'd moved through a full spectrum of emotions as I read those pages—from happiness, to sadness, to anger—and realized at one point I had dried tears on my cheeks. It was impossible to tell if every page was there, but I had to believe if he was willing to share the part about almost doing something with that girl, that he was telling me everything. Everything he needed to anyway.

He'd come here afraid to face me, afraid I'd reject him, and I'd done just that. He thought I was dating Colt, and yet he still put himself out there for me.

My heart squeezed.

Winding back through what I'd read as I drove, I felt so proud of him getting involved in the writing and directing.

Making a name for himself. Showing people he was capable of more. Man, and I was so sad for him when he talked about his father, proud he'd been trying to find out more, and understand more, in what I knew were difficult memories.

I came to a stop at the light on Atlantic and Palmetto and drummed my fingers on the steering wheel. The window was still down in my truck from last night, and the cool spring sea breeze helped calm my impatience. *How long could this traffic light possibly be?*

And his mother? I wanted to hug her for understanding him so much and getting him to open up the only way she knew how. I laughed through my tears. *A message in a bottle.* That's exactly what he was. He'd tried to open up to me and *I'd* been the one too afraid.

He'd hurt me. Nothing could be undone, but how I chose to move past it would change the rest of my life. I was still nervous about who he was, and what that meant for me. Especially now that I really understood how much he loved the craft of it. But I wondered if we could find a way to try and have a relationship separate from the *celebrity-ness*. We had to try.

Pulling into the driveway of Devon's gorgeous beach house, I saw the silver Jeep pulled in under the house. That didn't mean Jack was here, though. That thought sat menacingly in the back of my mind. What if he'd left?

I jogged up the stairs to the periwinkle blue front door, holding the white painted cottage bannister and knocked, my heart literally pounding in my ears.

Why was blood so hard to move when you were nervous?

After a few moments of thinking my head would explode or I'd get sick, the door opened.

Devon.

I tried not to let my deflating shoulders be too obvious.

"Hi," I said as he stood there expressionlessly. Very different from the Devon I'd met previously who'd seemed to be on my, or at least "our" side. The side of us getting back together. I'd be pissed off at me, too. I hated to think what they'd talked about after I kicked Jack out of my truck. Now that I really understood how Jack felt . . .

I shifted my weight. "Uh, is—"

"He's not here."

Stones formed in my chest, their weight pressing down on my stomach that was already churning with nerves and regret. I held onto the doorframe. *Please let him not have left.*

I must have looked like I was going to pass out.

"Ah, Christ," Devon said finally, shaking his head. "This is ridiculous. You two are ridiculous. He's under the house, beating the shit out of something. Just go past the Jeep. Could you do me a favor, though?"

I nodded.

"Give him the benefit of the doubt this time?"

I nodded again, not trusting myself to speak. Relief and a new jolt of nerves flooded my system, making me weak-legged as I turned and went back down the stairs.

Devon closed the door behind me.

I paused to gather myself, having no idea what to say to Jack, and heard the sounds of grunts and thwacks I hadn't noticed when I'd first arrived. Tilting my head to the sky, I filled my lungs deeply. *Nana, if you're out there, I hope you knew what you were doing when you brought me Jack Eversea.*

It was dark under the house. The space, which obviously reflected the entire footprint of the home, was huge. I paused as I entered, then passed the Jeep, letting my eyes adjust to the cool dimness. A faint mildewy smell that characterized life in the humid coastal South, wafted through the space. I trained my gaze on the direction of the sounds and could make out a figure, Jack, in the far corner through the concrete support columns sparring against a large black punching bag that hung from above.

The shadows were perforated with beams of sunlight slanting through the lattice-work covering all sides of the house. They landed like mini spotlights all over his muscled form, the rays bouncing off his wet skin. He wore only black gym shorts that clung with dampness.

He grunted and panted as his fists flew, his dark hair wet and brow furrowed. Sweat beaded and dripped to the concrete floor.

I continued moving forward, but stopped when I was about ten feet away from him, trying to force my dry mouth to take a swallow. He was so beautiful it was heartbreaking.

And he seemed so lost.

My eyes skated down his perfect form.

His bare feet glided back and forth on the dusty cement as he shifted his weight easily into every punch his upper body threw. He had a new tattoo on his foot. It made me uneasy to see it, to know there was so much of his life I didn't yet know or understand. But I wanted to. So badly.

His back was still to me when he stopped his current combinations and grabbed and hugged the bag, dropping his forehead against it. After a few moments I expected him to be done, to catch his breath and stand up, but he suddenly released one arm from around the bag and proceeded to pound out right hooks over and over again, letting out a loud grunt with each one. Sounds of frustration or satisfaction at landing the perfect hit, I couldn't tell.

He finally stopped, his torso heaving as he clung to the bag. His breathing was loud and labored.

"What do you want, Keri Ann?" he croaked.

I started.

He didn't raise his head from where it rested against the bag, just stayed frozen, panting with exertion.

A weird sizzle arced through my churning belly. God, I was so attracted to him. To every part of him. The strong arrogant side of him the world saw. And yes, to this visual and visceral display of maleness. But especially to the vulnerable part he'd had the courage to show me.

I reached behind me and drew the folded pages out of the back pocket of my cargoes, trying to keep my hand steady. "Are these real?" I asked, in a whisper.

His shoulders slumped. "Seriously?"

"It's just a question."

"Yes, they're real." He sighed.

"No, I believe you . . . I'm sorry. I don't know why I asked like that." My voice was breathy with nerves. "Will you . . . will you look at me?" I managed.

He didn't move for a moment. Then he tilted his face to the side and looked at me over his arm. His eyes were dark as they met mine. He blinked slowly then dropped his gaze to the pages I was holding. "I wanted to figure out a way to get those back before you read them . . ."

"I'm glad you didn't. Is this everything?"

He closed his eyes. "It's everything that matters. There's some stuff about my father you probably didn't need to see and . . . well, I also didn't explain what happened with

Audrey." He sliced his eyes back up to mine, as he finally pulled back from where he was clutching the bag. "I slept with her the day I found out she cheated on me."

"What?" I said even though I'd heard him clearly. I needed time to process it.

He waited, watching me.

How does someone react to being cheated on by sleeping with the enemy? An image of him being with her, naked, skin to skin, flashed through my mind, making me wince. Obviously, I knew he'd had sex with her to have thought the baby was his. But not *when*. And I knew he'd been with other people before me, it wasn't about that. But in this image it wasn't a faceless girl. I knew Audrey. I knew her beauty. And now that I'd read Jack's pages, I knew her ugliness at threatening *me* to get to Jack. But to sleep with her, knowing she'd just been with someone else? I saw them together in my mind, imagined he must have been . . . angry while he did it. My stomach rolled.

I felt disgusted. And dirty . . . like he'd transferred her on to me. "Unprotected?" I asked, although I already knew the answer.

He nodded.

I curled my arms around my middle.

Unwrapping the wrist-strap on the fingerless boxing gloves he had on, he straightened to his over six-foot frame and pulled them off. This Jack, this wary Jack, that seemed as if he was bristling with armor, was new to me.

"What do you want, Keri Ann?" He asked me again and threw the gloves to the side. "I know you're disgusted with me. I knew you would be. You should be. *I* am."

I dropped my eyes to his sculpted chest as it heaved.

A few hundred yards from where we stood, the sound of

waves crashing incessantly against the shore vied for attention against the sound of his still irregular breathing. Waves that were constantly changing and renewing the sand, bringing beautiful things and also ugly remains, and then washing them away again without regret. I sighed and looked away. There was dust floating in the beams of sunlight, a few boxes were piled up haphazardly in a corner next to me. I laid the journal pages down on one.

"You hurt me," I whispered and looked back at him.

He pursed his lips and squeezed his eyes shut for a few seconds then nodded once. "Yes."

"And I hurt you, too."

He didn't respond.

"I didn't . . ." my throat was dry again, felt clogged. "I didn't know I was able to do that." I hadn't really believed him until I saw it written in his almost illegible handwriting. "I'm scared, Jack." I inhaled deeply and steadied my voice. "Like I told you last night. I'm not ready to be out there with you, to have that define me. To have *you* define me."

He nodded and swallowed, wincing as if in pain. "I know."

"I've barely discovered myself," I whispered. "Who I am. What I'm capable of. What *I* want."

Tension radiated off him in physical waves, steeling himself against my words. He was so successful, so strong, so larger than life when the world turned its camera lens on him. But with me he needed to protect himself?

God, how did I have the power to make someone like Jack Eversea so vulnerable?

I held the power to crush him right at this moment. The knowledge was humbling and terrifying. Didn't he know I'd rather drown myself in the ocean than use that power?

Walking forward, my pulse beating a wild rhythm with

every step, I stopped right in front of him. I breathed him in, all his sweat and salt and exertion mingled together.

His jaw was tight and his vivid eyes flickered once as he held my gaze.

Moments stretched out, and our breathing became joined in rhythm. His finally slowing, mine catching up.

I had nothing left to ask him that would make me feel better about trusting this. Trusting him. This was the leap right here. This was the moment where I wondered if history was always doomed to repeat itself, and why I would make the same mistake again. I wished I could see the future in the depths of his green eyes, in the dilated pools of his pupils. I couldn't, so I dropped my attention to his full mouth, the curve of his lips, softly set against his hard, rough jaw.

"If you touch me right now," Jack rasped, cutting through the silence, "I'm taking it as a *yes* to us." He leaned his sweat-slicked body closer, and my heart fell right through me. "And I'm *never*," he drew the word out, "letting you go."

CHAPTER NINETEEN

I absorbed his roughly uttered words, their echo weaving its way around us, and my body began a distant throb. "Is that a promise or a threat?" I managed softly and raised my hand up between us. Heat flowed off his chest onto my palm as it hovered right over his heart.

He looked down at my hand, then back up at me.

I almost expected to see a quirk of his dimple, a Jack-ism to lighten the moment. I *fully* expected him to step forward into my hand and force us to make contact.

He did neither. "Both," he whispered. "But you have to make the choice, Keri Ann." His eyes grew fierce. "You have to know there's no going back. Don't do this unless you can take all of me. You know who I am. What I do. I can't hide it from you, and I'm not sure I can hide *us*. I'll try. But you have to give me all of you. If you're still with Colt, I need you to step back and leave. Don't come here unless you're free. I need you to be mine. Fully. All the damn way. Because I'm *yours*," he finished harshly. "Do you understand?"

God. How could I do this? How should I go forward? I couldn't agree to everything he was asking, could I?

My hesitation was reflected in the grim firming of Jack's mouth. His eyes clouded over.

"Wait," I managed before he took my hesitance as a negative. "I'm not with Colt. And nothing . . . nothing ever happened with him," I added. Not that it should matter.

A rush of air escaped him.

"But . . ." I dropped my hand away from where I'd been about to touch him.

Jack's jaw clamped down hard again, and he took a step back, before running a hand through his damp hair.

My palms itched to do the same. "You can't ask me to go out there, and . . . and *own* this with no thought for myself. *Please* . . . God, I know there are a thousand, *thousands*," I amended, "of girls who'd want to take my place, and wouldn't care . . . would crave what you're offering, but . . ."

"But I don't want them. I want *you*," he said, finally looking at me.

"I know," I whispered.

"Do you?"

I nodded.

"I'm talking about you and me. That's it. Just you. And me. There has never been a simpler," he shook his head and sighed, "yet more . . . impossible concept in the universe." He reached up and roughly grabbed two fistfuls of his hair before abandoning them in an unruly wet mess. "And you, Keri Ann? What do you want?"

You. "I want . . . I want to be more than I am now, on my own merit. I want not to be afraid that Joey and I will be the generation to lose the family home. I want to be respected and not pitied. I want to feel proud of myself and my abilities. I want to live a life where people are not watching and judging every action I take. And that's *your* life in multiples." I inhaled deeply. "I don't want people looking at you and wondering why you're with *me*. But, mostly, I don't want to imagine my life without *you* in it."

He blinked, seemingly processing each aspect of what I said, storing it away, but I knew what he heard was that I was saying yes. And I was. There was no way I was walking away from this. From him. I couldn't if I tried.

Pursing my lips, I blew out a breath. I really hoped I knew what I was doing here. If we failed this time, it would break me irreparably.

I reached my hands out slowly, hesitating before my fingertips made contact with his chest. "Just . . . *please* . . . can we do this slowly? Can you give me time? Can we try and be together without the rest of your world knowing?"

"Yes?"

"Yes," I nodded. "Please?"

I couldn't wait any more. We'd figure out the details later, and we'd do it together. I took a deep breath and pressed my palms against his damp skin.

Jack's eyes closed as he exhaled and canted forward toward me.

Sliding my hands around his ribs and up around his muscled shoulder-blades, I stepped into him.

His arms curled around me, drawing me against him. One hand slid up into my hair and pressed my face against his damp chest. A barely controlled groan came out with his next breath, reverberating against my skin.

I reveled in the feeling of his hot wet skin, his heart pounding beneath my cheek, my body pressed flush against his. So strong was the feeling of relief of being in Jack's arms, it seemed in that moment that nothing bad could ever happen to me ever again.

The scent of his raw masculinity slid into my every pore, and my face turned to press my lips to his salted skin before I could question it.

His body reacted beneath my touch.

Bringing both hands to cup my face, he tilted it to look at him.

"I'm going to kiss you," he rasped, staring at my mouth.

I nodded and moistened my lower lip in anticipation as he lowered his head. My pulse picked up a frantic beat as he closed in on me. I willed myself to calm, but my breathing hitched as it gathered pace. I slid a hand up and around the back of his neck, tugging his mouth closer, because he was taking too damn long to get to me. The last thing I saw was his dimple flash before his mouth met mine.

There was nothing slow and sweet about this kiss. We'd waited what seemed like forever for a kiss where there were no doubts and no questions between us. I opened under him, meeting the slide of his tongue and moaned at the exquisite sensation.

His lips were firm against mine, withdrawing and opening again, capturing my lips between his then sliding inside my mouth once more. Our heads shifted and moved, our mouths trying to find the perfect fit. The perfect rhythm. Trying to get closer, even though we were already drinking in each other. Neither of us seemed to want to stop and breathe more than the needy and necessary gasps that punctuated the moment.

I grabbed a fistful of hair at the nape of his neck, and as his lips moved over mine, sucked desperately at his bottom lip, grazing it with my teeth. My entire body was tuned to the kiss, focused on tasting him, the sweet mint on his tongue and the salt from his sweat, and every nip and pull of his mouth reached and pulled sensation from the very depths of my body.

"God," Jack rasped against my mouth, pausing between thorough kisses. One of his hands left my face and wrapped around my middle drawing me up and against him. Hard. "When you said slow . . . how slow?" His fingers dug into me, pressing me closer. The hand at my face moved down my throat, tilting my head back, making room for his hot mouth as it left mine and slid to my chin then my ear, causing goose bumps to break out over my already sensitized skin.

I said slow? A giddy laugh bubbled up my throat, and I swallowed, unsure how to answer.

"You have to guide me here, Keri Ann, or I . . . shit," he said suddenly and lifted me off the ground. Swiveling around, he headed for the lattice gate leading out to the pool area.

I squealed. "What the hell, Jack?"

"Kick your shoes off."

"What? Why?" I asked, winded from how tight he was holding me as he ducked out the gate into the bright sunshine. I glanced at the pool over my shoulder. "No! No way!"

"Nope, not the pool, it's heated," he said and hefted me up suddenly over his shoulder in a fireman's lift.

Gasping, I opened my eyes against his lower back. "Jack! What are you doing?" I yelled and slapped his ass.

He laughed, a deep rumble, and pulled my sneakers off, dropping them as he headed up and over the dune path, his bare feet sliding into the sand as I beat pointlessly at his back.

"Wait, Jack! I thought I said nothing public," I tried desperately, my voice breathy. His shoulder was digging into my belly. And Mrs. Weaton's breakfast wasn't feeling too settled. "Oh, God, I feel sick."

"Almost there, and no one's on the beach for about," he

swung both ways, not breaking a stride as he headed to the water line so I could look, "a few hundred yards each way."

His feet splashed into the waves, slowing against the resistance of the water then he pitched us both in with a splash.

I spasmed with the frigid cold as we both went under, and I scrambled to get my feet under me, coming up with a gasp. "What the hell, Jack? What was that for?" I coughed and spat out seawater.

"I needed a cold shower, and fast," he said, flicking the water from his hair with a swift head snap, and leaving it perfectly styled. *Guys*. "Damn, it *is* cold! Sorry," he said, reaching for me and pulling me against his still warm body.

"Idiot. Of course it's freaking cold, it's barely spring," I muttered, my teeth chattering. "Ugh! I hope it's *this* cold," I said, holding my finger and thumb about a half inch apart in front of his face.

He convulsed with laughter, his mouth wide, his dimples deep, eyes squeezed closed with mirth. Seawater dripped from the tips of his dark hair.

Damn. And his smile made him impossibly, and insanely, more beautiful. My chest suddenly expanded with emotion. The swoon effect was still in full force seven months later. I hiccupped a laugh that bubbled out in spite of myself. It was so contagious to see his happiness.

"Not with you around, Keri Ann." He winked at me and pressed me against him for proof.

I swallowed with nerves, even as a rush of heat seared a path straight through me, warming my iced down body from the inside. I gritted my teeth against the sensation, lest I pant like a dog or something equally embarrassing. My body quaked.

"C'mon," Jack said. "You're freezing. You're beautiful, but

your lips are blue and I can feel you shivering." He pulled away and, taking my hand, headed to the shore.

We started trawling through the waist-deep water toward the sand. My body felt heavy with the weight of my wet pants and t-shirt, and the breeze chilled me further. As we moved, an idea formed in my mind. I had to get him back for dunking me *after all*.

Just as we got to his calf depth in the water, I waited for the perfect timing of his step and flung out my right leg, hauling his arm to spin his body. His reflexes kicked in, and he grabbed me as he turned and lost his balance, pulling me with him as we both went down, me squealing, into the shallow water.

Jack let out a harsh grunt as his back hit the sand without much water breaking his fall. I landed on top of him, pounding the air out of both of us.

"Christ," he croaked and, closing his eyes, let his head fall back. "What was that?"

"Sorry. Me trying to get you back for dunking me?" I offered, sheepishly, my damp hair falling to the side of our faces like a curtain.

He opened his eyes and looked into mine. A small wave washed up our bodies then ebbed away, pulling the sand around us.

"Can I make it up to you?" I asked and lowered my mouth to his, kissing him deeply.

He responded, winding a hand up into my wet hair and holding me against his mouth. Gentle waves lapped at us every few seconds or so before a big one suddenly rolled up over my back. My arm was under Jack's neck and I jerked him up suddenly to get us out of the water.

"Are you trying to kill me?"

I laughed. "About every seventh wave is the largest. Luckily, the tide is going out, otherwise we'd be choking right now."

He blinked up at me then pitched over, rolling me onto my back in the surf, settling his weight between my legs and on my chest. Cold water forgotten, my heart tripped and heat spread through me.

"You know a lot about waves, huh?"

I nodded, instantly thinking of my wave sculpture. "I've totally dorked out on research. We're lying in about four inches of water right now, which means that the next wave that makes it this far before breaking will probably be eight inches higher than that. I'm thinking you'll be fine, but you've left *me* kinda vulnerable."

Another small wave lapped up our bodies and carved the earth beneath us, and I wrapped my arms around his bare back.

"Eight inches, huh? I could go so many different ways with this topic." Jack laughed teasingly, his green eyes bright against the flush on his cheekbones. "So, my beautiful ocean dork, how many waves 'til the big one now?"

"You're a little distracting. I have no idea," I answered honestly with a smile at his mischievous expression.

On cue, a larger wave rolled up causing me to lift my face closer to him. It also rocked Jack's body along mine. *Whoa.* I flicked my eyes down to his mouth. The way the rest of me was feeling, I needed to complete the connection. "And I may be a dork, but I'm *your* dork," I whispered. *Please kiss me.*

Jack's lids lowered fractionally and he dropped his forehead to mine. "God, you have no idea how much I like hearing that."

"What? That I'm a dork?"

"No, that you're mine."

CHAPTER TWENTY

The sand beneath my back ebbed and undulated with the washing tide, but it was a tiny distraction compared to Jack hovering above me, his body pressed against mine.

He was hard, smooth, and firm. Too hard. Intimately hard.

The earth at my back was fluid and rough. I was fully clothed, but the situation was making me feel completely bare and exposed. I turned my head and made out figures and a dog barking in the distance.

Jack followed my look. "We're fine," he said and bumped his nose softly against mine. "I think I'm pretty good at spotting if we're being watched by now." A cloud passed over his face as he said that.

"What?" I asked.

"Come on," Jack whispered. "It looks really great on postcards, but this making out in the surf thing is bloody freezing."

He climbed off me, and I grabbed his offered hand as he pulled me to my feet.

Without his body heat, the normally mild spring ocean breeze sliced through my wet clothes and straight through me. I shuddered.

He tugged my hand and we jogged back toward the house. Trying to move with cold, wet clothes and rough sea sand in every crevice was not a good mix.

"There's an outdoor shower under the house, and it has hot water," Jack promised as we made it over the dunes to the privacy of Devon's house.

"I hope you have something I can borrow. I'll have to get home to change before work tonight."

"Yeah."

We went past the pool and I grabbed my sneakers Jack had dropped. We re-entered the dim area under the house, and Jack led me to a small area hidden by more lattice.

Leaving me in the private enclosure, Jack took my dry shoes from me. "Will you get the water sorted? I'll be right back with towels."

After I got it just right, I stepped fully clothed into the welcoming scalding hot spray and tipped my head back to let the water wash over me. Wow, how did I let my life change so drastically in just a few hours? I was involved with Jack again. Fully. All the way involved.

I hadn't even talked to Jazz about the journal pages, and we consulted about *everything*. And Joey? God, I had no idea how Joey would react. Everyone's head would be spinning. Mine was.

Hearing a noise behind me, I turned as Jack let the enclosure gate slam closed behind him and placed a bottle of shampoo on the small shelf inside the fence. "Dry towels and change of clothes just outside," he announced and stepped closer, still only in his black shorts, placing his hands on my waist.

The water was hitting my back. He turned us and ducked his head under, letting the hot water wash the salt from his skin. Then he stepped out so we were both barely under the spray.

I leaned up to kiss him. I couldn't help it. I kissed him softly, nipping at his lips, and then drew back.

He grinned.

It was so weird to think I could probably do that anytime I wanted now. Some moments I would look at him and just see *my* Jack who I could kiss whenever I wanted to. Others, it would be like a filter dropped, and I saw Jack Eversea, movie star, a person I shouldn't even touch. It was an odd feeling.

He watched me curiously, his hands at my waist. Then he curled his fingers into my shirt and pulled up. "You should probably get the sand off your body."

I hesitated then smiled shyly at him and raised my arms, letting him pull the wet fabric from my skin. It smacked the floor as it dropped, and I stood in my small black cotton bra. Nothing lacy and sexy like I would have been wearing if I'd planned this moment. His face was broody and flushed and his eyes roamed over me. His mouth grew tight.

"Hey," I whispered. "I think since I'm sandy and all, I probably should take my pants off, too." I laughed.

"I feel like a horny teenager," Jack croaked.

I smiled and quickly undid my sopping cargoes and shimmied them off. I could just be wearing a black bikini, I told myself. But we both knew different. As soon as I was standing under the spray in my bra and panties, I was in Jack's arms. We were right back to where we'd left off. The water cascading over us tasted sweet in comparison to the salt of sweat and seawater.

Jack groaned and his tongue stroked into my mouth, bringing my body up to a fever pitch of longing. His arms were wrapped around me, and it was a heady feeling to have my bare skin pressed against his. Feeling the hard press of his arousal made me ache deeply. But it was also an instant reminder that we'd made love before and were probably going to do it again. I was nervous. And still thrown by what he'd admitted to doing to Audrey.

I shuddered, trying to reconcile the beautiful transcendent moments we'd shared—moments in which I'd experienced Jack being so tender and passionate with me—with the animalistic coupling full of anger and humiliation I saw in my mind's eye when I thought of him and Audrey together.

"Hey," Jack eased back and looked at me. "What's up?"

I hung my head, resting my forehead against his chest. I felt his heart thudding and heard the swallow of his throat.

He hesitated, and then wrapped his arms around my shoulders, kissing my wet hair. "We can take it slow, Keri Ann, I promise. We don't have to do anything you don't want to." He swallowed loudly again. "Ever. But please talk to me. Please. You're making me nervous."

I nodded against his chest, not really knowing what to say.

He pulled away then, and grasping my shoulders, turned me around gently to face away from him. I looked quizzically back at him over my shoulder, but he was reaching for the shampoo. He squirted some into his hand, and lathered it, then reached his fingers up to my hair.

Oh, yes.

I acquiesced and dipped my head back.

The smell of the piney shampoo flowed around us, the source of Jack's scent I remembered from when he was here last, uncovered. I was almost sad to know the mystery but closed my eyes with a barely suppressed moan as Jack's fingers slid against my scalp, massaging the lather in. There was nothing sexual, but everything sensual about what he was doing. It was confusing but too exquisite to question. He gently massaged and worked the lather through to the ends, his hands then sliding the suds down the exposed skin of my shoulders and back. I felt a tug at my bra closure and tensed as it came loose. Jack, still behind me, slid the straps off my arms and tugged the wet material forward and off my body.

I froze.

"It's okay, Keri Ann," he whispered. Then he gently pulled me back into the spray, letting it rinse my hair and washing the suds down my body. I realized I had coarse sand on my breasts as the water washed it down my belly.

Jack's tender, reverent ministrations seemingly without ulterior motive, were doing me in, melting my concerns away.

His hands never ventured around me. Instead, they slid down either side of my waist to my hips and tugged at my panties. My breathing stuttered, and an edgier warmth than that provided by the water sluicing over me, traveled languidly through me.

He pulled down, crouching behind me and I stepped out of them, my heart now pounding in the region of my throat. The thuds echoed throughout my body. We'd made love before, but this felt like the most intimate moment we'd shared.

He moved to the side and the water hit me once more. Then it stopped, and Jack stepped around me without turning and reached out the gate for a large white towel he'd brought. It unfurled, shielding my body from his eyes that didn't stray from mine as he offered it.

That was it?

Ideas raced through my head about ignoring the towel, or tossing it aside, undressing him as he did me, washing him, washing his hair . . . touching him. I looked back down at the towel, but in the end, I took it gratefully and wrapped it around me.

Jack smiled.

CHAPTER TWENTY-ONE

We were lying on Jack's bed. We'd been waiting for my clothes to dry downstairs, and they were done now and lying in a heap on the floor by the bed. Neither of us seemed to want to leave this moment.

I was wearing a sage green t-shirt of his that reminded me of the color of his eyes. Unfortunately, it had been clean when he'd given it to me so it smelled of detergent rather than *him* when I'd put it on, inhaling as I went, like a love-sick puppy. And I was wearing a pair of his boxers. They were black and a little loose. His waist was fairly narrow, despite his frame, so it wasn't too bad.

It was strange being in this room again. The memories of the last time I was in here, naked, giving him all of myself, flickered like disjointed images around the edge of every coherent conversation I tried to have between kissing him. And we kissed. A lot. "There are months 'til filming, right?"

"September, so yeah, about four months," Jack answered.

We rolled onto our sides facing each other.

He was bare-chested still, but wearing a pair of worn and comfy jeans. He must have seventeen pairs of them, I mused.

"What are you going to do here for four months?"

He grinned, his dimple teasing me. "Learn to fence. And annoy you, probably."

"Never. Anyway, why is it so long until filming starts?"

"There's the entire set to be built first," he answered. "Most will be built and stored in warehouses around Savannah. I'm not really part of that. SCAD students are doing some stuff too, a summer project I guess. They have to re-create the Pirate House. I don't think Savannah tourism could stand to have the original one blown up," he added in mock seriousness.

"I can imagine." I smirked. "But seriously? That's so cool. It's a pity I'm not already enrolled there, I'd totally beg to be on that project." I thought about the old weathered gray wood of the Pirate House and the doors and shutters painted *haint* blue to keep the ghosts out.

He smiled. "I had this crazy idea to turn the whole script kind of steampunk and magical, especially the ship *Revenge*, to make it different. I told Devon and he was all over it, so we've been re-working it with the scriptwriter. But mostly it'll translate in set design."

"You really love this stuff, don't you?"

"Yeah." He looked at me seriously and brushed a strand of hair behind my ear. "I really do. Books, movies, they were my escape growing up. It's only right that I be a part of creating that for other people now."

"I just wish it didn't come with all the bad stuff," I whispered, thinking of his lack of privacy and having to think through and second-guess every single action he took, even going out for a burger when he had no food in the house.

"Keri Ann, I don't want to *not* do what I do."

"I know. That's not what I meant. I can see how much you love it. I'd never want to get in the way of that."

Jack sighed. "I did almost give it up. When I was here last time I was so disillusioned, so controlled. I'm still working through all that, and after Audrey threatened all the things she did, I thought I should just walk away from it all. Give it up, so no one could coerce me any more. But, I realized giving it up wouldn't solve anything. In the end, the way I chose to handle what was dealt to me, getting out of the contract and getting the chance at the project in England, ended up being the best thing I could've done."

"*It's how you play your cards that makes the game,*" I said.

"Whose quote is that?" Jack laughed, rolling me onto my back.

"Actually, my Nana."

"A wise lady." He lowered his mouth and kissed me.

I didn't want to break the moment, but what he mentioned about Audrey troubled me. "You alluded to it in your journal, about Audrey threatening you. What did she do?"

Jack stiffened.

"I'm sorry," I offered. "I . . . I just really want to know. And you just mentioned it again, so . . ." I pulled my bottom lip between my teeth nervously.

He sighed. "Actually, part of why I didn't come right back was—" He sat up, pulling me with him, and faced me.

I folded my legs up and crossed my ankles.

"I did come back actually," he continued. "Got as far as Butler Cove, but I didn't stay. I couldn't stay. I found out Audrey had paid a guy to take pictures of me when I was here."

"Then? When you came back?" I was confused.

"No, before." He laced his fingers through mine. "Of us."

A thud of dread echoed in my chest.

"He got pictures of us that she threatened to make public as an excuse for why she cheated on me."

"Us?" I racked my brain to think of where we'd been public. Jogging on the beach? On his bike? What if they'd been taken at my home? The invasion made my stomach sour.

"She was going to put it all on you, Keri Ann. She was going to say *you* were why she had an affair. That's part of why I didn't come back. I wanted you as far away as possible from me."

"What pictures did she have?"

Jack swallowed.

"Jack?"

"They were taken here. In this room. Most were pretty grainy, you couldn't really see anything. But there were some clear ones of you and me standing right there." He motioned toward the French door and balcony that was now closed, although the blinds were open to the blue sky. "The morning after. I was hugging you from behind."

I remembered the moment, perfectly. My skin prickled as my blood pooled in my gut. "The grainy pictures . . .?"

Jack winced and nodded. "We had the light on in here."

I remembered him turning it on. Me wanting it off, but not because someone could have been watching. My eyes stung as tears welled.

"You really can't tell it's us, but that wouldn't have mattered. And really it was lucky she paid a local P.I. and not the paparazzi. They have far better equipment to capture a moment."

I let go of Jack's hand, clutching my middle and straightened my legs so I could lean my head down. I needed some blood back. "Oh God, I don't think I can do this," I finally managed and brought my hands up to cover my face.

How could I possibly? The idea that he would be a target for salacious pictures and stories was obvious, but it was just so opposite from anything I could want for my life. I'd known this all going in, yet I'd let it get so far. I'd willingly gone down the path with him back then, pretending what he did didn't matter because it wasn't the real Jack Eversea. The Jack I fell for. But the Jack I fell for was part and parcel of this crazy, voyeuristic society we lived in. And I'd walked right back in.

Jack pulled away and I heard a thud. I peeked through my fingers to see he'd slid to the ground, his back against the bed. His denim-clad legs were bent, his arms resting on his knees, cradling his head. The nape of his neck was stretched and . . . and I wanted to kiss it. I couldn't reconcile any of this. How I felt about him with how I felt about who he was.

"Where are the pictures?" I whispered.

"I own them. All of them," Jack muttered and took a deep breath, raising his face and letting his head drop back on the bed. "It was part of the deal. The deal I made with her and with my production company. She gave me the pictures, and I promised not to see you until the end of the contract term, which ran out last week."

He'd made a deal for me. To protect me. And he'd come here as soon as the obligation was fulfilled. *But Audrey?* "God, why does she hate *me* so much? What did I ever do to her?"

"She doesn't hate you. She hates to lose."

"Does everyone? How do you know she's done with this, this . . . *vendetta*?" I thought back to us on the beach earlier today and felt irritated that Jack had willingly put himself, *us*, at risk again.

"I don't," Jack admitted.

I let out a wobbly breath. "I can't—"

"I know," Jack interjected sharply and fisted his hands with frustration. "I know you don't want this. But I've done everything I can to make sure her part in this is done. I just can't promise about anything else. I just don't know." He got up and paced toward the offending window, glaring at it, his hands clutching his hair again. "Shit."

"Well, you invited it the other night by going public at the Grill. So it's probably just a matter of time before someone comes here to follow you around, or whatever it is they do. Stalk you," I added bitterly. God, I hated this version of me. This bitter, fearful, miserable version of me. Jack brought out my best parts and my worst parts.

I slid my legs off the bed and reached for my heap of clothes. I pulled his boxers off under the t-shirt and got my underwear back on as modestly as possible.

Jack paced back from the window to the door to the room, my exit, blocking it, but keeping his back to me as he clutched the frame.

Satisfied he wasn't looking, even though *I* was mesmerized by the fact I could outline every muscle in his back, I pulled his t-shirt off, put on my bra, and hastily followed with my top and pants. I sat back down on the bed and gathered up his borrowed clothes. "I'll wash these—"

"Don't."

I stopped. "Don't wash these?"

Jack turned around and grabbed the t-shirt and boxers from me, tossing them aside. "Yes, don't wash those, but I meant don't leave. Not like this."

"Jack—"

He sank to his knees in front of me, his hands on my legs, pushing them apart and making room. "I'll keep us a secret.

I promise. I want to tell the whole damn world, but I'll keep it to myself or kill myself trying, if it means I get to keep *you*."

I gulped down the ball that seemed to be lodged in my throat. "I'm not leaving you, Jack," I whispered, running a hand down his chiseled face, grazing over his stubble.

He closed his eyes.

"I wouldn't have come here today if I wasn't willing to deal with the bad as well as the good. You know that." I slid my hands into his soft hair and leaned forward, resting my forehead against his.

"Dammit, Keri Ann." He ran his hand up and fisted it in my wavy mass, pulling it tight. "How do you do this to me? I'm completely out of control. Since I met you, every emotion I have is tied to how I think you're feeling. I've never felt like this in my life."

"Same here," I breathed and curled my other hand around his thick forearm. "I think . . . I think this is new for both of us."

Jack opened his eyes and looked at me for several long moments. Then he kissed me, a long, but chaste kiss, and got to his feet. "I know you have to go." He offered me a hand. "Can I walk you home after your shift?"

I smiled, remembering the first night I'd met him, when he'd ended up doing the same. "Yeah, sure. I'll text you."

"Still have my number?"

"Yes." I laughed. "Though I thought of deleting it at least once a day. Still have mine?"

God, why did I ask that? If he said no . . .

"Yes," he answered, in a tone that suggested I was crazy. "And *I* thought about *texting* you at least once a day."

I wish he had, we could have avoided lots of misunderstandings. Then again, it could have made it worse. And I had no idea how we were going to move forward with 'us.' It was obvious he was more comfortable with his 'celebrity' than I'd assumed when I met him, even though he still didn't relish it. But just like I wanted to announce my relationship with Jack to all the people in my life, Jack obviously wanted to do the same. But the people in his life . . . were *the citizens of the whole freaking world*, with all of their judgments.

And never mind my upcoming enrollment at SCAD. I doubted they needed some tabloid sleaze-fest embroiling one of their students, especially when it involved a member of an upcoming film project they were working on at such high profile.

I was beyond grateful for whatever Jack had done to keep me out of the public eye, but how would I ever know if a situation like that was just round the next corner?

Today had changed *everything*. *I* had changed everything. *Everything* going forward was going to be a minefield.

CHAPTER TWENTY-TWO

Late Night Visitor: Are you done yet?

Late Night Visitor: Yet?

Late Night Visitor: Yet?

The three texts came in quick succession about five minutes after I arrived at work. I grinned like a loon and stuck my phone in the back pocket of my jean shorts.

"Someone's in a good mood tonight." Brenda eyed me with a smirk. "I don't suppose a certain Hollywood hottie has anything to do with it?"

"Shhh, seriously Brenda, you have to help me keep this quiet." I reached to help her unload the rack of clean glasses she'd brought through from the kitchen.

"Of course I will, hon, don't worry. It seems almost impossible to believe anyway, and I don't mean that toward you!"

I swallowed. Brenda was right though. It was insane that a celebrity of Jack's caliber would be in Butler Cove, our tiny tourist town where nothing exciting ever happened. And not only that, but he wanted to be with *me*. Boring old Keri Ann. "You shouldn't believe it." I agreed with her assessment of its improbability. "It's beyond nuts. Honestly, I know underneath it all he's a regular guy, but at times I just don't get what he sees in me. I mean he's . . ."

"Jack-freakin-Eversea?" she supplied.

"Yes, and I'm . . ."

"Probably the coolest thing to ever happen to him?"

I elbowed her playfully. "Thanks, Brenda."

She smiled and swatted me. "You should know that there were a couple out-of-towners in here today askin' 'bout him."

I cleared my throat. *Already?*

"It was lucky Paulie wasn't in, he would've been hootin' and hollerin' about it. Saying this was Jack's favorite place to eat in Butler Cove." She pursed her lips in disapproval. "He'll get a brass plaque at the bar, you mark my words."

"Unfortunately, you're probably right. He got his picture taken with both of them, and made them promise to come back in and sign it so he can put it up behind the bar." My belly tumbled over with dread. The conversation Jack and I had this afternoon about the pictures of us rattled through my mind. We were going to have to be so careful.

My phone buzzed my butt again. "Sorry, give me a minute," I said to Brenda and headed to the ladies' room.

Late Night Visitor: I'm bored. Do you have anything that needs fixing?

Me: Seriously?

Late Night Visitor: Seriously.

Me: It's weird to be texting again. You don't have any movie quotes for me?

There was a pause long enough for me to feel guilty about hanging out in the restroom instead of helping Brenda set up.

Late Night Visitor: But good, right?

Me: Yes, good.

I smiled and quickly texted Jazz.

Me: So . . . I have news.

Then I texted Jack again.

Me: I meant to ask you. I saw the new tattoo on your foot. A sea turtle?

Late Night Visitor: To remind me of you.

Me: Whatever. I've already said I'll date you, you don't need to lay it on so thick.

Late Night Visitor: Unfortunately, I'm totally serious.

I paused, trying to think of something quick witted to cover my surprise.

Me: I didn't realize you were in danger of forgetting me so easily that you needed help.

Late Night Visitor: You kill me. I wasn't. Maybe I just like to torture myself. We're not talking about this again.

Chuckling, I resisted the urge to reassure him that I was likewise in no danger of forgetting him either. But I resisted. For a split-second I gave in to the heady feeling of knowing I had Hollywood's sexiest man alive never wanting to forget me.

How I made it through the next few hours was beyond me. I kept wanting to haul my phone out and send another text just so I might get one back. I was losing it. The anticipation of seeing Jack later was killing me. Memories of our earlier kisses as well as the moment in the shower that I was now wishing I'd let turn into so much more, were outweighing all of my worries one by one.

The only break we'd taken from making out on his bed all afternoon was when he decided he should shave his stubble. I'd sat on the edge of the bath and watched him in the mirror as he lathered his face and neck and ran the blades over his skin. His eyes flicked to mine repeatedly as he worked, both of us knowing he was only doing it so he could kiss me again without making my skin raw. I didn't think I'd ever seen a sexier act than shaving in my entire life.

A tremor ran through me at the memory, and I touched my fingers to my still tingly mouth. I needed to focus on work, not Jack.

Luckily, it was a busy evening, and Joey showed up just before eleven as things finally wound down. He knew Jazz was usually here keeping me company, so it was surprising that he came.

Where was Jazz, anyway? She hadn't texted me back yet.

"Hey, kiddo," Joey said, slinging his leg over a barstool.

I smiled a goofy smile at him. "Hey. Where did you run off to this morning?"

"Went paddling. Needed to get some Lowcountry air through my head." He ran a hand through his dark blond hair and pointed at the Stella on draft.

I grabbed a glass and found myself grinning again. "How's the studying going?"

"Fine." He looked at me quizzically. "What's up with you?"

"What do you mean?" I frowned. "Nothing."

"Right," he said skeptically as I slid his beer toward him. "Where were you when I got back?"

I sucked on my lower lip. I wasn't ready to tell Joey yet, but I could hardly lie to him. "I went to see Jack," I said quietly, making sure we weren't overheard. The last patrons were leaving and Brenda was showing them out. She flipped the 'closed' sign and headed back to the kitchen.

"I see." Joey pursed his lips with a slow nod. "So you read his letter then, and whatever he wrote just erased the last seven months of his not giving a shit? Does it not matter what I, or any of your friends who care about you, think?"

"Of course it matters."

"God, I even hate to ask, because she probably cheered you on," he snorted derisively, "but what does Jazz have to say about you going to see him?"

"I haven't told her yet."

He raised his eyebrows in surprise. "But you're going to think long and hard before you get involved with him, I hope. I'm sure it was all very convincing, but you're going to think this through, right?"

I gritted my teeth in irritation.

"Right?" Joey pressed.

"Of course I've thought it through," I snapped. "I've done

nothing *but* think about it, Joey. But seriously, at some point I have to follow my gut and my heart."

His head bobbed back. "So you've already decided?"

"Yes, and I'd really like you to be happy for me. In fact, he'll be here in a few to walk me home."

He pursed his lips again. "He can walk *us* home, then. What about Colt?"

"What about him? Why don't you ask Colt about me and Jack? I think you'll find he gets 'us' a lot more than you do." I reached forward and took his arm. "Joey, I'm not going to lie, I'm scared out of my freaking mind about embarking on a relationship with him. But if anything goes awry, I'm going to need you to support us, not offer a bunch of *I told you sos.*"

"So why do it?" he asked, pained. "I'm not here, I can't protect you if it all goes to shit. And we really don't need to be raising our profile in this town. Or for you to be seen like one of those groupies, or whatever they call girls who hang out with actors, with everyone assuming he's onto his latest piece of ass. We need approval ratings in this town, not judgments." His eyes flicked away.

"What else is bothering you, Joey?" I managed, trying to stuff down my surge of bile at the idea of people seeing me like he'd just described. "This can't just be about Jack. If it's about the town, I already know they raised the property taxes on us. It'll be a struggle, but somehow we'll make it, or appeal to get them to lower the taxes a bit. Me seeing Jack shouldn't affect that. Anyway, we're going to keep it secret. You know I don't want to be in the spotlight any more than you do."

Joey sighed and drummed his fingers on the polished bar top. "I didn't want to freak you out, but I got a call from our insurance guy a few months ago. Apparently we're in a *storm surge one* area, and with all the freak weather events in the last few years, they're dropping flood insurance from our coverage, and we'll have to buy it separately. It's a fortune. And with our taxes going up too . . ." He blew out a breath and left the sentence hanging. He didn't need to finish it. With a huge insurance bill, if we could even pay it, there'd be nothing left to pay the taxes.

My mind whirled.

Brenda popped her head out from the kitchen. "Keri Ann, I have to head out. You okay to close up tonight? Hey, Joey."

"Hey," my brother nodded, distractedly.

I waved at her. "Uh, yeah, thanks, Brenda. See you tomorrow."

She disappeared, and I looked back to see Joey looking desolate.

"Keri Ann . . . long term, I don't know how we're going to keep the house."

I gulped a breath as my heart took a nosedive. "Why didn't you tell me before now?" I whispered.

"I am, now."

"No, I mean, before. You said you found out months ago. There's no way I can go to SCAD. We'll need every spare cent for the house."

Joey squeezed his eyes closed and then pinched the bridge of his nose between his thumb and forefinger. "I don't want you to give that up. It's your time, Keri Ann."

"But, Joey—"

"No, listen. There's a small amount left of Mom and Dad's money. We can use that to pay the insurance this year, and then *I'll* take student loans out, too. That'll buy us a year to figure out what to do. We've just got to hope I can convince the town to back us up on an appeal to the county about the taxes."

"What happens if they don't and we can't pay?"

"Well, then they'll auction it, and someone will be able to buy up the Butler House for the price of just the taxes, rather than what it's probably worth, being an historic home and all."

"I wonder who *that* might be," I said, then added grimly, "Somehow, I don't think we'll have much luck getting the *town* to back us on an appeal." The town council, and especially Pastor McDaniel, had been after our home for years. I guessed they finally devised a strategy to make it happen. Why did there always have to be a villain? And my poor friend Jasper had him as a father. I shuddered.

"Look, don't freak out yet. If we don't pay them we've got until *next* April before they consider the taxes delinquent, and then if they go to auction it won't happen until October. After that we have a whole year to redeem the house. So this is a ways away, okay? I just needed you to know what's going on." Joey hung his head. "God, I'm sorry, Keri Ann."

I came around the bar. "What for?" I said and stepped into his big bear arms.

"For not keeping my promise to look after you. I went off to school and left you to get your heart broken, to get involved with someone like Jack Eversea, *twice*, and now I probably won't even be able to keep our house for you."

Tears stung my eyes. I'd never heard Joey sound so distraught. "Joey, I don't know who you made that promise to, but you need to let it go. We're both grown-ups now. It's not your job to look after me any more. We'll figure it out, okay? We've got time. We'll figure it out," I repeated reassuringly and squeezed him hard, then pulled back. "And you didn't *let* me get involved with Jack, I did that all on my own, and it only happened once, I've never been *un*involved." I admitted the truth to both of us. "I need you on board, Joey. I think . . . I think this is *it* for me."

A throat clearing behind me made us both jump. I turned to find Jack, in a black ball cap, standing in the doorway to the kitchen, his eyes boring into mine.

CHAPTER TWENTY-THREE

"I came in the back way," Jack said quietly, his fingers stuffed in his jean pockets. His shoulders were hunched up under what looked like the sage green t-shirt I'd been wearing earlier.

My cheeks throbbed with heat and my chest expanded with embarrassment. How long had Jack been standing there listening to Joey and me? Long enough to hear my declaration? Perhaps even long enough to hear the pitiful story of the house. I couldn't tell by his eyes, but they looked intense.

"Hector said it was okay. Sorry to interrupt." As Jack stepped toward us with his hand out, his eyes finally left me and went to my brother.

That seemed to spur Joey into action. He approached Jack and took his hand.

Jack nodded at my brother, who matched his height. "Jack. We've never officially met. I apologize for that."

I bit my lip. The last time they'd seen each other in person was in Savannah, when I'd practically run into my brother's arms after I'd said goodbye to Jack. Not to mention Jack had just decked my brother's best friend.

"Joey. Good to meet you," my brother said and shook

Jack's hand firmly. Joey cut his eyes over to me a split second, and I knew he too was wondering how much Jack heard, and also acknowledging that he himself had heard me, understood what I was saying. We would talk about it again, I knew, but right now my brother was giving me his temporary blessing.

"I hear you're walking my sister home tonight." He looked back at Jack.

Jack gave a slight nod and winked at me. One of those twinkling, slow and sexy winks that melted my insides and made me instantly self-conscious that he'd done it in front of Joey. "If she'll still have me."

"I do believe she will." Joey raised an eyebrow at me, but seemed to have missed whatever it was I'd just experienced from Jack's wink.

"Yeah, uh, just give me a few." I quickly turned back toward the bar and tried to remember my close down checklist. "Joey, you finishing this beer?"

"Sure." He walked over and Jack followed. They both sat. *Awkward.*

"You want something, Jack?" I asked. *Please say no, so we can get out of here faster.*

"No, thanks, I'm good."

"Wow, I get it now," said Joey about twenty minutes later as we made our way home by the light of the almost full moon, chatting about everything and nothing. Joey, bless his heart, had politely been asking about Jack's movie and making conversation while Jack tried his best to look engaged. He'd grabbed my hand as we left, his first contact since he'd arrived. And now his fingers wouldn't keep still.

Hidden by the shadow of our bodies as we walked, Jack's fingers were sliding up my wrist, skating my pulse, down my hand, skimming my palm, and then sliding languidly between my fingers, as if they were my legs.

I couldn't breathe.

"Get what?" I managed to ask Joey and immediately cleared my throat, pretending my breathy response was just a vocal mishap.

"Being with you two is like being in the showers in the girls' locker room after volleyball practice. You have nowhere safe to look."

Both Jack and I burst out laughing, our moment temporarily suspended.

"Soooo not what I was expecting to come out of your mouth." I raised my eyebrows. "What the hell do you know about being in the girls' locker room after volleyball?"

"Oh, you have *no* idea what Colt and I got up to in high school," he said cryptically.

"God, and I don't want to. *I* played volleyball!" Well after they'd both left school. Thank God.

Joey laughed. "I don't think principal Holt could wait to see the back of *The Butler-Graves Offensive*, as he called us. On and off the field, we were kind of a nightmare."

"Joey was center and Colt was quarterback of their high school team," I explained to Jack.

They launched into a discussion about football and high school sports.

Jack had been at school in New York City and mostly played basketball but said he still missed Rugby from being in England, so they discussed the similarities and differences in that and football.

All the time he spoke, Jack never once let go of me, and

sometimes in a pause in the conversation or when Joey was talking, he'd amp up his sensual assault on me. He'd change it up completely like kneading gently as his hand slid down mine one moment, or scraping his fingertips over my pulse so lightly, I almost thought I'd imagined it. By the time we got to my back porch and he released me, I was on internal meltdown.

Joey shook Jack's hand, nodding goodnight to me with an odd look when I didn't follow, and went inside.

We stood for a few moments after Joey's departure, then Jack turned to me.

I ran my eyes over his large frame. "Are you wearing the same t-shirt I borrowed from you earlier?" For some reason the idea that I'd taken it off and he'd put it on thrilled me.

Jack nodded. "I like the way you smell."

And hearing him admit it was better.

"In the interests of keeping my promise to you," he said softly, "and keeping us a secret, I'm not going to kiss you right now. If anyone's following us, or watching, this would be a prime opportunity."

I instantly felt the sharp edge of anxiety clip the edges of my mood. The urge to look around and look for someone spying on us was almost too much to resist. I tried to picture what someone would see if they were watching us right now. Two people standing close together, face to face, but not touching. Total innocence.

But my hand still tingled from his seduction. So did the rest of me.

"I *want* to kiss you, but we're not doing it out here, and I doubt Joey would appreciate me coming in right now," he whispered with a sexy grin that quirked his dimple.

He folded one arm across his chest, and the other came

up and ran a thumb over his bottom lip as if in thought. Then he inhaled a short breath and speared me with a shadowed look from under his ball cap. "Right now this bottom lip I'm touching is literally aching to be on yours."

Oh.

He went on, "I'd like to slide my hands into your hair, then down your back, and pull you really close against me. You feel amazing when you're against me, do you know that?"

I wasn't sure if I shook my head or nodded, but my body definitely swayed toward Jack. I held it in check.

"Damn," I whispered. "When you decide to tell me what you're feeling, you don't hold back, do you?"

His hand lowered from his mouth to join his other arm across his chest. Anyone watching would never guess what was coming out of his mouth.

I was poised, waiting for his next words. Desperate for them.

"You feel so good against me, you make me want to strip you and slay dragons for you at the same time." His dimple flashed. "And do you have any idea how good your mouth tastes? How amazing it feels when my tongue slides over your lips and touches yours for the first time?"

I gave up trying to control my breathing. "Jack," I managed between two shallow breaths. I'd barely stopped a whimper escaping. My mouth felt dry, so I moved my tongue to find moisture and licked my lower lip.

"God, and when you do that? You fucking kill me." He breathed out. "I should stop talking to you because watching you react is about to do me in, and I may not be able to keep my promise."

"Don't stop talking." I half laughed, half gasped. "This

could be the best non-kiss in the history of non-kisses." My body was functioning on a deep, subsonic, resonating throb. It had started with his handiwork on the walk home and was now in the realm of desperation.

He shifted and winced and tightened his arms across his chest. "Okay," he said. "Although I may have been a bit ambitious about what I can handle. My threshold is a little low when it comes to you."

"So you can dish it out, but you can't handle it?" I asked, winking at him. "What were you doing to my hand on the walk home, Jack?"

Jack looked at me and sucked his lower lip into his mouth, catching it with his teeth before releasing it. "I was caressing your hand the way I want to touch your body." He paused.

I tightened my arms around my middle as if I could rein in the heat swirling through me.

"Slow, then fast . . . soft . . . then . . . rough." He exhaled an unsteady breath. "Gently . . . then really, really hard."

Holy shit.

The whimper escaped me before I could stop it. But I didn't care over the rush of hot lust sluicing through me from top to bottom with a roar like a waterfall.

Both of us stood in shock.

I was seconds away from combusting, and he hadn't even touched me.

By the look on Jack's face, he felt the same way.

CHAPTER TWENTY-FOUR

"If I don't turn around and leave right now, I'm not going to give a shit about what anyone sees or thinks," Jack croaked.

He stood a foot away from me in space and time, but he could have been inside me, given what my body was going through, or a thousand miles away, given the frustrated ache that went along with it.

"Come inside," I managed. "I don't care what Joey thinks."

"Yes, you do. *I* do. He thinks I only want one thing from you. In this split second of time, he wouldn't be far wrong. But I want more, a lot more." He exhaled and brought one hand up to the back of his neck. "Please. Go inside, Keri Ann."

Trying to get my head working through the haze of hormones that had been unleashed, I didn't respond for a few moments. Then I nodded and jogged up the stairs and inside without looking back.

I closed the door and sagged against it, my heart pounding in my ears. My body was a flushed and gooey mess of confusion and want.

Taking a deep breath, I tried to calm down. I was confused

because I'd been wanting to take it slow. But all of a sudden I was willing to throw my fears of having a public relationship with Jack aside. I couldn't reconcile the way I was reacting to being with him with the part of me that shied away from who he was and what he stood for.

The kitchen light was still on.

"You okay?" Joey asked, making me jump as he came around the corner.

I put a hand to my chest. "Yep, fine. You startled me. You gonna stay up and study?"

"Actually, no. Did you see the moon? It's almost full. I think I'm going to go for a full moon paddle. You want to join?"

It had been one of our favorite things to do growing up. It was always an even bigger treat for me, as I'd get to stay up late, and hang out with my older brother who at other times was too busy with friends and football to spend time with me. But I just wasn't in that mind-set tonight.

I sighed. "Nah, but you should go ahead. Actually you should call Jazz, she'd love it. She can use my kayak." I don't know where the suggestion came from.

Joey started. "It's late," he said. "She won't want to come."

"Are you afraid she'll read more into the invitation than you want her to?"

He turned away. "Maybe. Anyway, she's with someone now."

"Yes, yes, she is. So you could, I dunno," I rolled my eyes, "*go as friends?*"

"Come on. Come with me, I need to talk to you."

I did love a midnight paddle. "Just a short one, I'm beat."

He held his hand out. "Keys. I'll get the kayaks in the truck."

I nodded and fished around in my purse then tossed them.

Joey caught the keys and I stepped aside to let him out the back door.

"Joey," I said, stopping him before I changed my mind. "I want to be with Jack, and I'd really like you to get over your reservations about him, about us together."

"Look, Keri Ann. I get it, but I don't have to like it. As far as I'm concerned, he could and probably will, leave anytime, and you'd be right back where you were."

I swallowed my disappointment at his reaction. "Jack wouldn't come inside tonight, or even kiss me, out of deference to you. So I believe he got your message loud and clear. Thank you for being so protective, but . . . do you think you could tone it down a bit?"

"Go get ready, let's talk on the water."

We drove with the windows down. The spring night air washed over us, the smell of the marsh riding the wind.

"I'm not sure I trust him." Joey ruined the calm I'd finally collected on the ride to the parking pad under the bridge.

Instead of answering, I hopped down and pulled my kayak out the back. The normally inky dark of the island and its inland estuary was splashed with silver from the moon.

Working in silence, Joey held my kayak while I got in and settled myself. Then I leaned over and held his steady for him.

"Up the creek?" he asked.

I smiled. "As long as I have my paddle." It was always our joke when we decided to head away from the open sound. "Yeah, let's stay close."

I back-paddled and turned, waiting and drifting slowly. The water was black and eerie but beautiful with the light from the moon. It was a full moon high tide, so the water level was higher than normal. If we had an early warm snap, the mosquitoes would hatch in larger batches than usual in the water left behind.

As Joey pulled up close, we moved in silence, soaking up the peace.

I kept my eyes peeled for dolphins. It was the best part of full moon paddles.

Joey cleared his throat to warn me he was about to speak. "I know he's got a movie coming up here and all, but what about after that? I mean if you two are still together, what then? Will you just follow him around the world?"

Sighing, I tried not to get upset. "God, Joey, I don't know. Why are you worried about something so far in the future? We'll figure that out when we get there." I kept up the rhythm of my paddle strokes and my breathing.

"Why *aren't* you worried about it?"

"Because it feels right, because I feel like I'm supposed to be with him." I didn't think he needed to know about Nana's letter. That I believed she'd been involved in getting Jack and me back together. He'd never consider that anything but a coincidence.

"And you think if you give up your life and your dreams to follow him around he'll still respect you? That he won't get tired of feeling responsible for you all the time? He's not giving up his life for you, but you seem pretty wishy-washy about sacrificing not only *your* future, but this town's respect, and frankly my respect, and our family name."

Blood drained from my head, leaving a buzzing emptiness in its wake. A sharp prick of hurt stuck me in the back of the throat, and my eyes welled with tears. I pulled the paddle out of the water and laid it across me.

"Joey—" I tried, but it came out a whisper.

"I'm sorry, Keri Ann." Joey stopped paddling too and reached out the end to grab a hold of my kayak. We paused in the middle of the waterway. It was the dead of night, but the moon was like a spotlight on earth. His features looked pained. "I'm sorry," he said again. "But this is the way I feel. I don't think he's using you. He's seems like a pretty genuine guy. But I can't see the two of you together. I just can't. And I think in the end, you'll be the one hurt." He raked a hand through his hair. "God, do you even remember Mom and Dad? Mom danced, did you know that? I loved watching her dance. It was magical to me. She'd take me with her sometimes if I didn't have school. She was amazing. People told me she was good enough to be in New York, dancing as her career, but she met Dad and fell in love. He promised her they would find a city that had a dance company. He kept promising, promising. Then she had us and eventually all she wanted to find was a teaching job. If she couldn't dance for herself, then she'd teach others. But no. Dad kept fucking moving, and she eventually gave up. She just gave up."

I wanted to tell Joey this had nothing to do with me and Jack, but he'd never talked about Mom and Dad, and I wanted to soak it in like a desert rain.

Joey let go of my kayak and started paddling again. Slow and forceful strokes. I followed, pulling my paddle through the inky water.

"When I was nine or so," Joey said as I pulled up close, "you were twirling around the kitchen in this apartment we'd just moved into in Wilmington. You were so little." He smiled. "We were there for some other deal Dad was working on. A sales contract or something. And Mom, she . . . she started crying out of the blue. She was crying while you were dancing around the kitchen. I didn't know what to do. I thought we'd upset her, or something, or you'd done something wrong. I knew she'd been trying to get a job since we'd arrived, so my nine-year-old mind wanted to help her feel better, and I told her she should teach *you* to dance. She just looked at me, sobbing, and then stood up and went and pulled out all of her dancing stuff, leotards and ballet shoes, and threw them in this big metal garbage can that was outside.

"She threw all her stuff away," he said, shaking his head as if he still didn't believe it. "The way she was acting was so scary I screamed at her to stop, and you were crying at all the commotion. Before I knew it, she had set the whole lot on fire. The neighbors called the fire department. It was awful."

I sat in stunned silence. Tears streaked my cheeks. I felt the cool sting of the salt in the breeze.

We'd both stopped paddling again.

Joey was far away in his mind, his eyes glazed as he remembered. "Dad came home a few hours later, celebrating. He'd just 'closed' the deal or whatever. He didn't even know anything had changed or that anything happened that day. It all just went on business as usual. But everything was different. God, she was so different. She wasn't sad so much as she was just . . . nothing. I hated it. It was awful. And I hated that Dad never even noticed. I don't even know if they ever discussed it, the fact that she wasn't looking for work any more. That she never danced again." He took a deep breath. "I look at you, and you remind me of Mom so much. The Mom I remember when I was younger. You are creative and honest and good and beautiful, and if it is at all within my power to save you from a situation like that, where you'll give yourself up for someone else, then by God, I have to try."

He looked at me, his normally blue eyes dark in our current black and white world. But they glittered unshed tears. He let go of his tightly held paddle with one hand and clenched and unclenched a fist.

I reached for his hand and held it in mine. My heart felt like it was breaking. I'd never known. I was thankful not to have experienced her pain so keenly, but immeasurably more sad I had no memory of it at all. I had no images of the magical and dancing Mom Joey so obviously remembered.

"Please think, Keri Ann. I said it from the beginning, since I saw you together in Savannah, and God, tonight even, you guys have a kind of intensity that is insane. I'm not saying you're not grown up and can't handle it, but you know what I mean."

I nodded. "I do, Joey. I have all the same concerns as you do. I understand everything you're saying. I'm not going into this blindly. And I don't know how we're going to figure out being together and keeping it private. Or how I am going to be my own person and not be sucked into his vortex. I have no idea what the future will bring, and I'm shit scared that I'm going to make the biggest fool of myself."

Joey cringed.

"But no one can plan their life like that. You can't plan it for me, you can't protect me from hurt . . . and I don't want you to."

His shoulders slumped. "I know."

I thought of him and Jazz, but I knew he wasn't ready for me to draw the parallel. Perhaps he was scared she was *it*, and she'd hold him back. Or that she'd give up her plans to be with him, and he wouldn't be able to handle the guilt. "And you shouldn't hold *yourself* to that either," was all I said.

"So it really doesn't matter what I say, does it? I just want to protect you. I swear if he hurts you, he'll regret it."

Squeezing Joey's hand, I tried a smile.

"And he's Jack Eversea, for God's sake," Joey added, incredulously. "I mean, *seriously?*"

I managed a small laugh. "I'm so sorry about Mom, Joey. I don't remember." My eyes welled again. "I never remember her dancing. I'm so sorry you had to go through that. And that *she* went through that." I swallowed in an attempt to keep my voice from disappearing. "*And* that I never got to see her dance. She must have been beautiful."

"Yeah, she was," he said quietly. "And look, I didn't mean to say I'd respect you less if you and Jack got together. I'm sorry. I'm just worried."

"Yeah, well, me too. And I forgive you, even though you ruined the shit out of what could have been an amazing night paddle."

Joey chuckled. "C'mon, let's head back."

We drew our kayaks through the water silently except for the sounds of our breathing and the water trickling off the paddles. I kept my ears strained for the sound of a puff of air signaling a dolphin nearby.

As we got to the dock, all I heard was the low buzz of my phone where I'd left it with my sweater. I waited until we were on the way home, my head resting against the window frame, drawing the last bit of spring air for the night, before I read it.

Late Night Visitor: Take the day off tomorrow? I have plans for us . . .

CHAPTER TWENTY-FIVE

As soon as I woke up, I texted Brenda. I was only working the lunch shift today. Confirming she could cover me, and get some other help in, I called Paulie.

"You've never officially asked for the day off," he said gruffly. "Anything important?"

"I have no idea."

Then I texted Jack.

Me: What are we doing?

Late Night Visitor: Dev and I will pick you up in 45. Bring a swimsuit in case. Do your brother or Jazz want to come?

The surge of disappointment that I'd be sharing Jack with Devon, and also that he wanted to invite as many people as possible was so strong, I almost laughed at myself. Swimsuit?

Me: I'll check . . . again, what are we doing?

Late Night Visitor: Location scouting and looking for horses (don't ask).

Looking for horses . . . in a swimsuit. Right. I'd just started to text Jazz when another message from Jack popped up.

Late Night Visitor: Don't worry, I also have alone plans for you and me.

A giddy laugh escaped me, and I bit my lip down to hold onto my emotions.

Me: Didn't even cross my mind.

Late Night Visitor: Lucky you. It was all I could think about.

Me: I lied about that. Obviously. Me, too.

Late Night Visitor: I know.

Me: Arrogant.

Late Night Visitor: Confident.

Jack and Devon had pulled up in their silver Jeep, the top down, and Jack hopped out in aviators, wearing his uniform of dark ball cap, distressed jeans, and solid color t-shirt. He'd shaved and his strong jaw was grinning. *My, what beautiful teeth he has.*

My brother shook his hand and was introduced to Devon. As Jack pulled his seat forward so Joey and I could climb in, Joey stepped back to allow me in first. I gave him a shove. I wanted to sit behind Jack.

My brother rolled his eyes, and climbed in, then took the bag from me with our towels and stuff. He and Devon exchanged a couple of comments and talked about where we were going. I'd already told Jazz to meet us at the Marina as per Jack's additional instructions.

"Good morning," Jack murmured softly as I moved in front of him to climb in after Joey.

I glanced up but couldn't see his eyes behind his glasses.

"Yes, it is," I returned and settled myself in the seat, tying my hair up with a band.

Jack put the chair back and got in. I could see the smooth nape of his neck over the seat back. Seriously, was every part of him like the most beautiful thing I'd ever seen?

As soon as we were moving, his hand came down the gap between his seat and the door and touched me lightly on the ankle.

I pursed my lips, inhaling deeply through my nose. My chest began a deep steady thump, and I wanted to close my eyes and just revel in the feeling of his fingertips on me. Rummaging around in my brown leather purse, I pulled out my mirrored sunglasses and slid them on. I shifted my foot forward, and his hand closed lightly around my leg.

The Harbor Master at Palmetto Marina was salty and weather-beaten, with the palest blue eyes I'd ever seen. He also may have been the only person in the world who had no recognition of Jack.

Devon filled out paperwork for the charter boat, and then we bought enough drinks, sandwiches, and snacks for an apocalypse and headed down the jetty.

"Wow," I said, getting a good look at the large white yacht at the end. "This one?"

"Dang!" Jazz echoed my surprise. "This beats tooling around in Cooper's dirty old Carolina Skiff dropping crab traps. This has to be like forty feet."

We climbed on board, and Dan, the captain, who was also older and turned out to be the second person in the world to be completely oblivious of who was on his boat, gave us a tour and showed us where to stow our stuff. We all settled on the front sundeck, chatting over the sound of squawking gulls.

Cap'n Dan glided us slowly along the no wake zone toward the open sound, the cool salty wind whipping errant strands of hair into my eyes.

"I wish Monica was here," Devon said. "She loves the water. Loves being on a boat."

"Where is she?" I asked.

"She'll be here next week, we had a couple of projects we were finishing up."

"So what are we doing?" asked Jazz. "I'm happy to just lounge on the boat, but are we doing something specific?"

"I wanted to get here and check out the spots our locations department had listed," Devon answered her.

"So, you're just approving them or something?" Jazz asked.

"Well, normally we go with the locations people, but Jack thought we could make a day of it and check a few other places out ourselves." He glanced at Jack, and they exchanged a look.

Jazz caught my eye, and winked.

"Do you know anything about Marsh Tacky horses?" Jack asked me.

"Well, they're local and in danger of extinction. I think there are less than three hundred left," I offered.

He nodded. "Yeah, they date back to the Spanish colonials and are really sturdy and good in swampy water, so they'll be perfect for the movie, we think."

"That's right," Jazz said, lying back on one of the white cushions to get more sun. It was chilly out on the water despite the clear bright sky. "I heard they have Marsh Tacky races on the beach on Daufuskie Island. It's coming up in a few weeks, I think."

"Yep, that's where we're headed," Devon said. "Normally they come on a barge the morning of the event from surrounding stables."

"Damn, that must be a sight to see," Joey added.

Jack twisted his ball cap around to the back. "I spoke to a local guy who keeps a few on the island." He dropped his shades a second and caught my eye. "So that's what we're headed to do today. Race horses on the beach."

"Oh my God, seriously?" Jazz squealed. "That is so freaking cool!"

Not to mention apparently quite dangerous, and the sum total of my riding experience was . . . nil. I swallowed nervously. *Wow*.

Daufuskie Island was only accessible by boat, making it uniquely sheltered from massive development. The stable owner's land was right next to the beach, nestled among massive pines, palmettos, and ancient, sprawling Live Oaks strewn with Spanish moss. We could see the ocean glittering through the pines from where we were standing on the crunchy brown pine straw that carpeted the ground.

"It's typical that someone from California would be the one to show us what a freaking amazing part of the world we live in," said Joey. He nudged Jack as a local *Gullah* boy walked a chestnut stallion over to us.

Devon left us to speak to the stable owner about permission to film and get the skinny on the logistics of using the barge to bring film equipment.

"Who dun' gunna rai dis 'un?" the boy holding the horse asked us in his *Gullah* dialect. He looked about twelve, young but sinewy under his deep dark skin.

The horse was handsome and strong looking. Jazz and I both found ourselves stepping back a bit as the boy tied its lead rope loosely on the split rail fence.

Jack looked at my brother blankly.

"Oh, sorry. He asked who wanted to ride this horse first."

"I think you and I should race first," Jack said. "Show the girls how it's done. Maybe make a wager."

"This guy wants to date my sister," Joey told the boy and then pointed at me.

The boy looked at me, then at Jack. He jerked his head for Joey to follow him, and they exchanged a few murmurs, before the boy ran off over the pine straw.

"What the hell was that about?" I asked Joey.

"He said he's getting me a faster horse."

Jazz snorted with laughter.

"Uh, Joey," I said, my eyebrows raised in amusement. "When was the last time you rode a horse?"

"What? You think I can't beat this pansy-ass actor?"

Jazz lost it, doubling over with giggles. "Did you—"

"You're on." Jack aimed my brother a serious look before Jazz could finish. "If I win, I get to stay here on the island tonight with your sister. Alone."

I gasped out a breath then clamped my jaw shut.

Jazz promptly stopped laughing. "Shit, that was hot," she murmured at me.

No kidding.

Joey seemed to be weighing it up. Then his horse was led out of the barn. A muscly black horse that skittered sideways and pulled on his lead. "It's a deal."

We followed behind as boys and horses were led down to the beach and into the bright sun.

The race, which was marked out with rope, was to comprise a four hundred yard sprint, followed by a wade into the water around a small buoy, and then back. I was nervous to watch. It was notoriously difficult to maneuver the Marsh Tackies around turns without falling.

Jack toed off his shoes and socks, sliding his bare feet into the sand. He gathered his t-shirt behind his head, giving me a peek at his beautiful stomach. *Oh yes, please please take it off.* Then he pulled it over his head, leaving me with a dry mouth and sweaty palms.

My brother followed suit.

Jazz made a soft sound next to me.

Where Jack was chiseled and lean, Joey was no less fit but slightly broader with thicker arms and shoulders.

"Oh my . . ." Jazz got her phone out. "I've got to get this on video. It might be the hottest damn thing I've ever seen. Like, ever. I'm rarely speechless, but this might just do it." She began singing a sultry song for my ears only. Words all about how that face and that body made her want to party. *No kidding.*

"How do we get on without a saddle and stirrups?" Joey asked.

Jack walked over and created a stirrup with his hands for Joey and helped him up. Then he walked back with a smirk, held onto the mane of his horse, and leaped up onto its back in one smooth motion.

Oh. My. God.

Jazz squeaked. "I think I just orgasmed."

"Shut up, Jazz," I managed, and swallowed thickly.

"If I win?" asked Joey, looking a bit disgruntled and more determined than ever. His horse skittered to the side, ignoring the soothing tones of the boy holding his leading rein.

"You won't. There's too much riding on it for me. 'Scuse the pun." His eyes found mine.

I held Jack's eyes a moment before he winked and looked back at Joey.

My brother flushed. "If I win, you can stay on this damn island *alone*." He glared at the stablehand who was standing next to them as the Race Starter. "When you're ready."

My eyes roamed down Jack's bare torso to a tendril of black ink sneaking out over the waistband of his underwear that was visible above his worn blue jeans. The tattoo that covered his scarred skin caused by his father. His hands were curled into the mane, his biceps flexing. His powerful leg rested on the side of the chestnut horse, ending in bare feet and the tattoo of the beautiful little sea turtle. Jack had marked his body four times . . . once to cover his painful childhood memories, once to celebrate the leap in his career to megastar, the thin chain of ink on his ankle I'd never asked about, and once . . . to remember me.

I didn't get a chance to think on that further as a loud, "Hah!" rendered the air and both horses were smacked on their rumps and took off.

Jack immediately leaned in, gripping the horse with his entire body, muscles rippling. But Joey was on a much faster horse, and what Joey lacked in style as a rider was more than compensated for.

The black horse looked to be pulling into the lead. Joey threw a look over his shoulder at Jack, his blond hair whipping into his eyes.

Jazz mewed next to me. "Go, Joey," she yelled, her phone pointing straight ahead.

"Are you seriously cheering for me not to get laid tonight?" I laughed incredulously. "Go on, Jack!" I screamed out.

"Didn't realize you were ready to ride the horse again, so to speak." She giggled.

"Maybe I've changed my mind."

"But seriously, this is like the hottest thing I've ever seen."

We both looked at each other, and then screamed and cheered for our respective guys.

Joey reached the end of the first sprint and turned the horse into the water. It waded into the surf. On the turn, however, Joey had slipped down the side of the horse and was now battling to get himself righted. Jack came in after him. They made it around the buoy, the horses almost to their flanks. I don't know why I hadn't taken a picture before now, but I slid my phone out of my back pocket and aimed it at Jack, taking a shot just as he pulled into the lead ahead of Joey.

He leaned down close to the horse and dipped his head in the water, wetting it. And then stayed down, urging the horse on as it emerged out into the shallow surf and then the sand. With a squeeze of Jack's now waterlogged and dark blue thighs, the horse took off again as soon as it hit dry sand.

Joey was out of the water too now, and his horse was gaining. Joined by a couple of spectators from the stable and Devon, who'd just sauntered up, Jazz and I yelled and jumped up and down.

I was impressed with Joey's riding actually. He'd done some riding growing up and had a job at a stable one summer, but I didn't think he'd actually be able to pull off bareback racing.

And Jack? There were no words for how I felt about what I was witnessing. It was a purely physical reaction.

Joey got within a head of Jack, and I screamed louder, my voice breaking as I jumped up and down. They crossed the finish line in front of us, Jack narrowly keeping his lead.

A cheer went up from everyone just from the sheer joy of the spectacle.

CHAPTER TWENTY-SIX

$\mathcal{B}$oth Jack and Joey slowed their horses a ways further down the beach and slid from their mounts, panting and grinning as they grabbed each other in a handshake, and then bumped shoulders with a back slap.

Their joy and exhilaration was written all over their faces. All wagers and tensions forgotten.

As I watched, grinning like an idiot, they sauntered back, talking. Jack grabbed Joey's hand again, and as the stablehand led the horses away, pulled him in, saying something in his ear. Joey nodded, flicking his eyes to me, before shaking Jack's hand and clapping his shoulder again.

Then Jack turned to me and just pointed. His eyes were dancing, his dimples fully deployed, and I ran. I ran to the sound of catcalls and whistles and launched into Jack's arms.

"Oof," he croaked then groaned as my legs wrapped around him and I hugged him tight. We hugged like that for several long minutes, the briny smell of surf and Jack's warm body permeating all my thoughts.

"That was incredible," I said finally. "It's safe here right?

To hug you? I mean this place is isolated, and I'm not sure the locals are going to be posting pictures to the Web."

"Yeah," he murmured in my ear. "That's why I want to stay here with you tonight. That okay?"

"I suppose," I said coyly. He pulled back to look at me and I quickly added, "Yes."

"We don't have to do anything." He bumped his nose against mine. "I just want to be with you for a night and not have you worried about anyone seeing us. The boat can take everyone back, and return in the morning to get us back before your lunch shift."

I hugged him tight again and unwrapped my legs. He lowered me to the ground, and we headed back to join the others. None of us raced like the boys had, but we all took turns riding along the beach and walking in the waves. Jazz and I agreed it was without a doubt the coolest day ever. Jazz looked like a gypsy princess with her long print shirt hiked up to her thighs as she rode and colorful bands around her ankles and wrists. To my satisfaction, Joey couldn't keep his eyes off her. I looked up from the horse I was riding in the surf with a huge grin and caught Jack taking a picture of me with his phone.

All was fair I supposed.

After the horses, we went back out on the boat. Changing into swimsuits, we ate our sandwiches and explored the perimeter of the island. We stopped as close as the boat could get to a small sandbar that had emerged with the low tide, and after much persuading and cajoling from everyone else who'd already jumped overboard into the frigid water, I did the same.

"You realize there are tons of bull sharks around here, right?" I said, my voice all wobbly as we made it to the sand.

"All kinds of sharks," Joey said, shaking his head. "And dolphins and stingrays and whales."

"And snapper and cobia and flounder," added Jazz, cuffing Joey on the knee. "Doesn't stop her being afraid of sharks. Idiot."

Jack took my hand, and we all flopped on the sand. I shifted and laid my head on his leg. His fingers stroked my hair. I sighed contentedly.

I could feel Joey watching us, as he had all day, and wondered what he thought, and what exchange had taken place between him and Jack after the race. He also seemed perturbed that Jazz kept up constant conversation with Devon, asking all sorts of things about the movie business and the ins and outs of production and basically ignoring my brother.

"Are we staying in the hotel here?" I murmured to Jack, wishing I could kiss his lips.

Jack shook his head. "A cottage."

"What do we do about food and overnight stuff?"

"That's all been taken care of by the company handling the resort cottage rentals. They brought stuff over this morning, I think. And I asked them to buy overnight stuff, too—toothbrushes and what not."

"Wow, you thought of everything." I smiled and closed my eyes. The thought of what lay ahead for us kept a steady drumbeat of anticipation in my veins as the afternoon slowly ticked by.

We all caught some sun as it lowered, and full bellies and the sea air made everyone sleepy. When the tide began encroaching on our borrowed strip of sand, it was time to get to the boat.

I couldn't wait to get everyone on their way so Jack and

I could be alone. Back onboard, I pulled my white jean shorts on over my bikini, and then stared at Jack's face behind my mirrored glasses.

Sometimes to avoid the Jack Eversea, movie-star effect, I had to break his features down into individual aspects of beauty, just so I could see *him*. The angles of his cheekbones that sometimes seemed harsh, the small crease lines at his eyes, the full lips, and the tiny scar in his left eyebrow that I felt anchored to as a reminder he was a real guy beneath what he projected to everyone else.

We pulled up at a dock. I hugged Devon, Joey, and then Jazz, and Jack and I hopped onto dry land and waved them off.

I looked around the open piney area and saw a golf cart. "That our ride?" I asked, keeping my voice steady through sheer force of will.

The golf cart had the keys in it and a map of the island with a marked trail. We got in and headed down the dirt path through the trees that seemed to run parallel to the water's edge, even as we got to a bend in the road, where the island jutted out then turned to face the open sound. Here, the trees stood closer together almost hiding a small cottage near the shore. "This should be it," I said, double-checking the map.

Painted white, and stunning in its simplicity, the board-and-batten cottage looked like a marketing tool for *Southern Living Magazine*. It had a seamed metal roof jutting over a deep front porch, complete with two rocking chairs facing the sound. A glossy grass lawn ran down to the sandy edge of the water. There were lanterns strung in one of the small, pink-flowered crepe myrtle trees near the house and some hurricane jars with candles set here and there.

"Wow," I managed.

Up on the porch, we could see inside the glass French doors and the two windows on either side. There was a silver ice bucket with a bottle of champagne and two glass flutes set on a small bistro table by the window.

And I could see a bed. A huge bed. I glanced at Jack, who was wearing a lopsided grin, his eyes cutting away as he turned and knelt down, feeling underneath the mat for the key to the door.

He found the key and stood up, turning to me. The sun was low in the sky over the water, casting a golden glow.

I stepped forward and slid my hand up around the back of his neck and his eyes flickered closed. Pulling his face down, I gently touched my lips to his. My other hand ran down his arm until I reached his hand that held the key. I squeezed and urged his arm up, letting him know I was impatient to get inside with him.

He smiled against my lips and unlocked the door.

Stepping inside the open plan cottage, I breathed in the smell of clean laundry and cedar. A small kitchen area was tucked in the back corner behind the open living room with stone fireplace. The walls were cream painted shipboard siding, lending a casual feel to the elegantly decorated room.

The only windows were the ones facing out to the front porch and the sea beyond, dressed in elegant white ceiling to floor drapes.

I turned slowly and headed to the left side of the open space where a low partition separated the bedroom area from where a large white Victorian clawfoot tub nestled, open to the view.

"Wow," I said again, and then froze staring at the bedside

table. "Oh my God," I squeaked when I recognized my drift-wood lamp-base Faith had sold in her shop.

"What?"

I went over and sat on the edge of the white bed, running my fingers over the lamp gently. "This is mine. Wow."

"It's beautiful," Jack said and came to sit next to me.

I smiled at him. "This place is beautiful. Thank you."

"You're beautiful." He swallowed. "I hope you don't think it was too presumptuous of me to do this so fast. Just because we're here, doesn't mean we have to, you know."

"I know." I smiled. He'd said that like three times.

"I'll bring our stuff in. I think there's more to the bathroom than just that tub, maybe back behind here somewhere," he said, indicating the wall behind the bed. "You go investigate. Maybe we can shower then see what we've got to eat in the fridge."

I nodded, and he headed out to the porch.

There was indeed a bathroom back there with a massive walk-in shower lined with white subway tiles and multiple showerheads. I reached in and turned it on, letting the water heat and wandered over to the mirror above one of the marble-topped vanities. I was flushed from the sun and my hair, as I pulled it out of a messy bun, was a kinky mess. When Jack told me I was beautiful, I believed him. Fully. I felt beautiful when he looked at me.

His mention of us showering conjured all sorts of images, and while he probably meant we should shower one after the other, all I could think about after our outdoor shower was us in there together.

We had this one amazing night here, away from prying eyes and judgments. I had no idea what our relationship would look like going forward, but we had this moment.

Seven long months I'd spent missing him and wanting him and fantasizing about various scenarios. And some had been sexual, there was no point denying it to myself.

I took a deep breath. "Jack?"

He came in, carrying a black toiletries bag and dumped it on the counter. "Yeah?"

"I-I was thinking . . ." *Gah.* My throat was so thick with nerves, I sounded like I needed speech therapy. And my cheeks were hot. My eyes flicked over to the shower involuntarily.

Jack followed my look then looked back at me. And I saw the thought cross his mind, his eyes narrowing, his nostrils flaring slightly. His Adam's apple bobbed roughly as he swallowed. "What were you thinking?" he said roughly.

My shaking fingers found the buttons of my shorts, and I popped them open, and then shimmied them down my thighs until they dropped. I stepped out of them and toed off my shoes.

Jack's eyes tracked down my legs then back to my hands, waiting to see what they would do next, I guess. The steam from the warm shower filled the room.

I reached for my t-shirt and pulled it off and stood in my bikini. "I was thinking, you did such a good job of washing me in the shower before, y-you could do it again?"

Jack's mouth closed in a tight line, and his hand gripped the counter, white knuckled.

"Get undressed, Jack," I said softly and reached for my bikini tie at my neck.

"Stop," he said harshly.

I froze.

He let go of the counter, and reaching behind him, pulled his t-shirt over his head. "I want to do that."

Gulping, I obeyed.

"Get in the shower," he rasped, his eyes intense.

The hunch that I'd released some kind of animal in Jack was strong. And rather than trepidation, it sent a rush of hot want through every single part of me. I nodded with a small smile as I entered the shower. Stepping under the warm spray, I turned to watch the vague outline of Jack through the foggy glass as he took off his shoes and shorts. Despite the moist humidity and the water streaming over me, my mouth went dry at the sight of Jack stepping into the shower completely naked and aroused.

Wow.

The sight of his muscled form with the hideous tattoo, beautiful but ugly for its significance, caused my nerves to ratchet up. My eyes traveled back up to where he was watching me intently, his green eyes boring into mine.

A small crease between his brows let me know he was also nervous. Maybe he was nervous this was all a big tease, or that he might step over some kind of line and go too far with me. I didn't know.

Picking up my sopping hair to expose the knot of my swimsuit, I turned and presented my back to him. "Can you take this off me now, please?"

His fingers touched my neck and spine. The top gaped forward and I pulled it off, letting it smack the floor of the shower. He stepped in close, his arousal hard at my back, causing an involuntary shudder to run through me. His hands slid around my belly, and after a brief hesitation, up and lightly over my breasts.

I clenched my teeth at the shock of sensation.

Holy shit.

I let my head fall back.

Reactions cascaded one after the other, a relief of having

his hands on me. It wasn't nearly enough. How did I let him know how much I wanted him?

Sometimes the look in his eyes was completely at odds with his slow and gentle touches.

I *wanted* him to lose control. I wanted to see Jack at his most primal. I wanted to be the object of his lust. Of his love, not his pain or revenge.

Hearing his breath in my ear, I came to a decision.

CHAPTER TWENTY-SEVEN

$\mathcal{J}$ grabbed the miniature shower gel bottle and poured some in my hand and moved away, sliding around behind Jack in the shower. Exchanging places.

Lathering up the soap, I slid the suds over his muscled back, massaging my hands over the slick and tense terrain, and up into his hair, using my nails to scrape lightly over his scalp.

"What are you doing?" He hissed in a breath, dropping his head forward into the spray. His hands came up to brace on the wall as the water sluiced over him. "Damn, that feels good."

Smiling, I got some more gel, the scent of rosemary and bergamot swirling with the steam, and ran my hands down his back again. I glided over his buttocks then, as I felt him tense, and swallowing my nerves, round to the front of him where I grasped his firm thickness in my hand.

Jack's hand immediately clamped down on my wrist, hard. "Christ," he gasped, his voice breaking over the word. Then he moved, spinning me toward him, lifting me through the hot spray and back against the cold tile wall that took my breath. I barely got a chance to see his flushed face and beautiful eyes before his mouth took mine.

Grasping his neck and his head, I hung on, returning his fevered kisses, lashing my tongue against his. Tension coiled tightly in my body, a mass of heat that seared me from the inside out, a scalding ache that begged to be eased.

"Please," Jack whispered as he pulled his mouth from mine. "Please, stop me," he repeated before seizing it again. He pressed himself between my legs where I literally ached for him.

"No fucking way," I managed through a whimpered gasp.

Immediately Jack pulled back, looking at me in shock, and then bursting into a chuckle, his dimples creasing his cheeks. He kissed me again. "I seriously never know what is going to come out of your mouth. You kill me."

"Yeah, well, you're killing *me* right now. I need these bikini bottoms off. Stat."

Jack snorted, and his shoulders heaved with silent laughter as he stepped back to lower me to my feet. Then he knelt down and pressed a kiss to my belly.

I inhaled and held my breath, my fingers tangling in his thick, wet hair.

When he looked back up at me, he was still smiling.

I watched, mesmerized, as he grasped the sides of my bottoms, and just as he had in the outdoor shower at Devon's, when I hadn't been able to watch him, peeled them down my legs. When they hit the floor, I stepped out of them.

As I looked down at him, he held my eyes. He seemed to be communicating some kind of challenge, maybe expecting me to call this off. Perhaps he felt nervous. *I* was. But there were other feelings that were a lot stronger. Running a hand back up my calf, he pulled my knee forward and then, when I still didn't stop him, hooked my leg over his shoulder.

Shock and arousal sent a startled whimper past my lips.

He cocked an eyebrow, then continued running his hand up the inside of my thigh. Okay, I didn't think I could watch this, but I sure as heck wasn't going to stop him from doing whatever it was he was thinking of . . .

"Oh God," I whimpered as his fingers found my slickness and didn't even stop before sliding inside me. I closed my eyes, my head falling back and hitting the shower wall.

Jack's breathing was as quick and shallow as mine.

"Don't get shy about watching now, Keri Ann." Jack's voice was rough. I peeled my eyes open and looked down at the expression on Jack's face. I'd never seen a more desperate and restrained set to his mouth. It added a thick layer of intensity to the already building sensations that were spiraling through me at the drag of his finger, his thumb circling me.

My breath started coming in pants.

"Fuck," Jack rasped. "I could come, just doing this to you."

His words shocked me, yet thrilled me at the same time. "So do it then," I breathed desperately. "I don't want to be feeling this on my own."

Jack groaned. "You're not . . . I promise." He reached down with his free hand.

I willed my eyes to stay open. To watch him.

Oh my God. I didn't think I could ever see anything sexier. *In. My. Life.*

Then, with a sound like a starving man, he leaned forward and replaced his thumb, that had been dancing a rhythm over me, with his hot mouth and I shattered apart, gasping and shuddering against the tiled wall. I cried out as the sensations went on, a long wail, and I pressed against his mouth, my hands in his hair holding him against me. Wanting it to never stop.

"Oh God, Keri Ann," Jack ground out, and his entire body jerked. My hands left his hair and I slid down the wall to join him on the floor, reaching to cover his hand with my own, to be a part of his release.

He grabbed my face, kissing me deeply, then we wrapped our arms around each other, holding our still heaving and convulsing bodies.

The shower water, now running cooler, poured over us.

Jack, in fresh shorts and a t-shirt, since he'd actually known we had a sleepover ahead of time, and me just in the fluffy white robe I'd found in the bathroom, made ourselves comfortable on the wicker love seat out on the front porch. We elected not to use the rocking chairs, as cute as they were, so that we could sit together.

We'd found chilled local shrimp and cocktail sauce in the fridge, and we were now feasting on them, along with the champagne.

I felt heady and decadent and not entirely sure I wasn't in a dream.

Even though the sky was still light with leftover sun, we'd lit the hurricane jars and citronella candles that surrounded the deck in an effort to keep any early mosquitoes away.

"Thank you for sharing your journal pages with me," I said, broaching a subject I'd been meaning to get to. "What does taking the piss mean? You said the rain there 'takes the piss'?"

He chuckled. "It's a British term for taking the mickey, or teasing. Like it's not really rain, it's just insulting you by pretending to be . . ."

"Hmmm. It sounds like England is a tough place for you

to spend time in. You seem . . . darker there, than how you are with me. Here."

Jack took a sip of his champagne. The glass looked so delicate in his strong hand. He set it down on the table. "I am, there. But really, I have been like that for a while. I . . ." he took a breath and looked at me with a strange lopsided grin, his brow furrowing as he tugged on the crown of his hair. "I'm no good at expressing this stuff. I know I seem different with you. I notice it too, but I feel more *me* than anytime else. Does that make sense?"

I shook my head slowly side to side.

"I guess you just make me believe that there's a world without bullshit, where I can just be me. I'm so on guard everywhere else, so tense. About everything. In the world I live in, you can never take anything at face value. Every decision I make could be the one that tears down everything I've worked for. It could be a movie choice, but worse, it could just be a wrong place wrong time, or one bad word. One minute they love you, the next they hate you. There were times, in the early days, I took stuff, a line of coke, a pill or whatever just to be able to put my face out the door and be 'on.' Or a *tranq* just to fall asleep at night. It changes you."

My hand itched to touch him, so I rested it on his forearm.

He looked at it a few moments. "I spent a lot of time in England, trying to reconcile things that happened there with my father and who he was and . . . why he burned me, and all the other . . ." he winced, "shit he did. I wrote a ton of stuff about it in that journal, nothing you needed to read, believe me. But . . . I've been turning it into something. Like a screenplay about him, who he was, what he did. I don't want to honor him or anything, or do anything with it, I just needed to see it laid out as if it were a movie, as if it were a script, so I could process it, you know? See it objectively. And know that without my past I wouldn't be who I am today."

"So in a way it was kind of good that you went? Like it was meant to be . . . I think there were parts of you . . . you needed to knit together."

He nodded and stared out toward the water.

"Even though I totally hated that you didn't tell me what was going on and didn't come back here, I get it."

Jack turned to me. "Come here," he whispered, taking my champagne flute and setting it down next to his. I shifted closer, but he slid an arm around my waist and hauled me astride his lap. My robe was large and tightly belted, but it could hardly survive that move and revealed a lot of thigh. Jack glanced down and swallowed. "Shit, didn't mean to do that. Now I'll be distracted."

I laughed softly and covered my upper thighs as best as I could. When I looked up, Jack was gazing at me seriously.

He reached a hand up and brushed a stray lock of my hair from my face. "I'm sorry I didn't tell you everything when it happened."

I blinked slowly. Then gave a single nod, accepting his apology, but waiting for more.

"I never left you for *her*. It wasn't *her*," Jack said softly. "I was in shock for a while, back then when I thought I was about to be a father. I just wasn't going to let a child of mine grow up without me. And I must have known deep down the kind of person Audrey was, that she'd never let me be fully in her child's life if I wasn't *with* her. I came here right after I found out she lied." He shook his head. "Remember I mentioned I ended up at that gallery on Hilton Head Island where you had that exhibit?"

"Yes, but you never said how." *Or why you didn't come see me*. It still hurt.

"Dumb luck, I guess. I saw a thing about it on the magazine I was given with the rental car. I drove straight there. Seeing that piece you did . . . that wave . . . really affected me. It was so beautiful and so painful to see. I realized how much being with me could hurt you."

I sat frozen, afraid even my breathing would stop him talking.

"Not just how much I obviously hurt you by what happened, but also that being with me, being seen to be with me could damage you professionally. Which is something I totally understand."

Shaking my head slowly, I wanted to argue, but he was right. It was a different take, but still the same issue I'd already voiced to him. About being with him as his girlfriend.

He put a finger to my lips, stopping me from making any objection. "I was already thinking about not seeing you for those reasons, and only those reasons, but I drove to Butler Cove anyway. I wanted to see you. Apologize or something, I didn't know really. Maybe be selfish and go after you anyway. And then Sheila called, she's my publicist, and told me about the pictures."

Just being reminded of the pictures sent my belly lurching violently.

"I was freaking driving toward you and seriously about to bring a shit storm to town along with me." Jack shook his head and closed his eyes. "I couldn't do it. I turned around. I couldn't do it to you. And I literally promised not to go anywhere near you until the contract was done." He shifted, looking up at me.

I stared at him. I couldn't believe he'd been here, so close, and just turned around. My heart hurt. Even though he'd done it to protect me.

"Audrey also made some claims about my temper, saying she was scared of me. She was trying every angle. She had a video of me hitting Colt, and I'd lost my mind and punched the wall at my place when I found out about the pregnancy being fake," he added at my look. "The publicity would have been a nightmare if anyone thought the reason my hand was in a cast was because I . . ."

I tried and failed to hold back a shudder. Yes, it would have been grotesque sensationalism. *Jack Eversea in violent outburst with Audrey Lane.*

My heart felt wounded for him. I just couldn't imagine someone deliberately hurting him, and worse, I couldn't bear the thought of what he must have felt to be so utterly betrayed. Reaching my hand out, I ran my fingers through his hair and skated my fingers around his neck to his jaw. Then his lips. His lips were so soft. Leaning forward, I kissed him softly.

He cleared his throat. "So Peak used that. They pacified Audrey by telling her they needed me on something out of the country. In England. God, I didn't want to take it. I didn't want to be back there. But my main contact at Peak said if I didn't take it, they might not back the *Dread Pirate Roberts* project. I'd already told Devon I'd do it, and we have other investors who'd pull out if Peak wasn't involved."

Jack took one of my hands and placed it on his chest. "And part of me wondered why you'd want to see me again anyway."

His shirt was warm and soft, and I could feel the steady thump of his heart beneath my fingers. "I thought of contacting you so many times, but I didn't know how. Can you imagine if you'd gotten a text or a phone call from me out of the blue? And what would I even say? Every day that went by, it became harder to even contemplate that as an option."

"It's okay, Jack," I whispered, because truly I didn't know what else to say. He was right, a random phone call from him would have made me mad as hell. And even though I didn't like it, it all made sense to me, but unfortunately invited a few more unwelcome thoughts. "Are, are you going to be in a contract for the *Dread Pirate Roberts* movie?"

"They're going to try, I'm sure. But the female lead hasn't been cast yet, and I'll make sure she knows the deal about you and me."

"I'm probably going to need a firm 'no,' Jack." I raised my eyebrows.

He laughed. "Of course, it's a firm 'no.' No relationship contracts, period."

"So what *is* the deal about you and me?"

"You exist, therefore I am?"

I snorted a giggle. "Is that existential Jack talking?"

"No, it's real Jack. And real Jack has very real, like crazy, crazy, real feelings for you that might actually scare the shit outta him a little."

I knew the feeling. "Why are they so scary?" I whispered.

The last colors had faded from the sky, allowing the candles to cast their warm glow and leaving Jack's eyes in shadow.

"Partly because I don't know that you want real Jack and his crazy life and everything that goes along with it," he returned. "And I'm not sure, going forward, how to keep that separate. It could still hurt you."

It was my biggest fear, too. A hurdle to tackle tomorrow when we headed back to reality.

At least we had tonight.

CHAPTER TWENTY-EIGHT

*J*ack and I talked for hours as stars pierced the sky above the now dark water, and continued talking as the full moon rose. At one point, I made to leave his lap, thinking he was probably uncomfortable, but his hands tightened on me. "Don't," was all he said.

So I didn't.

We talked more about his timeline for the movie, and he asked me all about the long process of getting into SCAD. I told him about my successes over the last few months and how it was hard to believe people actually wanted to see my stuff, let alone buy it. There were times when I felt like everyone was humoring me, maybe doing a favor to Faith who had been so supportive of me by putting me in her boutique and setting me up with my first gallery exhibit.

"Never lose your humility," Jack told me. "But you need to own your gift."

"I know. I'm not used to being so unsure of myself." I ran my fingers through his soft hair, feeling the languorous effect of the champagne. "There's only two things that have ever made me feel that way. My art and you."

"Your work is beautiful. And you don't need to be unsure of me," Jack whispered. His hands came to cup my cheeks and draw me down, pausing with his face inches from mine. His eyes, heavy lidded, were on my lips.

It occurred to me that the moment in space and time before lips touch, the small exquisite sting of wanting, a beat of thirst, of yearning, was the most underrated part of kissing. There should be sonnets and epic poems written about the space before a kiss, and the thrilling rush that comes with the moment of contact.

My mouth moved greedily, sliding, and grazing his captured bottom lip with my teeth, soothing it with my tongue.

A low sound rumbled through Jack, and his hands were no longer so gentle as they gripped me, seeking and kneading, finding my back, my thighs, pressing me closer and fumbling with the knot belting my robe.

Our breathing picked up pace, but not rhythm, as it labored between now deep kisses and heart-pounding want.

Jack's mouth slid down my neck, sucking at my skin, igniting my nerve endings in a flare that raced down to my toes. "I need to get you in a bed." His hand slid inside my robe, across the skin of my belly and around to my back, his movement baring me to him. One shoulder of the robe fell back. He drew away, his nostrils flaring, raking his hooded gaze over my breasts and down to the juncture of my thighs as I sat astride him.

I reached down and undid the button of his cargo shorts then pulled the zipper down, revealing the strained fabric of his boxers.

His mouth parted slightly, and I heard the sound of his dry swallow. "Like, now," he rasped.

"Are you going to do your caveman thing again?" I asked and giggled, because he was already moving to stand with me in his arms.

Wrapping my legs tight around his waist, I hung on as we dipped sideways through the door and nudged it closed behind us. I closed the curtains, one handed.

He backed up to the bed and sat down heavily. His mouth was instantly on mine again, and I lifted up and tucked my knees under me so I could take his t-shirt off and press closer. I wanted my skin against his.

The hard ridge of his arousal tortured me. I rocked forward, and he immediately responded, his hips bucking and pressing hard against my wet heat.

"God," he breathed out roughly, pulling his mouth from mine.

Shimmying back, my breath choppy and shallow, I dropped to my knees on the floor.

"What are you doing?" he whispered, and the telltale flush across his cheekbones told me all I needed to know. His carved abdomen tensed.

"Getting you naked." I grinned and helped him take his shorts and underwear down. Then moved between his knees.

"This," he croaked and clutched the edge of the mattress, "may be the hottest thing ever. You realize I'm going to picture you sitting here like this whenever we're not together?"

"Just sitting here?" I raised an eyebrow, and then reached out and grasped him. "Not doing this?"

"Shit," he hissed, his skin flushing further.

I leaned forward. "Or this?" Out of the corner of my eye, I briefly saw his knuckles turn white as I took him in my mouth. I think he literally growled, and one of those white-knuckled hands fisted in my hair as he surged up and moved with me. His reaction shot a bolt of reciprocal lust straight down to the pit of my belly.

"Fuck," he rasped. "I don't think I can do this." He pulled me up. "I won't last."

He fumbled in his discarded shorts pocket for protection then pulled me back astride his lap, kissing me deeply.

I throbbed with anticipation.

"Take your hair down," he whispered. His hand ran up my spine then skimmed around to my breasts, grazing over the sensitive peaks.

I gasped, arching forward, needing more, and getting it as his hands palmed and his mouth followed. He sucked me into his hot wet heat.

Shakily, I let my hair out of my bun, letting it fall damp and heavy down my back.

Jack pulled away and watched me. His fingers flowed over and around my belly. They skimmed my inner thighs, reaching between us, sliding over my slick and sensitive flesh, easing inside me and triggering whimpers from my throat.

"You're so Goddamn beautiful, Keri Ann," he murmured. Then he lifted me, one hand pressed to the small of my back, and guided me over him.

Oh God.

I was so ready, so wanting, but I'd also only ever done this once with him.

"This okay?" he whispered brokenly, his eyes searching mine. Rigidly still, his shoulders under my fingers were quivering.

I got the feeling he was physically struggling not to surge up into me. I nodded because I couldn't talk over the emotion clogging my throat.

His hand skated up my spine into my hair, and he wound it up in his hand and kissed me.

As my tongue found his and slid deeply into his mouth, he pulled me down, easing me onto him. Taking me.

It was just too good, and we'd waited so long. The feel of him inside me filled my entire being with sharp and exquisite needles of ecstasy. My skin was on fire, every nerve-ending I possessed experiencing it firsthand. I pulled my mouth from Jack's just so I could focus. So I could try and hold onto the cry that seemed about to be torn from my throat.

"Shit," Jack hissed and then groaned. "You feel so good."

He rocked his hips, and I opened my eyes, my teeth clenched, as the sensations barreled through me with his movement.

"How could you possibly feel this damn good?" His eyes implored me desperately, like I could answer him. As if I'd woven some spell over him.

I didn't know. *I'd* certainly never known anything like this. Even the unbelievable first night we'd shared paled when compared to the depth of emotion that was attached to the feel of Jack beneath me. Jack inside me. Jack holding me and sliding in and out of me as I moved on him. And God, I was moving. I couldn't help it. I was propelled by a need so strong, I couldn't catch my breath over it. "God, Jack . . ." I sobbed out, no longer able to hold anything back.

The climax when it came, ripped its way through me so fast I barely heard Jack as he held me tight to his chest murmuring calming words and sliding his fingers through my hair, keeping me anchored to him.

Afterwards we moved into a tangle of naked flesh, limbs, and sheets, his mouth making love to mine, and then finding my aching nipples. I arched into his kiss, his arms under the bow of my spine, holding me up. His hands and mouth roamed the landscape of my body, searching out all my secrets, creating future fantasies, and coaxing me into a trembling mess of hot torturous need that only existed for some kind of release.

"Please," I managed at some point.

"I want to go slow for you," he breathed. He settled between my legs, and I flashed back to our first time, when we'd made love in this same position.

My hands raked through his messy, dark brown hair, and I lifted his face to mine. "I don't," I said. The imaginary images of him and Audrey were fading with every moment we spent together, but I wanted them gone. I wanted it to be *us* I saw when Jack was wild and not gentle. "I like slow . . . but also fast," I murmured, echoing his words from the other night.

His lower body surged against mine, hard and heavy against my thigh, so close to where I was aching and needing. Again.

"Soft, but also rough," I scraped my nails over his skin and up into his hair. He hissed in a breath, his green eyes darkening, watching my mouth, waiting for the words he knew were coming. "Gentle . . . then really . . ." I closed my hand firmly in his hair and swallowed, building up courage, looking him straight in his eyes. "Really . . . hard."

Jack expelled a rush of air, sharp and deep. Seconds passed, his mouth tightening like he was struggling for control.

I moistened my lower lip and caught it between my teeth, a little nervous at my own boldness, waiting for what he would do.

He lifted his body, a dark carved shadow in the low lamp light and took my hands, pinning them on the bed either side of my head. Eyes blazing, his mouth curving into a lopsided grin, his knees pushed my legs wider. "You asked," he said finally and slammed into me hot and hard.

I cried out, but he didn't stop.

I didn't want him to.

He knew it.

Jack was fierce, and glorious. A face etched with determination, with need, and with an aching reverence that had me shuddering beneath him. An animal, yet also a man. A driving force of nature whose eyes blazed as his skin glowed with sweat, and in that moment, and that moment alone, I became a woman. I was no longer the girl he knew. I was a woman who'd forged her own future, made her own choices, had experienced heartbreak and first love and now demanded to be made love to as an equal. I had wants, I had needs, and right now my need was to watch Jack Eversea, my Jack, my sweet, vulnerable, yet closed and guarded Jack, lose it.

Surging and arching up, I wrapped my legs around his waist and matched him, stroke for stroke. The feel of him overwhelming, and so right.

His eyes closed and his hands gripped mine tighter, his weight pressing them into the bed and his body quaking. "Jesus," he growled.

"Look at me, Jack," I whispered through my labored breathing, echoing his words to me when we'd first made love.

He obeyed, his eyes almost black, his pupils so large, and I felt him slowing.

"No, I need you, Jack. Don't . . . don't stop." *Please. Don't ever stop.* I arched up further, tilting my hips, the momentum coming from some deeper, primal part of me.

"Ahh, God, Keri Ann, I—shit." He gasped through clenched teeth, his thrusts coming faster. Harder. "I can't," he managed. One hand left mine and thrust under my spine, yanking me up to him so our bodies were flush, skin against slick skin.

The contact made me shudder and cry out, igniting the fuse inside me and pulling me with him as he lost all semblance of restraint. My hands both suddenly free, I clutched his back and my fingers dug in, holding on as we moved, straining against, yet pulled willingly into the tide of release.

Daylight piercing through the slits between the drapes found us still wrapped around each other. I came awake slowly, taking stock of our surroundings and the feel of Jack's heart-beat thudding steadily against me. Images of all the things we'd done last night, interspersed between sleeping and more talking, replayed through my mind, sending another wave of longing through me. That thing where he'd flipped me onto my belly and run his tongue down my spine . . . *God.* And the things he said . . . I felt like a goddess to Jack. A worshipped, fall-to-his-knees goddess.

He'd never called me any term of endearment, like baby, or sweetheart, always my name. Over and over, my name. Like a prayer falling from his lips. It was raw. A reminder with every sensation that it was *us*, right there in that moment. *Me* that was making him feel the way he was feeling.

Jack had been right, our being together was as real as it got. It was more than real. It made everything else, every thought, every idea that didn't include him, seem muted and faded. How on earth was I going to exist as anything but an extension of *us*? How the hell were we going to keep this secret?

"Stop thinking so hard," I heard Jack's muffled voice next to me.

I gulped guiltily then laughed. "Sorry, I didn't realize I was so loud."

His head emerged from half under a pillow, his hair sticking up in all directions. Damn, that wasn't fair.

I sat up and instinctively pulled my own hair back and secured it with the band I kept around my wrist then quickly covered my bare breasts with my arms.

"Are you joking?" he asked with a grin, reaching out and pulling my arm away. "That's the most beautiful sight I can imagine waking up to."

I swallowed, feeling heat bloom in my cheeks, and sank back under the covers with him. "I think I'll have to take advantage of that gorgeous clawfoot bathtub. I'm aching in muscles I never knew I had."

Jack leaned up on an elbow and turned my face to his, kissing me softly. "Sorry," he murmured with a grin that said anything but. Then he laid his head down and just watched me, his hand tracing lazy circles over my neck and chest.

I looked back at him, counting the tiny bright flecks among the sea of iridescent greens surrounding his dark pupils. "Sometimes your eyes are translucent like green sea glass and other times they're dark, almost gray, like a deep forest," I murmured. "And sometimes, like now, they're like pools I want to throw myself into." I smiled at my own ridiculousness.

His hand that had been lazily tracing my skin now took mine and pressed it firmly against the hard smooth skin of his upper torso, like I could ease an ache for him.

My own heart lurched up to thump heavily in my throat, making it hard to breathe. I swallowed, not trusting myself to speak, hoping he could see in my eyes what I couldn't get out of my mouth.

And hoping I was strong enough to handle this beautiful man and all he was offering and not let my fears break both our hearts.

CHAPTER TWENTY-NINE

Jack and I sat on the front porch before we left, eating our scrounged-up breakfast of eggs and biscuits. The latter he'd looked at curiously before declaring them freaking awesome. Biscuits were cookies in England, apparently.

My eyes were on the beauty of the ocean before us, but my mind was awash with worry about my art opening. Still being nervous of the attention and not having anything to wear to it was trivial compared to my new concern of how Jack could be at the event without eclipsing everything I'd worked so hard for.

"I've been to some amazing places all over the world," Jack murmured, his eyes on me. "And all I can think about is how much I want to take you to each and every one of them. See them all through your eyes, be there with you . . . make love to you in every single one of them."

His dimple flashed, and he cut his eyes away.

Warmth pooled low in my belly, but it came along with a shiver as Joey's words came back to me. Would Jack expect me to follow him around the world? Not that I didn't want to go places with Jack, I did. But . . .

The breakfast we'd just eaten began to feel like cement the more I considered his being with me for the event. I should want him there at the party. I should want him there for the support. I should want him there, even to help with my fear of attention, because truly, who would give a shit about a small town waitress and her sculptures when they could focus on Jack? That thought gave me pause. So I was nervous of the attention, but yet I didn't want Jack to overshadow me? I was so confused.

The added concern of the house and how I would even go to SCAD added its weight to my churning thoughts.

"What's wrong?" Jack's voice broke through my thoughts. And I hated that we'd shortly be leaving this cocoon of privacy. "How do you always know when something's wrong?" I asked, cocking my head to look at him.

He shrugged. "Honestly? I seem weirdly attuned to what's going on with you. It affects my mood." He glanced at me then got up and stuffed his hands in his jeans pockets. Leaning a shoulder against the pillar, and turning to the view I was so mesmerized by, he shrugged. "Right now, I'm starting to feel anxious and on edge. And since I know I'm not afraid of golf carts, or boats, which are both in our near future, I can only assume I'm catching a vibe." He winked.

"I know I've talked to you about being nervous to be seen with you. What that will mean. What that will look like . . . for me."

"Yeah," he murmured. "I get it. Living in a fishbowl has been my life for six odd years, and to be honest, I'm still not used to it."

"So how do we do this?"

He blew out a breath.

I stared at his profile and the lump in his throat moving

as he swallowed. His shoulders, which had made to shrug again, stayed up in an expression of tension, muscles outlined through his thin white cotton t-shirt.

I waited.

Then his face transformed, and he pointed out straight ahead. I followed the direction of his hand and looked in time to see another splash and dark glossy fin. A pod of dolphins frolicked just off the shore, not a hundred yards from us.

I jumped up and grabbed his hand, and we jogged to the water's edge, the grass cool and wet under our bare feet. There was no sand here but rocks that had been placed to stabilize the coastline.

The dolphins swam in a group, first one way then the other, all shining backs and blowing mist, undulating and vanishing in turn.

"Wish I had my kayak," I murmured.

Jack slung an arm around my shoulders and tucked me in close, dropping a kiss on my head.

"You know people get bored and move on to a new story quickly, right?" he asked, continuing our earlier conversation. "I mean, if we just do this and go out there, it will suck for a period of time. People will want to photograph us together, photograph you. Ask about you. But then when there's no drama, it will get easier. It won't be gone, but it will get easier."

My heart rate picked up a panicked rhythm. I shook my head. "I don't think—"

"Let's not think about it right now. Okay?" He turned me to face him, threading his fingers through my hair and tilting my head back.

I blinked up at his beautiful face and tried to calm my heart.

"I'll do whatever I can to keep you out of the madness, I swear," he said softly.

I nodded, and he kissed me softly, wrapping me up in his arms. It wasn't the madness I was nervous about. It was the fact that that's all I'd be known for.

We locked the cottage behind us and left the key for the cleaning service. I hated to leave. I wasn't sure when Jack and I would next get to spend time like that again. We headed back toward the dock on the golf cart.

It looked like the boat was already here. And Jazz was on it, pacing.

"What the—"

"Oh my God, you guys," she screeched, leaping off the boat onto the dock. "I've been calling like a maniac—"

"What? Why?" I said, as we headed toward her.

"It's a freaking nightmare. Jack," she speared him with a sharp look. "Why don't you tell me which 'source close to the actor' knows about Keri Ann? Because I'll freaking cut them."

A rush of cold ice poured through me as my blood drained. "What?" I repeated, but without sound. My ears rang and my vision turned black at the edges. Orange juice and coffee turned into a vile mix in my belly.

"What the hell are you talking about?" Jack asked.

I stared at Jazz, hoping beyond all hope I was reading the wrong thing into her question. But I saw her face, and I belatedly noticed the pages she held in her hand and was now shoving in Jack's face.

As Jack's expression of shock confirmed my worst fears, I stumbled backwards.

"Fuck!" Jack yelled and grabbed his hair, sinking down to his haunches. Then he lifted his head and turned in slow motion to look at me, his face bleak.

My stomach heaved.

The pictures? The thought flitted through my mind.

Jack nodded. He looked destroyed. God, and in pain. He'd been betrayed again, but all I could think about was me right now.

Jazz stepped past him and marched to me, her face a mask of concern and rage mixed together. I shook my head, like if she didn't get to me and show me, then it wouldn't be real.

"I don't want to see them, please don't," I said as Jazz got close. She wrapped me up in her arms. I buried my face in her vanilla hair.

"It's bad," she whispered against my ear. "Really bad. It's a reporter. He showed up and spoke to Joey this morning, gave him this, he wanted a statement from you. Joey would have come here himself but didn't want to lead him to you, so he called me. You can deal. Okay? You can totally handle this."

I peeled back.

She grabbed my face, morphing into a pillar of strength as she realized I wasn't coping. "Seriously. You can deal with this. You've gone through worse."

I nodded, though I didn't know what I was agreeing with.

Behind Jazz, Jack conversed briefly with Dan, the captain of the boat, then started talking on his phone. He paced back and forth and kicked an imaginary object. I wanted to wrap him up in my arms for having to always go through this. I wanted him to wrap *me* up and tell me it was all a joke.

Taking a deep and bracing breath, I looked back at Jazz. I needed to see it all and know what I was dealing with. What *we* were dealing with, I corrected myself.

"All right, show me," I said to Jazz. The buzzing in my ears from nerves and dread made me feel off-balance.

The moment I saw the pictures of Jack and me from seven months ago, just as Jack described, my stomach finally rebelled. I turned, making it to the edge of the dock. As I looked down, the churning coalesced into a sharp spasm and I gave in to it, opening my throat and throwing up my breakfast and my worst nightmare into the marsh reeds and black pluff mud.

Nice.

Belatedly, the words accompanying the picture joined the throng of torture in my head. I wiped my stinging eyes and grabbed the paper from Jazz.

Jack approached, holding a bottle of water.

The headline, *Audrey loses baby in grief over Jack's cheating ways*, was followed by a messy timeline dating back well before I'd met Jack. I was one in a long line of conquests, according to the article, but held particular significance because I caused such a rift in their relationship that she'd lost her baby. And in her grief she'd sought comfort and solace from the director of her new movie. *Whatever*. But it was all so . . . *believable*.

"Look, I can talk to him," Jack said to whoever was on the phone. He handed me the water but didn't look at me.

Please look at me.

"Have Sheila and my lawyer reach out to him. See if we can come to some kind of deal before he turns the story in. He can't use the pictures without being sued. I own the rights. And I can promise you, I'll sue the fuck out of him. But realistically, he'll use them, then retract, so he'll still get impact."

"I can't believe one girl can be such a bitch." Jazz grimaced.

"Yeah," Jack murmured. "She just waited until we were out of the contract and did exactly what she'd wanted to all along." He turned toward the boat, looking out into the distance.

He hadn't touched me since we'd left the cottage. I felt the loss of it keenly. At the same time I felt so irrationally angry and irritated with him, I felt if he touched me, I'd cringe.

"We need to get to Savannah," Jack said to us, as he ended his phone call. "Devon will pick us up. I'll arrange to meet this guy there instead of back in Butler Cove. Then maybe you guys can get home without him bothering you." He headed toward the boat.

God. Was this going to be my life?

"How's Joey?" I asked Jazz, my throat raspy.

She pursed her lips. "Mad as a yellow jacket. He said Jack swore to him this wouldn't happen."

"When did you do that?" I asked Jack's back.

He shrugged, not turning around. "Yesterday. On the beach."

Please look at me, I willed him again, to no avail.

We climbed on the boat and Jazz's phone buzzed. She paused to pull it out of her back pocket. "Oh shit buckets," she said.

"What?"

"That Ashley girl is telling everyone she made out with you, Jack. Apparently that photo of you guys she posted on Facebook a few days ago has gone nutso, and now she's making all sorts of shit up."

"Great," I muttered tonelessly as my chest grew tight. I couldn't even look at *Jack* any more. He'd said he would keep me out of the craziness, and while I knew he couldn't help Audrey's actions, his stupid night out with Devon had just made it all worse. And to be honest, a part of me blamed him for Audrey, too. Surely, her prior behavior should have alerted him to how unhinged and spiteful she was. I knew I was being irrational and that Jack was hurt, too. We should be dealing with this together . . . but we'd both just closed off from each other. It was agonizing, yet . . . I couldn't help it.

I sat in the back of the boat on a soft white vinyl cushion as we sped across the inland waterway, making for a Marina at Tybee, just south of Savannah. The normally freeing feeling of being out on the water felt like a death knell.

Feeling Jack's eyes on me finally, I could practically hear him begging me to look at him, but I was afraid he'd see accusation in my eyes now. I took another sip of water as Jazz came and sat next to me, sliding an arm around my shoulders.

Jack got up with a sigh and made his way to the bow of the boat.

Shit.

The idea of Ashley going around saying she and Jack had done stuff just about gave me hives. It didn't matter that I knew they hadn't. Perception was fact. I shuddered. What about when he was away on a movie and this happened? Would I be so sure it wasn't true then? Did I fully trust Jack? Was I a secure enough person?

I couldn't imagine how this relationship was going to do anything but bring out every single ugly insecurity I had.

I'd promised Jack I'd take the bad with the good, but I wasn't sure I was strong enough for this.

CHAPTER THIRTY

Devon met us in Tybee in the Jeep. Jazz had apparently gone to him first after Joey's call to tell him what was going on, and it had been his suggestion for us to divert to Savannah. He was of the opinion that it was easier to stay incognito in places where people didn't expect us to be. And not knowing what the reporter's timing was for the story, it seemed to make sense.

After Jack's and my obvious breakdown in communication, he ended up on the phone nonstop for the remainder of the boat ride to the marina in Tybee. From what I could tell, first with Sheila and his agent, and then with a lawyer they must have conferenced in about drawing up papers for a potential lawsuit.

In the end, Jazz and I decided to use our time in Savannah wisely. We asked Devon to drop us downtown in order to make another attempt at dress shopping.

Since we were there and all.

My brother was coming to get us later in Jazz's car because we didn't dare have him drive his car or my truck in case someone wanted to follow him.

It was a weird, creepy cloak and dagger situation. I was sure a lot of people would get off on the danger element . . . I didn't find it remotely exciting. It made me daydream about what it would feel like to pop a Xanax. And I wanted to smack Jack for acting like he was the only one affected.

With barely a word from us to the guys, and not one word from Jack to me, we climbed out and headed into a department store. I tried to shake off the horrible lonely feeling I had at Jack's standoffish-ness. And I knew I'd done the same to him.

"This isn't working," Jazz moaned as she stared at me around the changing room curtain.

"Tell me about it," I agreed morosely with her assessment of our dress choices. It wasn't that they were *all* awful, but how on earth did I pick something for such a momentous occasion. That I could afford. That didn't look like I was going to Prom.

First of all, I'd never been to a grown-up black-tie affair. Secondly, I was a guest of honor. *Gulp*. And thirdly, there might be an A-list Hollywood celebrity in attendance. And I was going to be portrayed as his arm-candy. And with the axe of a tabloid exposé about to fall, I was in major anxiety–mode.

"So, look. What's the worst that can happen?" Jazz always enjoyed playing devil's advocate.

"Uh . . ."

"'Cos, I'll tell you how I see it." She posed against the doorframe to the changing room, hand on hip and head cocked to one side. "Insanely handsome Hollywood god brings free publicity to extremely talented, but relatively unknown artist." She bobbed her head back quickly to make sure we were still alone and cocked an eyebrow at me. "Oh, and he worships the ground she walks on. Did I cover everything?"

"Fine, Jazz. I know." I rolled my eyes at her. It did sound fine when she put it like that. "But you know me."

"Yep. Yep, I do."

"And he acted horribly this morning," I grumbled.

"Of course he did. He'd just promised Joey he would avoid this, and it happened anyway—and within hours. He must feel like shit. Not that it's okay."

"And what about all this Audrey crap? It makes me look worse than a random hookup."

"Whatever. You don't and won't look like a random hookup if he's still with you, right?"

"Fine," I huffed. "But you know the thought of being known as Jack's arm-candy or latest 'piece of ass' as Joey so eloquently put it, is not high up on my bucket list."

"Well, it'd be on mine."

I raised my eyebrows.

"Kidding," she added. "No seriously, I'm kidding. He's hot as shit and *be still my beating heart*," she slapped a hand on her chest. "The boy really wants to be with you. But you're out there trying to make something of yourself. He's got to understand that, right?"

"Yes, not to mention that being Jack's girlfriend will totally eclipse the point of the evening, which is to establish myself as a legitimate artist."

She cast a disapproving look over the latest sateen and chiffon number I had on. "Whatever you decide to do, we have *got* to find you a dress. You look like a pastry."

I knew I looked pretty bad, and that swirl of lemon yellow

cast a sickly glow to my skin. We'd tried it on in desperation. *You never know . . . some things look better on.* "What the hell kind of pastry looks like this?"

"I don't know. I try not to look pastries in the eye for fear they'll jump down my throat," she said, seriously.

I snorted.

"You look like I *imagine* a pastry to be, all sweet and puffy and shit. Definitely not screaming 'artistic ingénue with hot Hollywood boyfriend.'"

"I give up." I groaned.

"You can't. We just need help." Jazz whipped out her phone and began texting.

"Who?" I asked.

"Didn't you say Colt had that gorgeous friend who set up your spa appointments. She'll know, right?"

"Money, Jazz. Money." I stripped the awful concoction from my body and pulled my jeans back on.

"Puh-shaw. It's an investment."

"Whatever." I pushed past her out the changing room as she bent over her phone, thumbs moving in a blur. There was no way I was spending money on a dress at this stage with all the other financial obligations I had looming ahead of me. I hastily texted Colt and told him to ignore any and all texts from Jazz, that I had it covered.

"Just think," Jazz continued, oblivious. "You won't have to pick your own dresses for Jack's industry events, you'll have the hottest designers vying for the honor."

I froze for a moment. *God. Really?*

"Seriously?" Jazz rolled her eyes as she noticed my expression. "Sometimes I think you were dropped on this earth out of the belly of a mothership. How does that not excite you?"

I just shook my head.

We still had ages to kill before Joey was due to get us, so Jazz and I took a walk over to our favorite coffee shop, Sentient Bean, overlooking Forsyth Park. I had a latte, she had a black tea with local honey.

"So, you practically floated off the golf cart this morning before I burst your bubble." Jazz cast me a sideways look.

I turned my head and looked out over the park and the long line of stroller brigade mommies who looked to have just finished a long workout. Yes, I should focus on the good stuff that came before my worst nightmare unfolded.

"I'm still floating," I sighed through a small smile. "It was amazing. The place was so gorgeous." I told her about the bedside lamp being one of my pieces. "But beyond that, we really talked, you know. About us, about everything. But not about how to deal with all this stuff, obviously."

"You just talked? Shit, all that romantic seclusion and sizzling tension, and no sex?"

"Jazz!" My skin flooded with heat. Not because I didn't usually share with Jazz, but because my mind was immediately filled with all the intimate things Jack and I had done.

"Wow. That good, huh?" Jazz shook her head. "All the luck. Seriously."

I swallowed and shook my head as if I could dislodge Jack for a second. *As if.* "I thought you and Brandon were, you know, aren't you?"

"Dang, K. How are you doing it if you can't even say it? Repeat after me: *having sex.*"

"Stop deflecting, what's going on?"

"*I'm* not the one deflecting, but . . ." Jazz sighed and shrugged her shoulders. "Meh."

"Meh? Like *meh* you might be, or *meh*, the sex is *meh*."

"The sex is most definitely *meh*. We are definitely done.

He's sweet and everything, but honestly, my most important erogenous zone is my mind. When my mind is looking at him like he's a poor lost puppy, I can promise you it's the furthest thing from erotic. Not that he doesn't try hard," she added.

Joey had clearly ruined her. He'd made her fall for the stubborn, overbearing, alpha-male type.

"Let's go see Mrs. Weaton when we get back," Jazz suggested suddenly. "She's bound to have some vintage beauty hidden in her closet. Her past is so mysterious, don't you think?"

"Wow. Brilliant idea," I said. "Something vintage would be perfect."

Over the moon to have Jazz and me crowded into her small vinyl-covered kitchen, Mrs. Weaton fussed about as Jazz probed her with questions. "Well if you must know, I dated Montgomery Clift in the early fifties," she declared and looked at us expectantly.

Jazz glanced at me. "Name rings a bell," she tried and searched him on her phone. "Wow, so you *also* dated an actor. He was hot!"

I looked over and admired his dark hair and sonnet-worthy cheekbones.

"Oooh. Let me look," Mrs. Weaton implored.

Jazz turned the phone around to her. She sighed with a touch of sadness, reaching a shaky finger out, and then dropping it at the last moment. "Yes, he was. So beautiful and so tortured. Reminds me a lot of your Jack. Oh, he was so dreamy. Broke my heart, of course, when he started dating Elizabeth Taylor. Although he said it was all for show. What a beautiful couple they made." She sniffed. "Anyway, a sad soul he was. A brilliant actor, the likes of which I've never seen. He lived in those characters, taking them all on board." Her eyes took on a faraway look. "He had a terrible car accident and never was fully himself again. Both his looks and his mind were forever altered." She eased her thin frame into a chair and placed a plate of cookies down in front of us.

Jazz glared at the plate and gave in immediately. It was hard not to eat anything Mrs. Weaton made.

"*I* still thought he was beautiful," she went on in her trembly voice. "I saw him once before the end, at a party in New York City. 'Iris,' he said, 'you were always too good for me,' and he kissed the knuckles on my left hand." She rubbed her bony fingers softly over them, her eyes glistening. "I never saw him again. He died a few months later. Heart attack, they say, but I think he was addicted to the pain medication after his accident. I think . . . he couldn't deal with living such a public life and feeling like . . . less."

My eyes filled, and Jazz swiped a quick finger across her cheek.

"Maybe he died of a broken heart because he couldn't be with the love of his life," Jazz said, always the romantic.

"So very, very tragic," Mrs. Weaton finished with a watery smile at Jazz's words. "Anyway, I have something that may work. I wore it to that party in New York, actually. It was *my* mother's from the twenties. Come help me."

Jazz and I helped Mrs. Weaton pull open the large cedar trunk at the foot of her bed. "I should have hung these all up, but I'd rather they stay in the trunk and not be moth eaten."

We took turns pulling out layer after layer of tissue paper and plastic wrap and laying them on the bed, their contents indiscernible but for a hint of color here and there. Barely disturbing the packaging, Mrs. Weaton peeked in each one. Finally, I gingerly lifted a heavier-feeling package out, and she nodded.

We unwrapped it to find a gorgeous sheer flapper dress, completely see-through, made of thin tabard netting with hundreds of thousands of tiny jet beads intricately embroidered all over it down to a beaded fringe. "It was hand beaded. Everything was in those days," Mrs. Weaton said. "You can wear any color slip underneath. I wore a skin color one. I might still have it or something similar." She winked. "That sure did turn a few heads."

Jazz cackled. "You hussy!"

"It's perfect," I said, in awe.

Mrs. Weaton went to a drawer and pulled out a champagne colored slip. I took my shorts and tank off and tried the slip and then the dress on, with Jazz carefully lowering it over my head. "Are you sure you don't mind?"

"Wow!" said Jazz.

"Honey, I hope it brings you all the love and glamor in the world. I couldn't imagine it going to a better home. This dress was meant for you."

I hugged her sweet-smelling, bony frame as hard as I dared, my chest filling with emotion. "Now, I just have to get over my fear of having Jack there as well as feeling like an imposter who tricked people into thinking I have a talent."

"Yes, you do have to get over that, honey," said Mrs. Weaton into my hair, patting me fondly. "You are extremely talented."

Jazz pursed her lips and raised her eyes at me. *Told ya* her expression said.

After getting changed again, we said our goodbyes and

carefully carried the beautiful dress over to my place. I was relieved to have one less thing to worry about before the event the next evening.

My phone buzzed with a text from Jack just as we got into my house. A lump formed in my throat.

Late Night Visitor: Hope you got back safe.

God, we hadn't spoken all day. He'd barely looked at me and hadn't once touched me since we found out about the article. Now his short emotionless text left me swinging out in the cold.

Me: We did. How did it go?

There was a long pause before my phone beeped again.

Late Night Visitor: I was mostly unsuccessful talking him out of it. But he may keep your name out for now . . .

Me: That's great. Wait, for now?

Late Night Visitor: Yes . . . if he gets an exclusive on our relationship . . . I'm sorry.

Dammit. Panic flooded my system again. Part of me wanted to end things with Jack. It was too hard. But that felt about as possible as carving my heart out of my own chest with a blunt object. However, people had been known to hack their own arms off to save themselves.

Me: We should talk. In person.

Late Night Visitor: Dev and I are staying in Savannah for now, won't be back til late tonight.

I watched as a new bubble emerged on the screen, showing me Jack was writing something else. Then it disappeared and no text came.

My chest squeezed. I wanted to tell him I missed him. I wanted him to say something—anything to help ease this ache, this feeling that we were eons apart from each other emotionally. I wanted to say something funny and sweet, but all inspiration was gone. I was panicking and I knew it. I'd spent an amazing night with Jack, and suddenly the reality of today had made it all seem like an impossible dream. How could we possibly have a future together that I would be able to handle?

Having had to blow off my lunchtime shift once again today, I headed into work for my evening one. I'd told Brenda about the reporter over the phone and apologized profusely. The possibility I wouldn't be able to work at the Grill much longer without feeling like a curiosity at a county fair weighed heavily. As soon as it was common knowledge I was with Jack, I'd need to reassess, but I needed the money. Now more than ever.

Brenda was there, and a girl named Lisa, who worked most summers, and had been in sporadically over the winter months. She'd had to cover for me the last few days. Normally off-season, one waitress could handle lunch but business had picked as it got closer to the season. The excitement of Jack and Devon hadn't quite calmed down yet, either. It didn't help that a couple of the local newspapers had picked up the story.

"Uh, Keri Ann." Brenda nabbed me as I headed to the kitchen just after nine. It had been a busy evening and was only now starting to clear out. She nodded at the bar where a middle-aged gentleman with a long sleeved black crew tee and black rimmed glasses sat staring at me, his finger running absently up and down the side of a frosty water glass. His dark hair was thinning, his face bland.

"I think that's the reporter," Brenda murmured. "He was the one in here the other day asking about Jack."

A wave of nerves broke violently inside me. There was no point running from this guy. He clearly knew who I was.

"Okay, I'll be right back." I took the dirty items I was carrying through to the kitchen. Hector had his back to me and steam was billowing out of the huge industrial dishwasher. I joined him, and we worked quickly together as I helped him put in another load.

I knew Hector felt like he was personally responsible for Jack and me, having had a front row seat since the first night we met. "I need luck tonight, Hector," I said. "There's a guy out there waiting to talk to me and make me look like a . . ." I searched around for an egregious word that he'd understand. "a *puta*."

There. The Spanish word for *whore* should suffice, considering how serious the situation was.

Hector hissed through his teeth and turned to me, crossing himself. "No. Miss Keri Ann." His wrinkled gaze was serious. "You have angels fly over you. *Todo estarà bien*."

Except he said "*Un-Hells*", instead of angels, which totally made me smile despite the gravity of my mood.

He smiled back and pulled me in for a hug.

"Okay." I blew out a breath. "Here I go."

CHAPTER THIRTY-ONE

𝒮tanding on the dock at Broad Landing in the gray early morning light, I waited for Jack.

I'd sent him a text after work last night and told him I'd met Tom Price, the reporter. Tom seemed like a nice enough guy at first. I'd introduced myself to him promptly after exiting the kitchen, which seemed to surprise him.

"I guess you were expecting me to run?" I'd asked him.

"Maybe," Tom Price replied. "They either run or they want the publicity or money for the story. So that tells me a lot about you, though I didn't expect that."

I shrugged. "I don't want that either."

"Somehow, I believe you. So why are you talking to me?"

"Would you like me not to?"

That seemed to flummox him for a moment. "I think I like you," he said.

"Enough to keep my name out of the story?"

"Probably not that much," he admitted, his brown eyes blinking like fish behind the lenses of his glasses. "Besides, it's my editor who makes the final call, not me."

"Do you enjoy what you do?" I asked.

He smirked. "Are you always this direct?"

"I try to be. So *do* you?"

"I don't think I've met anyone quite like you in the course of my job before."

"I could say the same. But you still didn't answer my question."

"I'm supposed to be asking you questions."

"So ask. I may not answer, but I won't lie." My virtue or my downfall, I never knew.

He'd furrowed his brow. "I'm recording you, is that okay?"

I looked at the cell phone lying on the bar top. "Something tells me you don't usually ask permission."

He laughed, revealing tobacco stained teeth. "Okay. Are you having an affair with Jack Eversea?"

"No," I said. Then at his frown, and because I'd already seen the proposed article and knew there was no way to hide it, I admitted, "But I am having a relationship with him."

He smiled, a slow smile, like a cat. "Thank you," he said. "That's all I needed." Tom Price slid his cell phone off the bar and stood. "I'm going to tell you this, Keri Ann Butler, because you seem like one of the good ones . . . and I can see why he likes you."

I swallowed. Something told me I'd just royally messed up. "What?"

"If you hang around with the Jack Everseas of the world, don't speak to people like me. *Ever*. And don't expect to be known for anything other than the attention he chooses to give you. When he's done with you, you will cease to exist, for him and for everyone else."

Shells and gravel crunched behind me and I heard Jack clear his throat. His mere presence passed a current through me. I'd missed him, not having seen him since we got back from our secluded island getaway and been faced with our first major hurdle. A hurdle I felt like we'd both failed to clear.

His warm fingers curled through mine, and I squeezed them. I smiled in spite of my grim mood.

Jack turned me to face him, hands on my shoulders. His dark brown hair was messy, like he'd been tugging on it or sleeping under a pillow.

My fingers itched to slide through the glossy locks and pull his rugged face and full lips down to mine.

His eyes roamed my face, and he must have had the same thought, because we both moved into each other, our lips meeting, the relief of touching him gliding through me in a ripple of longing. "Good morning," I managed through kisses.

"I missed you," he breathed.

Jack's arms roamed my back and I pressed against him, curling my body against his larger frame. Seeking comfort. "Me, too."

"God, I'm sorry I reacted so badly yesterday morning when we found out. I felt like I'd failed you, I did fail you, and I couldn't bear to see how upset you were."

"I'm sorry too, Jack. And I'm sorry Audrey keeps trying to hurt you."

"She's the last person on my mind, trust me. It's you I'm worried about. And how this affects *us*."

We hugged for a few moments. Then I pulled back to look at him seriously. He seemed about to say something else.

"I don't want you to come to the art opening party, Jack." I spoke in a rush, before I chickened out, before he said something to change my mind. I steeled my nerves. I was probably going to say this all wrong. "I just don't want you there—"

He flinched.

Shit. "And now after . . . this story, after Ashley even . . . if they see me with you, people will think the worst of me." I wished I didn't sound so childish and petty. So selfish and uncaring. It was so out of character for me, and I knew it.

"No they won't. Because I'll tell them you're my girlfriend."

My eyes stung with tears. "I already did. I admitted to Tom Price we were having a relationship. I probably wasn't supposed to do that from the way he acted. I guess you didn't confirm it for him."

"I didn't, I never do." Jack shook his head. "But it doesn't matter. Don't let him get to you."

"You may be used to this circus," I swiped at my eyes, thinking about Tom Price's words and how they cut right to my fear of being just Jack's girlfriend, "and ignoring what people say about you, but I'm not. You said you would try and keep me out of the madness. How does showing up to an event with me fit into that? I'm so nervous about the event anyway. There are people from SCAD coming, and maybe some press. I don't want to be worrying about what people are thinking." Then the more sordid aspect made me shudder. "And if I'm supposedly your girlfriend, what will people think you were doing with Ashley? Especially if Audrey's story hits." I thought of England. "Especially with your reputation. I'll just be the next one in a long line."

"My reputation?" Jack swallowed. "Yeah, I guess I deserved that. But you know, Keri Ann, there's always going to be an Ashley. Someone saying they know me, or did something with me or whatever. Please. Please be strong enough to choose *us* over this."

He was right. "I want to, Jack, I'm going to try to be strong enough to deal with that. But as it stands you're asking me to give up my own identity, one that I'm only just discovering. My mother did it for my father, and excuse the cliché, but she lived a life of quiet desperation. That's what Joey sees for me with you, and I understand now. That's what you're asking of me. To never be recognized as my own person, always to be talked about in reference to you."

He grabbed my shoulders. "Even if people talk, it won't last forever. At least not with the same intensity. I know I promised to keep us secret, but I'm no longer in control, thanks to Audrey."

Panic washed over me.

"It's going to be impossible actually. I wish—"

"What?" I hiccupped a sob. "So you just want to go on business as usual and stick me in the slot of Jack Eversea's latest romantic interlude? Since your next movie is filming here, how convenient you have a local girl all lined up to take care of your lonely nights. And bonus, she gets to cash in on your fame to get some publicity." I breathed out roughly, already regretting my words and the bitterness in my voice. The way I'd just reduced the amazing thing we had between us to a cheap and shallow anecdote. I didn't need a tabloid to do it, I'd just done it myself.

Jack's eyes were dark.

"God, I'm sorry," I said, and wiped my eyes. "I'm so sorry. You know that's not how I feel about us."

"I don't think I really do know. I know that you're scared." He shoved a hand bleakly through his hair. "I wish you weren't afraid to be with me." His eyes settled on mine, and he looked so sad. "People use me all the time. They use my name and my status for everything. Being seen with me, wanting me to use or wear their product, their clothes, talk about it, wanting me at a party to raise their profile." He sneered, his mouth twisting. "Over and over again.

"But for *once*." He kicked at the ground. "For fucking once, I want to do that for good, for something *I* choose, beyond the bullshit. Even beyond the charity stuff I do and money I give away to this and that, even the freaking sea turtles."

"You give money to the sea turtles?" I interjected. The first orange sun rays glinted off his glossy brown hair.

"Since I met you, yes," he said dismissively then looked at me intently. "I want to be able to use who I am to help *you*. I want to help you pay for SCAD, I want to save your house for you."

God. Mortification burned me from the inside out. He must have heard the whole conversation I had with Joey.

"And I know you won't let me," he went on before I could react. "You have too much pride, you'd think I felt sorry for you or something. I don't. Not even fucking close. Yes, I want to go to your party," he said fiercely. "If you don't want to use my name then I want to go and be there for you, as your boyfriend, not as Jack Eversea. I know this is the biggest thing you've ever done. And I'm so proud of you even though I have no right to be."

"But you can't be there as my boyfriend and not as Jack Eversea," I said quietly, my eyes casting down to his chest. "They're the same thing as far as everyone is concerned."

"You're right, and what's wrong with that if it means more people show up and more people pay attention to how damn talented you are? And no, since we're being honest," he ground out, "I don't *want* to keep us a secret." He jabbed his chest, hard. "I'm just a guy in here. A mostly insecure, when it comes to you, depressing idiot, who has created this life of grand illusion. But it *is* my life. Without it, I wouldn't have you, but with it, I can't really be with you?" he asked. "It makes no fucking sense. I want you to see it all for the sham it is and look through it to *me* . . . I want your brother's approval only because I realize I'll never fully have you without it. I also want *you* to not give a shit who's watching. I want you to be proud of being with me and not care about what people might say about us." He pointed to his chest again. "Because *I* don't care what people say about us."

My eyes stung sharply before filling again and blurring my vision. All my joy and happiness at being with Jack—and fears enough to cancel the good stuff out—swirled blindingly together.

"I don't think I'm ready," I said in a small voice.

"What are you saying?"

"I need, I need time. I wish I could pause *us*." I cringed as Jack stumbled backward. "Please, Jack. Please try and understand. It's going to be hard enough for me to take this professional step without worrying about whether people are there for me or for you." I crossed my arms over my chest. "I-I need to do this by myself. If it goes well, I need to know it went well because of me and only me. And if it doesn't, then it doesn't."

"It will, regardless," he said, with exasperation. "But you're punishing me for something I can't control!"

Silence, brittle with tension, arced between us.

Then Jack's hands were on my face, his thumbs sliding under my eyes as I closed them, and a huge wave of emotion shuddered through my chest in a sob. "I'm sorry."

I'm an ugly cry-er, and that alone should have stopped me, but it didn't. I cried and cried, my shoulders heaving, until

Jack had me pressed against his hard chest, his hand in my hair, cradling me. Soothing me. Whispering to me like a child. Even though I should be the one soothing, even though I was the one punishing him for something he couldn't change. I hated being so pathetic, it wasn't me. It had never been me. And that made me cry harder.

I wanted to run. I wanted to run back to the past before I put myself out there and before I'd met Jack. I wanted to go back to the bland waiting period of a life un-begun. Back when dreams were just concepts and not the sinuous, glittering sirens they were now, taunting me to take a leap off the edge for them, to risk dashing myself on the rocks if I did something as stupid as try and grab on to them too tightly. I couldn't imagine how their smooth promises wouldn't slip through my fingers.

"God, please stop crying, Keri Ann, you're killing me."

I pulled out of Jack's arms, swiping my cheeks and nose with the back of my hand.

Nice.

God, my relationship with Jack had fully deployed every terrifying emotion I was capable of, and in the process I'd hurt him. I'd hurt the person I loved with my whole heart.

"You are so beautiful, so talented, so honest. And you are strong. Let me be part of your life, and be brave enough to be part of mine. I know you can be, I've seen your strength. Please believe in us." His voice broke.

I stood, mute, letting his words pour over and through me.

He sighed deeply, agony and frustration reflecting in his eyes. "I'll stay away if that's what you want. But know I'm only doing it because you're asking. We're going to have to figure this out. Unless I give up what I do and who I am, this is *always* going to come between us. I know I told you I could keep you out of it, or try, but I've realized I really can't. You need to choose *us* anyway, Keri Ann."

Jack giving up who he was? Never. Imagining him without his passion was like me deciding never to create anything ever again. It wasn't going to happen. But Jack being Jack meant having to put up with the Audreys, the Ashleys, and tabloids, the Tom Prices waiting in the wings to pick up a whiff of scandal.

It probably also meant him leaving for filming projects for months at a time. And if I went with him, what did that mean for my life? What kind of life would I be living if I could just jet off to be with him? Not a conscientious student, that was for sure. And one day, if he was done with me? Then what? Who would I be then?

Who was I without Jack? I needed to be sure now, and I needed to set the boundary now, otherwise I'd always be swallowed up by the tidal wave of who he was, and his life. I'd always only be an extension of him.

. . . And cease to exist . . .

The reporter's words, and Joey's story about Mom, shuddered through me.

All the reasons I'd rejected Jack when he stood in my kitchen were still valid and so very, very real. Yet somehow, I'd suspended them, and let Jack in, and fallen more deeply for him than ever. Now I was hurting us both.

"And Keri Ann?" He slid a hand behind my neck, tilting my face so he could land a kiss on my forehead. "However well you do, it's always going to be because you earned it, and you deserve it, no matter who shows up to the party. You have the talent, you just need to believe it."

I stood in Jack's arms, the cool early morning breeze ruffling through our hair, letting his strength and his certainty flow into me and trying desperately to believe it.

Then he let go. "Just . . ." Exhaling deeply, his jaw tensed tightly, the muscle twitched over and over. His expression was tortured. "Just . . . try and remember," he swallowed and grabbed my hand, pressing it against his chest. "Whatever anyone sees on the outside . . . this is yours in here. Please, God, don't throw it away."

CHAPTER THIRTY-TWO

The morning of my art opening dawned beautiful and sunny. A complete contrast to my mood. I was worried about the evening ahead of me and weighed down by the thought of how I'd left things with Jack.

He'd left me standing on the dock. I'd watched him walk away and climb into the closed Jeep and done nothing to stop him.

Over breakfast, Joey and I scoured the Internet to see if there was any story out there, but there was nothing. I felt like my head was on a guillotine.

"I checked, too," Jazz said when she arrived to pick me up for our trip into Savannah. "There was nothing."

We were spending the day at the spa where Colt's friend Karina had set up my appointments. I had begged and pleaded over the phone to bring Jazz, and they'd finally said she could come and they'd try to fit her in for either hair or makeup. I was reluctant to go at all, but Jazz speared me with a sharp look. I could see she wanted to say something like I might be photographed, so I needed to look my best. But in the end she settled with, "It would be a shame to ruin Mrs. Weaton's fabulous dress with mediocre waitress hair."

I thumped her on the arm, and Joey laughed at us as we made plans to meet back at the house. The Westin was sending one of their vans to pick us up. Colt and his date Karina were going to meet us there.

The day passed in a blur. I was primped and prepped. My hands, my feet, my hair, my makeup. I did agree with Jazz that, after hearing about my dress, they did an awesome job with my hair. It was waved and swept down over one ear then tied in a beautiful swirl, low on the side of my head. They used a tiny silver band that peeked out across my forehead before it hid back in the smooth, silky do. I felt like an old-timey Hollywood starlet, and I actually felt good. I didn't enjoy the amount of spray they had to use to keep it from coming loose, however. The makeup was flawlessly done. With deep kohl swept eyes, I hardly recognized myself.

"Wow," said Jazz when my chair was turned around.

"Wow, yourself," I said. They'd curled large cascading waves into Jazz's long blonde hair and tied half of it up with a loose and elegant braid. She would be wearing a red floaty dress that was sure to hit my brother like a blow to the head.

My heart thudded in a melancholic stupor when I thought of not sharing all this with Jack. I gritted my teeth and swallowed down the sadness.

We drove home, with the windows up, barely moving for fear of the painted illusion sliding off of us. We turned the radio on full blast, and listening to *Blondfire*, tapped our fingers and toes in muted enthusiasm.

At five, the three of us stood in our kitchen drinking celebratory Prosecco out of Nana's old wide-necked champagne glasses that I'd managed to find and dust off.

"Here's to the first of many evenings celebrating my talented sister's artistic endeavors." Joey, dressed in a rented tuxedo, raised his glass and we drank. I'd told him he didn't have to wear black-tie, but he was adamant.

"Yoo hoo!" Mrs. Weaton called, entering the kitchen dressed in an elegant violet dress. "Don't start without me!"

"Mrs. Weaton, I thought you were going to call me so I could escort you across the yard," Joey admonished and leaned down to kiss her papery cheek.

"Oh, honey, the dress is fabulous on you," she crowed toward me. "Look at you stunning girls."

"Thank you." I smiled. The dress really had turned out perfectly. I was about as comfortable as I could imagine being, considering I was about to step out in public and embark on having a public persona. It occurred to me then, if I was going to be successful, I would have my own critics to deal with. Sure, it would be on a smaller scale than Jack's. But people's opinions, good or bad, factual or misguided, of me and my art were going to be a reality, regardless of Jack being in my life.

"Are the rest of them here yet?" Mrs. Weaton asked.

"Liz had a babysitting problem. Cooper, Vern, and Jasper are meeting us there. So is Colt. So I guess it's just us four." I shrugged. "Let's sit on the porch and wait for the van."

As we stepped outside, the black mini bus from the Westin pulled into the driveway, the low-hanging Spanish moss brushing over it. And another car showed up behind it and out climbed Paulie, Brenda, and Hector.

"What?" I stuttered. "Who's running the Grill?"

"That's the first thing you think of?" said Paulie stiffly. He was dressed in a tan, wrinkled suit, and his gray hair was combed neatly into a low queue. "You seriously think we'd let our very own Keri Ann go and take on the world without our support?" He puffed. "Stuck a sign in the window."

My eyes welled.

"Nope, no." Jazz flapped her hands madly in front of my face. "No you don't!"

"Sorry." I sniffed, then laughed through my tears, and gingerly hugged everyone.

"Faith's coming, too," said Jazz. "We're all going to be here to support you, okay? But for God's sake don't ruin that makeup. Let's blot."

It was surreal to stand in the crowded and cordoned-off area of the foyer at the hotel and be surrounded by things I'd created with my own bare hands. Some I'd formed idly, some carried memories and impressions of all my pent-up emotion.

After being greeted by Allison, the events coordinator and then Mira, the curator from Picture This who had offered to handle any transactions for the evening, I was introduced to the arts and culture editor for a local newspaper. Then a few minutes after that, a very nice lady handed me a thick business card and told me she was from *Moss & Magnolia Magazine* in Charleston and would love to do a feature on me. I was buzzing, knowing what a high-end magazine it was, showcasing the best of the luxury southern style living. I think I nodded mutely at her.

"Did I totally fluff that?" I asked Jazz as we moved on.

Jazz assured me I'd been sweet and charming. After a few more introductions and tense smiles at cameras, I pulled Jazz over to the middle of the room, to the calm area in the eye of the storm, to breathe. The music from the string quartet in the corner was barely noticeable under the hive of conversation bouncing off the polished floors.

My wave sculpture, a monument to the lowest point in my relationship with Jack, sat under a spotlight that made the single piece of red sea glass glow. I felt connected to it about as strongly as I felt it was completely foreign to me. Something I didn't recognize but knew intimately. Very disconcerting.

"Wow," Jazz said. "It was always beautiful, but seeing it here on display, under the spotlight, makes it just . . . wow. And why won't you sell it again?" She snatched two toothpicks with something delicious smelling on the end from a passing waiter and handed one to me.

"It's all about Jack. It'd feel weird to have it owned by someone else."

I felt a tap on my shoulder and turned around to find Tom Price had slunk up behind us. "Hello again," he purred, pushing his glasses up between his eyes.

A shudder ran through me, and I stared, speechless. *Really?*

"Jessica Fraser," Jazz stuck out her hand. I quickly slapped it down without thinking. Tom Price raised his eyebrows, and I could imagine Jazz was doing the same.

"Tom Price," he said to her.

"How did you know I was here?" I finally managed.

"Oh, *little orphan Keri Annie*, your life is public now. Or is this artistic endeavor of yours just a hobby? Hmm?"

I swallowed.

"I just came to let Keri Ann know," he looked at Jazz, then back at me, his brown eyes unblinking, "that the story dropped tonight."

I heard Jazz practically growl next to me.

"But you should have some time to enjoy your evening, your success, or what have you. Where is Jack, my boy, anyway?"

"You mean you hoped he'd be here so you could get some updated pictures of them together?" Jazz snapped.

"Well, yes. I didn't come for the unimaginative finger food," he said, twiddling a toothpick between a fat thumb and forefinger. "But I'll settle for a picture of just Keri Ann. I would have thought he'd be here getting you some additional exposure. Although I did overhear someone saying a New York critic is here. A friendly phone call from Jack perhaps, calling in a favor for his girlfriend?"

"Well, that's blatantly untrue." Jazz narrowed her eyes at him.

"Does that matter though, really?" Tom Price canted his head and drew the last word out like a piece of slime.

My face scorched with impotent frustration.

"But I wish you luck, Keri Ann. Truly. Excuse me." He turned and moved slowly through the throng, for all appearances like a sweet gentle man admiring some art.

"He really is despicable," I said quietly, my fingers trembling.

"Let's get you some champagne and calm those nerves."

"Do you think it's true?" I asked Jazz. "Do you think Jack pulled favors to get me some press?"

"Honestly?" she handed me a glass. "No. I think the gallery did or word of mouth." Jazz paused. "But if he did, I wouldn't blame him. I'd do the same for you if I could. I love you, and I want you to succeed. If it was at all within my power to show your talent to the entire world, I would." She looked at me seriously. "And if it was within my power, and you didn't let me do that for you, I would be really hurt . . . I'd feel like you didn't value me."

I swallowed, thickly, raising my glass for a calming sip. The champagne tasted like sand as it passed my thudding heart and splashed into my belly. "I should eat something more substantial," was all I said.

We found Joey, standing next to Colt and Karina, by the food table. Colt and Karina looked really, really good together. "Thank you so much for including me, Keri Ann," Karina kissed my cheek in greeting.

I introduced her to Jazz. "Well, thank *you* so much for your help in getting us presentable." I laughed lightly, but inside my mind was whirling, going over and over everything Jack said, and then what Tom Price said. I was a public figure now. Granted a teeny tiny fish in a tiny pond, but I was still putting myself out there. And I was cutting Jack out of it completely. Did I want him to cut *me* out if and when he got recognition for his work? I'd want to support him and share it with him.

Before I'd met him, I hadn't even self-actualized as an artist. So much had changed in less than a year. Where would I be if Jack *hadn't* turned my life upside down?

People *would* say what they wanted about me as an artist. I would never, nor could I ever try to, control it. Some people would like what I did. Some wouldn't.

The thoughts crashed into one another noisily, but all pointed at the same thing. Jack.

Hell. I needed to go somewhere private and text him. Just tell him I was thinking about him or something. Or maybe just to please come here and be with me, and screw what anyone said. I missed him with a physical ache.

All the joys and successes of the evening were like castles being built on loose sand. I was grateful to have the support and love of all my friends, but I finally understood what

Jack had meant when I first met him, when he talked about the void beneath the success. The hollowness beneath what he did. He was asking me to give it all meaning, be his foundation, his anchor, and I wasn't willing to let him be mine.

Mira approached me as I was lost in thought, mindlessly nodding along at something Cooper or Vern had said. Our whole group was together, devouring the food, like they'd never seen any before.

"Keri Ann," she said with a confused smile. "Someone put in a bid to buy *Ever Broken Sea*. I thought I should let you know."

My eyes widened in surprise. Jazz, standing next to me, overheard. "I thought it wasn't for sale."

"Well, Keri Ann told me if someone offered the exact price," she waved her hand, "this obscure amount she told me about back in December, that she'd sell." She looked at me expectantly.

"What amount?" Jazz asked.

I sighed. "The exact amount I still owe Jack for the floors he had refinished at the house. I haven't paid him anything since December so I still owe him. But I mean, it was down to the penny." I furrowed my brow at Mira.

She smiled wide, presumably grateful to finally know the story behind the odd request.

"And he figured it out," Mira said with satisfaction. "I met him when he came into the Gallery before your exhibition opened," she explained. "It was the day you set it up, actually. He was mesmerized by it, the moment he walked in the door."

"Oh my God, I could just die. This is so romantic," Jazz slapped a hand to her chest.

"How is this romantic?" I asked Jazz and scowled. "I owe him money, and now he's paying me so I can pay him?"

"For God's sake," said Jazz. "Get out of your own head, Keri Ann, and give the guy a break. He wants to be here for you and you won't let him. He wants to help you, and you won't accept anything. He loves that piece you made so much he doesn't want anyone else to own it. And he knows how your mind works well enough to figure out your silly puzzles." She grabbed my hand. "And he loves you enough to play by your rules, anyway."

There was silence for a few moments between all three of us. A silence that allowed me to feel the full weight of the bucket of reality Jazz had just dumped on me. Even Mira got a dreamy look on her face and placed her hand on her heart.

I clutched my middle, nodding blindly.

"Sooooo . . . I should or shouldn't call him back?" Mira finally asked.

Fumbling, I tried to get my phone out of my small evening bag. "*I'll* call him."

"I mean are we making the sale? There'll be some disappointed guests who were told it wasn't available. I've had a few people ask me."

"Yes," said Jazz. "We're making the sale, she just doesn't need his line tied up right now."

"Gotcha. I'll have to be careful how I handle that. There's some high-falutin' folks here tonight who won't take too kindly to being told it wasn't for sale, when in fact, it was. I'll have to figure something out."

I finally got his number pulled up and to my ear, even though my hands shook. Maybe I should have gone somewhere private . . . I motioned to Jazz, cocking my head to indicate I was walking away, and pressed my hand against my other ear to drown out the crowd.

There was suddenly a weird lurch in noise level around me in the foyer, an electrified moment, and I heard some voices die down as some gasps and squeals came from across the polished floor near the concierge desk.

My phone slipped away from my ear as I saw Jack.

CHAPTER THIRTY-THREE

It was Jack like I'd never seen him. Dressed in a tailored black suit, a crisp white shirt open at his throat, his hair raked carelessly back from his face. He was devastating. Like the stop-dead-in-the-middle-of-a-bookstore-to-stare-at-the-magazine-cover, devastating. And he was thirty feet away from me, in the flesh.

His face was an easy smile, a wink of sparkle and charm, as he took a proffered pen from one of the two concierge girls who'd left their posts. His strong hand raced across the paper and he handed it back. A crowd was forming, but I saw his mouth move and his hand immediately going to his breast pocket, withdrawing his phone.

His lips curved into a smile as he looked down at it, a dimple flashed, and his eyes immediately moved past the throng and found mine.

I was still calling him.

He moved the phone to his ear, looking at me expectantly, ignoring the small group around him, waiting patiently. People were holding cell phones up to get pictures. The photographer hired for the event couldn't pass up the opportunity either.

I drew the phone back up to my ear and heard his breath.

"Hi," he said quietly, seriously.

I shivered. We were in a room full of people, and I felt alone with him.

"Hi," I returned, suddenly at a loss for words. The odd thought that we'd never had a conversation over the phone floated past.

His lips quirked, and he raised an eyebrow. "You called *me*?"

"I wanted you here." *After all.*

He breathed out. "And here I am."

"I see that." I raised both eyebrows, asking him the unspoken question. Why did he show up when I'd asked him not to?

"Well," he folded an arm across his chest, then he lifted the phone briefly from his ear, and I heard him apologize, that he would be right with everyone. "Well," he said. "I heard there was an art opening tonight with a very talented artist, and there was something there I wanted. And it was the craziest thing, but I was talking to my assistant, and something she said helped me realize a way I might get it. I decided I should probably come in person."

"You couldn't have called?"

"I could, but I wanted to make absolutely sure I didn't lose my chance," he murmured, his voice laced with meaning.

"You seem to make a habit of ignoring my requests." I smiled and closed my eyes a moment. "You clean up nice," I added with a smirk and opened my eyes to him again.

He tilted his head back and laughed, probably dropping a few panties nearby. "You look stunning."

Heads near him seemed to suddenly get that he was talking to someone he could see and turned in my direction. I moved, looking away reluctantly, and angled my face to hide the phone.

"I'm glad you called," he said.

"I'm glad you came," I returned.

"Give me a few moments here, and I'll come and find you."

Hanging up, I belatedly noticed Sheriff Graves in civilian clothes managing the crowd around Jack. I guess Jack had offered him some extra hours as his bodyguard.

Wow, bodyguards. That was another aspect I hadn't even considered. I blew out a pent-up breath.

Jazz pulled up next to me with Mrs. Weaton. The arts and culture writer from the local paper stood to my left, looking like she was in a complete flap. Her eyes darted back and forth from Jack to her phone as she frantically typed texts I could easily guess at. Far from annoying me, I found it kind of amusing.

"Well, I'll be. It looks like Christian Grey just arrived," Mrs. Weaton sniffed.

Jazz almost snorted on her champagne, and I giggled.

"What, you don't think an old gal like me enjoys a saucy book?"

"Not at all," I said, seriously. Jack had eclipsed every single book boyfriend I'd ever had from Darcy to . . .

"Christian Grey?" Jazz asked haughtily. "Methinks more Gideon Cross. That man can wear a suit."

"How about just Jack-freaking-Eversea?" the reporter next to me said, butting into our conversation.

I raised my eyes at Jazz. "Yes, Jazz, how about just Jack-freaking-Eversea?"

"Well, *you're* certainly getting used to the idea fast." Jazz nudged me with her elbow.

"The champagne helped," I said. "Let's give credit where

it's due. And his romantic gesture. I appreciate you pointing that out."

"What romantic gesture?" The lady next to me interrupted again. "Sorry, Shannon Keith, we met earlier. *Arts and Culture*."

"Hey, Shannon," Jazz said. "Romantic because he just bought her central piece."

"Oh. Wow. I thought that wasn't for sale. And wait, that's cool, but why is that romantic?"

I glared a dagger at Jazz, which she purposefully ignored. "Because he wants to date her. Because he's *in love* with her."

"Jazz!" I yelped.

"I think I'll go get another of those mini-crabcakes before they're all gone," said Mrs. Weaton.

"What?" asked Jazz. "It's about to be public. How about somebody gets to hear the real story? Anyway, it looks like that dick-splat Tom Price left and missed the best part of the night. Idiot."

Shannon's eye glided back and forth between us then glanced back at Jack who just happened to look up and straight at me. She swallowed. "This story is going to make my career, isn't it?" she whispered in awe.

"Probably." Jazz grinned. "It's certainly going to make my night."

"Ladies and Gentlemen," Mira announced, taking over the microphone near the string quartet. "Thank y'all for coming this evening and celebrating the unique artistic talents of these local artists." She reeled off my name with several others, whom I'd met when we first arrived.

There was a polite smattering of applause, along with a gruffly yelled, "Yeah!" from the direction of my friends.

My cheeks heated as a few chuckles responded around the room. I looked across at Jack and Sheriff Graves who were a few feet away. Jack's hands were stuffed in his pockets, a large, elegant stainless steel watch peeking out against his wrist. His skin looked amazing against the crisp white of his shirt. A few buttons were undone at his neck, and his collarbone had suddenly become the sexiest part of a man's body in living history. I couldn't believe that the creature in front of me was Jack. My Jack.

We had yet to greet each other in person.

He winked at me, and his eyes dropped to my mouth. He'd finally made it into the cordoned-off area where the event was happening, allowing him a little more room to move without being accosted. Most of the elegant patrons of the arts that circulated herein were above indulging in such public displays of adulation.

Hotel security had been stepped up and two police officers who'd arrived and shaken hands with Butler Cove's sheriff took their call to action very seriously. They now stood guarding our party and sending loiterers away.

"I'm sure you've heard by now," Mira went on, "or been offered a bidding paddle by Allison, our events coordinator. I believe Allison could conjure up a pink elephant if we asked her nicely." She paused for laughter. "We are changing the format of the evening slightly. Up until now, Miss Butler has been reluctant to sell the central piece of this exhibit, entitled *Ever Broken Sea*. She has agreed to auction it this evening, however. I'm sure those of you who've asked about it will be happy to hear this. And it just so happens I have my auctioneer's license." She chuckled.

Mira assured me she would use the price I had on it as our reserve. I merely went along with it, as I was still in shock that the evening was going so well, that people wanted to write articles about me, and that there were *high-falutin'* people here at all.

And Jack.

I was still in shock over Jack. Being here, being in my life, being on the cusp of going public with our relationship. It was almost too freaking huge to contemplate.

The bidding started at one hundred dollars. Jack kept his paddle tucked under his arm and watched me as I nibbled my lip.

An elderly couple, the man tall and gaunt with an air of old money, his elegant wife with a sleek gray bun and wearing an understated black dress, seemed the most interested. All of a sudden Colt raised his paddle, taking the bidding up over a thousand dollars. He winked at me. Joey clapped him on the back, clearly in cahoots.

As the bidding climbed higher, my heart pounded. It hovered at the reserve price for two long seconds, and then Jack tipped his paddle almost imperceptibly. I wouldn't have noticed except for Mira's acknowledgement of the bid. I held my breath.

The older couple paused, then the wife nodded again.

"Holy shit," whispered Jazz next to me.

Shannon was scribbling away madly.

I gulped. The whispering reached disturbing levels as people looked at Jack and watched him watching me.

The elderly couple finally realized Jack wasn't giving up.

"Going once, going twice," Mira intoned.

Jazz squeezed my hand.

"Sold!" There was a collective sigh, a release of anticipation.

I grinned, I couldn't help it. Even though I wanted to tell

him he was an idiot for wasting his money. Then I giggled and let go, happy tears clouding my eyes, and met Jack's smile.

"Well, unless people try and say you planted the other bidders, I think that just proved anyone wrong who says you'll be riding Jack's coattails." Jazz laughed.

"Ha, probably not. But you're a good friend, Jazz. I love you."

"I love you too, K."

Jack went to shake the hand of his co-bidders, and I received hugs and back pats from all my friends. Even Hector, who was wiping his eyes with pride. I hugged him fiercely.

Mira approached with Jack and a photographer. "I need a picture with the artist and the high bidder." She smiled.

The whole gathering seemed to be watching us.

I wondered if Jack and I should pretend not to know each other. I mean, we probably shouldn't just hug and kiss right now, but I wanted to throw myself against his tall frame. He looked so damn sexy in his suit. I blushed as my mind went immediately toward being alone with him later. Oh my gosh, there'd be a later, right?

Take a deep breath, Keri Ann.

I smiled.

Jack reached out for my hand, and I slid my fingers into his warm and rough ones, feeling them tighten around me. Then he lifted them to his mouth, and keeping his eyes on me, brushed his soft lips over my knuckles. My cheeks, already flaming, throbbed as more blood rushed to my face.

"I'm telling you there's something about that dress," Mrs. Weaton trilled at Jazz.

We posed for pictures, Mira between us, then she stepped away, and I temporarily stopped breathing as Jack's hand snaked around my waist, pulling me close for Shannon's photographer. He smelled so good. Expensive. Sexy. Masculine. *Mine.*

I introduced him to Shannon.

"Shannon's going to write the true romance version of you guys," Jazz said. "You just missed that donkey, Tom Price. He was here again, making my girl feel like a stardust-chasing slut."

"Is that right?" Jack returned smoothly and looked at Shannon. "Are you a freelance writer?"

She nodded as if with Jack resting his attention solely on her she couldn't get her mouth to work. I knew the feeling. She finally found her voice. "I'm writing for the local paper, but I'm a paid contractor for stories outside of what they've asked me to cover."

"I'll get us somewhere we can talk then, as soon as things wind down," he said. He tucked his mouth in by my ear, setting my nerves ablaze. "And maybe after that, I can get you out of that dress," he whispered.

He pulled away, and I motioned his ear back down to mine. "Only if you keep your suit on."

Jack exhaled sharply, and clearing his throat, swiftly left my side.

"What was that about?" Shannon asked.

"He had spinach in his teeth," Jazz answered for me.

CHAPTER THIRTY-FOUR

The evening took a while longer to wind down, especially after the unexpected excitement of Jack's presence and the impromptu auction.

I circulated once more, with Jazz as my support, thanking people for coming. When I approached the elderly couple who had bid against Jack, they greeted me warmly and introduced themselves.

"I'm sorry you missed out on *Ever Broken Sea*," I offered. "But I do hope you had a lovely evening. I really appreciate the support."

"Well, actually we aren't going home empty-handed." The wife smiled. "We're enthusiastic supporters of SCAD students. I understand you've been accepted to start in the fall. Congratulations. I think you're very wise to go through that program and not use your early success as a reason not to build a foundation and contacts. Being an artist is a business, not a whim these days. To be successful takes more smarts than luck. But something tells me you are going to be extremely successful."

"Thank you, Ma'am." I smiled.

I said goodbye and made plans for phone conversations with a few more people. And then when Allison motioned for us to follow her, I quickly hugged Joey and my other guests. Colt offered to take Joey and Jazz home. I'd be riding with Jack.

We moved to a small conference room. Jack gave Shannon the details for his publicist and his assistant. Then he advised her to go ahead and submit the story of my successful evening without our relationship angle if she wanted us to continue being cooperative.

I looked apologetically at Shannon, although she didn't seem to have a problem with his directives.

He advised her to show us the article first for approval, and if it was good enough, his publicist, Sheila, would put her in touch with some national monthlies instead of having it run just in a local paper.

Shannon gulped and nodded.

I felt oddly detached from the conversation as if we were talking about something affecting complete strangers, not Jack and me. There was almost relief in letting him handle us as a couple in public. After all, if anyone had prior experience, it was Jack. And watching Jack in no-bullshit mode was kind of hot.

From the way he'd handled tonight, I knew he was going to do his best to only have his notoriety work for me, not over me. Regardless of what Tom Price splashed all over the Internet.

Jack reached out and took my hand, sliding his fingers through mine as we sat side by side talking to Shannon about revealing our relationship.

I realized I also had a choice not to let the craziness in.

I was a fighter.

I was strong.

I would protect what I had with Jack, and he would protect me in turn, the best he could. I'd never trusted him more than in that moment.

Shannon left, and Jack and I were led through the now emptying foyer between Sheriff Graves and another officer, and then outside and into the back of a waiting black limousine.

I swallowed as I slid over on the cool leather seats, careful not to tear the beads on my dress. "Whoa. Where did you get this? A bit fancy for the Lowcountry, isn't it?" I looked around the interior.

Jack laughed. "I wasn't sure if I'd need room for your friends on the ride back." He slid in next to me.

Sheriff Graves poked his head in. "I'll ride up front with the driver . . . give you all some privacy on the way to the airport."

"Wait, what? Airport?" I stared at Jack as the sheriff closed the door.

"Don't be mad, okay?"

"I can promise you if you start any conversation with that phrase, it's a racing certainty I will be. What the hell, Jack? Are you leaving already? I thought we were going to face this stuff together? It's not fair you won't be in Butler Cove if the Tom Prices of the world start coming to harass us. They'll only focus on me! Please don't. And stop smiling. I'm serious as a damn heart attack right now."

My heart pounded and my cheeks throbbed. But unlike what usually caused these crazy physical reactions in the presence of Jack, this time I was *mad*.

Jack's smile broke free into a bellow of laughter.

Smacking his knee, I made to move across the vehicle to the bench seat.

He grabbed my wrist tightly.

"Let go," I whined.

"No." He laughed again. "Just let me explain." He leaned forward and pressed a button. Then talked into the darkness. "Hey, can you drive around the island a few times? Our flight's not scheduled for over an hour, and Keri Ann needs to get changed."

"Sure thing," came a voice. "Overtime?"

Jack smiled. "Of course." He released the button then he turned on a dim sidelight so we could see each other better. At least, I assumed that's why he did it. A John Legend song poured softly into the interior.

Smooth.

"Get changed?" I asked, belatedly recognizing a small duffel I'd bought for a camping trip to Hunting Island a few years back, sitting on the seat. "How did you get that?"

"Jazz might have been in on it . . ." He winced.

My mouth dropped open.

Wait. "*Our* flight?"

He nodded. "I wasn't sure when the story was going to drop so I asked Jazz to help me in case you needed to get out of the spotlight at a moment's notice."

A fizz of nausea swirled low in my belly. "Where to? God, never mind. And what about *them* having to deal with it? Is this what you usually do? Of course it is. It's how I met you. Is this what . . ." I swallowed. "I can't just leave! Is this how *we'll* have to be? How will I work, keep a job?"

Jack reached for my hand again, and I wrenched it free, lurching away from him. "How will I go to school?" A strand of the dress caught and snapped, tiny jet beads poured down over my feet. "Shit." I tried to grab the strand and stop them, making it worse. Tears pooled in my eyes.

"It's okay, we'll fix it." Jack's hand closed over mine where I held the dress. And he moved to the edge of the seat opposite me, spreading his knees and leaning forward.

"Okay," he said gently. "Let go, I've got it." His hands took over from mine and tied a small loop knot in the strand, stopping the flow of beads. Then he reached down to the floor between his feet and carefully picked them all up. I reached down to help. "I've got it," he said again.

I watched him, looking at his bent head, his soft hair, his strong hands making sure he had every last one. I fought a battle with myself to reach out and touch him. I knew I was panicking again about being with him. I just couldn't see what our relationship would look like.

"You can't always swoop in and buy my art, you know." I cleared my throat. "And if I can't afford to go to school, or we lose the house, you can't step in and save me. You know that, right?"

He sighed. "It's just money, Keri Ann. Do you have any idea how much money I make? It's meaningless unless I do something meaningful with it."

"I can't, I won't owe you like that. We are not doing a repeat performance of that auction tonight, as fun as it was."

"You have too much pride, you know that? And you wouldn't be owing me. If you were my wife, for example, why would you owe me?"

The breath I was taking as he spoke stuttered and hiccupped in my chest. Shock flooded my system, making me light-headed.

Jack continued picking up tiny beads. He transferred a handful into the inside breast pocket of his jacket.

I raised a trembling hand to my chest, putting my chin down. My flight response jumped to attention. We had to stop the car. He needed to take me home. My breathing picked up a panicked rate.

Then I felt his hand snake into the hair at my nape tilting my face up to look at him. "Just breathe, Keri Ann. It's going to be okay. We're going to figure it out. Take it one step at a time. But right now, until we know what the reaction to this story will be, we should go somewhere." He brushed his thumb over my bottom lip then dropped his hands down. "And maybe it will be nothing. And maybe I just want to be alone with you."

I stared into his deep, dark green eyes, my vision blurry. I needed to get back the feeling of calm I'd had earlier, when I felt such trust in him. I did trust him. I didn't want to leave him. But God, be his wife? I blew out a slow shuddering breath. We'd need to talk about that. A lot. Way, way in the future.

He watched me, waiting for my reaction. He seemed to know he just freaked the hell out of me. And after an evening like the one we'd had, he couldn't blame me. But God, I wanted this man. I wanted him to look at me the way he did, forever.

Giving in finally to the urge to touch him, I reached forward, sliding my hands through his hair.

He stilled, closing his eyes.

Then he exhaled slowly and reached for my calves, lightly running a hand over my skin. His fingers worked the small buckle of my silver sandals at each ankle, and then slipped each heel off my feet.

Moving up my calves, he gathered my beaded dress up past my knees. "Kneel down," he murmured, leaning back and creating space between us. His eyes were dark, somewhat unsure. "Let me help you get your dress off."

I did as he asked, kneeling between his dark suit-clad thighs, feeling the vibration of the car beneath me. He gingerly lifted the delicate beaded dress over my head leaving me in just the champagne-tone shift beneath and carefully laid the dress out on the long bench next to him.

My tears spilled over even while I smiled.

Jack's concerned face furrowed further. "Shit. I've got whiplash. Are you happy or sad right now? Please help me out here."

"God, both. I don't know." I laughed. "The things you do, the way you make me feel, it's incredible. You set my worries and fears alight until I feel they'll burn me alive. Then I find them floating away like sky lanterns. You asked me if I could be proud to be with you. It was never that I'm not proud of you. If anything it's the other way around, most of the time I don't understand why you want to be with *me*." I hiccupped.

"How can you not know?" He looked at me earnestly. "That's like asking why we breathe air. Because it's the way we were made. I'm telling you, that's how it is for me. The way I feel about you was never a decision. It just was. I was made to love you. I never fell, I was already there. From the very first moment."

He swiped a tear from my cheek. "Do you know that you're beautiful even when you're crying?"

If he kept talking like this, I would be a sobbing mess with my heart bleeding through my chest. "Just, just kiss me, Jack."

He smiled and, cupping my cheek, pulled my face toward his but stopped a breath away. "There was a time when you asked me not to."

"Yes, well. You certainly corrupted *that* girl."

He grinned.

Leaning forward, I ran my hand up his fabric-covered thighs, feeling the hard tension under my fingers. Then I touched my lips to his.

I moved over his mouth gently, reveling in the feeling of his lips and responding with a jolt of arousal as his impatient tongue swept into me, his hand twisting into my hair, tugging the bun loose.

"You looked incredibly beautiful tonight, but I'm done with your hair being up," he whispered against my mouth. A hand swept down my spine and lower until it reached the back of my bare thigh. Then it inched back up under my slip. "And I kept imagining you were naked under those beads."

Heat sluiced through me in a wave, pooling into a heavy throb. My hands curled hard into his thighs.

"Is there any chance I corrupted you enough that you'd let me make love to you right now?" Jack rasped.

My heart pounded. "Now? Like right here?" I looked around at the dimly lit interior, my eyes wide.

He nodded then sat back.

"They'll hear."

"No, they won't."

His warm, rough hands slid my shift up, over my lace panties, to my waist. He hissed out a breath then pulled me up and astride his lap.

A nervous, prickly heat swept over my skin and chest. I felt bare and exposed against his fully clothed body.

My nerves fizzled as I watched his face, saw the flush on his cheekbones, the flare of his nostrils, the tight set to his mouth. He looked at me like I was his end and his beginning.

I traced a finger down his neck and over his rough Adam's apple as it moved heavily. I undid a few more buttons of his white shirt and slid my hands against his hard chest, feeling his heart matching my own in powerful thuds.

Jack simply watched me. Waiting.

Then I went straight for his buckle, undoing it with jerky movements.

"My left pocket," he whispered, his breathing labored as I touched him.

I nodded and my fingers shook as I felt around for the package. Jack stilled my hands and took over. Readying himself was far from a clinical reality to making love. It was the most erotic thing to watch. To know what we were about to do.

I shivered.

Then he sifted his hands through my hair, looking up at me. I held his gaze. "We don't have to do this. I don't want you to be nervous. Or feel self-conscious. We have forever, we don't need to—"

I lifted up, moved my panties aside, and eased down on him.

Jack let out a guttural roar from deep in his chest and surged up, clutching me. Wrapping his arms around me, his head against my neck, he pulled me so firmly down upon him, that I felt like my whole body would explode from the depth of him.

I gasped.

"Oh, God," he groaned against my skin, and his mouth opened on me.

Holding still, his body shuddered and trembled under my hands.

I rocked forward gently.

Then we moved. Both of us together. His fingers gripping my hips.

At one point he managed to work my slip up off over my head, and I tore the jacket back off his shoulders, spreading his shirt, needing to feel his skin against mine.

Looking up at me, he tilted his head as I clutched his shoulders then his hair, pulling it into disheveled tufts.

"I love you, Jack," I whispered, brokenly, something within me unwinding with the admission I'd never made out loud.

He squeezed his eyes closed a moment.

"I love *you*, Keri Ann. I love you so fucking much it's literally a physical ache in my chest." He breathed out, roughly. "Whatever you want, I'll do it. I'll give you whatever you need. My life. Forever."

"Jack." My eyes stung.

His hands at my hips dug in, and he rocked harder beneath me. I bit down on my lip to keep my reactions in check, watching his eyes as they glazed, darkened, clouded with passion, pooled with emotion.

I was reading my future there.

I wanted to close my eyes and revel in the sensations that were racing through me, tightening in an ever increasing spiral, but I couldn't look away.

The sensations, they became bigger than us. And suddenly the wave was crashing over me, pulling me under and spinning me, tumbling me head over feet, over and over. I gasped, trying to find air, and my eyes finally squeezed shut under the onslaught so I could only feel Jack go rigid beneath me. Feel him cling to me like he would never let me go.

I had no idea where we were going. Tonight or tomorrow, or any day for the rest of my life. Or how we would manage all of our hopes and dreams.

Mine.

His.

Ours.

But we'd do it together.

EPILOGUE

JACK

Four years later . . .

My heel is bouncing up and down nervously. I sit in my office next to the glass sliding doors that lead out to the patio and the ocean beyond, at a beautiful old desk Keri Ann found. The desk was hauled out of a boarding school refurbishment in England and is eerily similar to desks I'd sat at once, etched with names, dates, holes and fountain ink. Deep grooves probably carved with the sharp point of a school compass in a boring math class, and some, I was sure, the result of an ink pen nib that probably didn't make it past that moment of its highest sacrifice. My favorite part of the desk were the initials carved with a date of 1961. An arrow pointed up to it with the words "my dad," and then whoever the boy was had crudely carved his own initials below with the date 1983.

We were in England three years ago meeting my mother when she found it.

I glance back up through the glass to where she is sitting on a lounger, soaking up some vitamin D from the winter sun and wrapped in a cream cashmere sweater I bought her and lied about how much it cost.

Keri Ann flips through each page. She hasn't looked up in three hours. At some point I know she'll need to move, stretch, eat, pee, I don't know. Her face has rippled from anguish to anger to tears, nervous lip-biting, and a small smile here and there. I wish I could exactly calculate which words she's reading that cause each of these emotions, but I can only guess by how far through the script she is. At one point she threw it down and lay her head back, staring up into the sky. Now she's nearing the end.

I nearly went out earlier and asked her which part she was on, and if she was just bored and tired, or reacting to what she read. Managing to stop myself, I settled with pretending to work on something at the desk that had inspired me to finally finish what she was reading but stayed where I could see her.

Her hand moves up to her mouth and her eyes are watery. I lay down the pen I'm holding, since I'll probably break it if I don't, and wait. Abruptly, she flings the pages down, her eyes finding mine, and gets up from the lounger coming to stand at the door. I realize her cheeks are wet.

"He was such a monster," she whispers. "But you made me pity him." Her eyes are confused.

Nodding, I reach out a hand and she accepts it. I pull her gently inside so she stands between my knees.

Sliding her hands through my hair, a light scrape that sends a shiver racing over my skin, she pulls my head against her.

Breathing her scent in, I wait to see if she has anything more to say and feel her curve her head down to rest on mine.

"My heart hurts for that little boy. He must have been so scared that night, but he was so brave. I can't believe he got away and ran. Then to be chased . . . by his father, by a person children are supposed to love and trust, and know that if he got caught . . ." her voice breaks. Yes, all the untold horrors that boy might have looked forward to, what he'd even woken up to that night . . . that he'd never see his mother again might have been the least concerning. Keri Ann's chest heaves with emotion and anguish beneath my cheek, and I squeeze my arms tight and hold her.

"I *was* scared," I say finally when she calms. "I was terrified, and I made it. I survived him."

"And you made me cry for *him*, too. I almost didn't want him to end his life, but I felt his relief. Oh, God. It's brilliant. I hated it. It's the darkest story I've ever read. And so much more painful because it's you." She reaches for a tissue from the box she placed on my desk.

I loosen my arms and tilt my head up to look at her beautiful face filled with such torment. A tight knot around my heart loosens slightly. I've been terrified to let her read the script I wrote, even letting Devon read it first.

Production on *The Missing Earl* begins in eleven weeks.

In England.

Devon says he's never fast tracked something that quickly in his life.

"But are you sure about this? Playing the part of your own father? And telling the world who you are?"

It was Devon's idea, and when he first suggested it, I balked. I was shocked and horrified, and truly didn't think I had it in me. The more I thought about it though, I realized it could only be me. And really it will be the hardest role I've ever played, that anyone could ever play. But I know I can do it.

I will do it. Moreover, I know with a quiet certainty, I'll do it brilliantly.

I nod.

"Why did you wait so long to let me read it?"

"I was nervous," I say truthfully. I like Keri Ann thinking the world of me. I don't want her not liking something I've written. The fact she thinks it is good absolutely humbles me. Relief washes through my veins. The publicity will be big though. "And look, if you would rather I didn't announce it's about me, I won't. It's enough for me that it's out there. It will only add extra publicity to our lives."

"Publicity that will help an incredible movie become even more important and mind-blowing? Of course you need to own it. You need to tell people it's your story." She smiles. "I can handle a bit more publicity. And since it will be on you rather than me, perhaps it will give me a break from "*ring watch*" and "*baby bump watch*.""

I try not to react to her observation of ring watch and baby bump watch. I feel like I've been doing the same as the press for three years . . . watching and waiting until she's ready. *I'll* be on "gay watch" soon.

"But we'll be in England," I remind her. "The paparazzi are worse there, it seems. Are you sure?"

"Yes, I'm sure," she responds to my concern. "Your mom and I will be fine. Besides, I want to go and visit the coast again. There's so much sea glass there. I get really inspired when we're in England."

Every time we go there, Keri Ann insists we stay with my mother and Jeff rather than one of the fancy hotels I push for. I always concede, knowing it makes Mum happy, too.

Making muted love to Keri Ann in the guest bedroom, trying not to be too loud, always drives me nuts and makes

Keri Ann giggle. I smile thinking about it and lift her sweater revealing her soft belly. Kissing it reverently, smoothing my lips over the silky skin, I inhale the soft fruity scent of her.

She pulls back and runs her hand through my hair, tilting my face up again. "I'm so proud of you," she says seriously.

Pulling her face toward me, I capture her lips with mine, feeling her soft sigh, and slip my tongue into her warm mouth. God, I love kissing her. "I'm proud of you, too," I whisper against her lips a few moments later. And I am. She dealt with the fallout of being blown up into a tabloid scandal with the most poise and grace I've ever seen, and continues to earn nothing but respect and starry eyes from the public who now look at her as some kind of Cinderella instead of the sleazy gold digger Audrey had planned. She's sweet and funny to the people who want to take her picture and gracious to the ones who deserve to get a fist in the face.

I don't know how she does it.

I fall more in love with her every single day.

And she never wavered in her desire to get her degree. I proudly attended her graduation earlier this year. I ended up setting up a scholarship fund at SCAD for local artists. She was, of course, a beneficiary. She didn't speak to me for two weeks when she found out it was my money.

I finally got through to her that it was an anonymous fund, and that the selection committee couldn't have possibly known. She won it fair and square along with two other deserving students.

I really enjoyed exacting an appropriate apology from her, one that we both enjoyed. She didn't need to know *I* had designed the selection criteria as specifically as they would allow.

The best part was that I started the fund with money we

won suing Tom Price's magazine for printing the pictures he had no rights to. I'd warned him, he did it anyway, and I'd taken great pleasure in putting him in his place.

Shannon Keith, the journalist who was at Keri Ann's first big exhibition, has become a friend. Her story ended up going a long way toward neutralizing the public view of what Audrey planned, and after several local residents corroborated the timing and basically made Keri Ann look like Mary Poppins, it was almost over.

The final blow to Audrey's plan, however, came six months later, when her assistant whom she'd always treated like yesterday's garbage, quit and went straight to the tabloids. She exposed all of Audrey's scheming. She described her rages, tantrums, and dirty secrets. One of which was that she'd overheard Audrey and my ex-agent strategizing about a fake pregnancy. It coincided with me being nominated for an award for the movie I'd shot in England, and it was catastrophic for Audrey's career. She's been in some small art house movies recently, and I hear she'll be making an appearance on *Dancing with the Stars* next season. Maybe that will help.

"When's everyone arriving?" I ask Keri Ann, suddenly thinking about the time. How much longer do I have her alone, to myself?

"A few hours. The boat is due at six p.m. Katie's going out to meet it. I think we've done about all we can for the ceremony. Now we should just relax and enjoy everyone being together for the weekend." Keri Ann sighs with contentment. She loves having everyone together, and *I* love seeing her so happy.

I'm amazed that I feel so at home in a place with which the only link I have is her. "I'm glad I convinced you to let me build a place here where no one can bother us unless we invite them. But I'm thinking we may have to get permission for a helipad, just in case. Then we can come and go more easily."

"A helipad? Are you nuts? That means a helicopter. I'm not getting into a helicopter!" She shuddered. "You got me on airplanes, let's be happy with that, okay?"

I chuckle. I'd had to get her drunk on champagne when we got on our first plane together the night of her art event. It had never occurred to me she'd never flown before. By the time we landed in Tahoe for a few days, she was a mess.

"But yes," she interrupts my memory. "I'm glad you built this place, too. I know Joey would be fine with us staying at the Butler house any time we wanted, but it's nice here, and so many memories." She winks.

"We," I corrected.

"We what?"

"You said *I* built this place. *We* built this place."

She smiles and shakes her head. "What am I going to do with you?"

"Take me to bed for a quickie before everyone arrives?" I ask hopefully and cock my eyebrow in a way I know she loves.

"A helipad," she says again, incredulously, shaking her head and not taking my bait.

"What's the big deal? Another resident here has one on the other side of the island."

"Then I guess you should make friends and use his," she suggests. "Anyway, if we have a helipad, someone uninvited may be tempted to land on it."

She has a point.

"Do you think anyone knows there's a wedding happening

here?" she asks, the thought of uninvited guests obviously sending her mind down a certain path.

"Nope," I assure her.

"Hmm," she muses, "I wonder if we should have ours here, too."

I stiffen. My heartbeat trips, and I realize I may have stopped breathing. "What are you saying?" I manage, hoping I seem curious and not desperately hopeful. It's useless, I realize, as the hope surges through me and makes me light-headed.

She gives me a wide smile, and my heart seizes. "Just getting everything ready for the wedding this weekend made me realize how much I want it to be us, and once I started thinking that, I literally couldn't stop." She laughs at my surprised expression.

I've never pushed her. I know how much she needed to be her own person, have her own identity. And it's been tough for her to achieve it and tough for me to sit on my hands and not help her. I'm so damn proud of her.

I've been ready to be a father, too, since the idea was unwelcomingly thrust upon me by Audrey years ago. The idea that I could create life and a family with this gorgeous, sweet, and incredible girl, grabs hold of my heart and mind every time we make love. Although, we've been scrupulously careful. But I *want* to create a small Keri Ann. A small person, whether a boy or a girl, with all of Keri Ann's grace and beauty, strength and unflinching loyalty. And I want to love that creature and keep it safe from monsters and create a family like I've only ever dreamed could really exist.

One step at a time, I remind myself.

"I'm relieved," I struggle to joke with her, when all I want to do is fall to my knees at her feet. She's finally ready to marry me. "However," I add gravely, "*you're* going to have to be the one to wait now."

Her forehead cinches up and her eyes grow wide.

"Yeah. You don't think I'm just going to ask you and be done with it, do you? You're gonna have to sweat a little," I say, warming up to my Machiavellian side. I'm going to make this torture.

"What? And give me time to change my mind back?" she asks innocently, and my blood falls to my feet.

Her warm hand runs over my cheek.

I grab it, bringing her palm to my mouth to kiss it. "Don't rob me of doing something romantic for you. Besides, you pretty much just did the proposing. At least let me save my pride and *pretend* to be the one doing the asking."

"Did I?" She slaps a hand to her forehead. "I guess you're right. Well, don't wait too long," she whispers.

My heart beats heavily. I thought I was always ready, but perhaps now that I'm facing my past, and my father, I'm becoming whole. Maybe it was good that we waited. Before I change my mind, I try something. "I . . ." I struggle to remember the exact way a British title should be spoken. ". . . William John Rhys Thomas, who would have been the twenty-first Earl of Huntley had he not been declared missing and presumed dead, a.k.a Jack Eversea . . . am utterly in love with you, Keri Ann Butler."

"Well, *Earl Huntley*, I think I prefer Jack. You're too big for your britches as it is, you can't expect me to start calling you *Lord*." She laughs softly, in a single moment relieving me of the gravity of a name and a past, and takes my hand. Sliding it back under her sweater, my fingers take the lead and run along the skin of her belly.

Suddenly, there is poignant significance in such a simple

caress. The swell of primal urge to plant my seed is almost dizzying. She leans down again and kisses me.

When we stop, I'm breathing hard. "But we should probably get a head start on creating an heir," I joke between kisses, my hand still resting on her belly, staking my claim. "I've heard it can take some time."

She looks down at me. Her blue eyes are startlingly bright today. "I guess I'm ready for that, too."

My hand stops its idle caress, and I flick my eyes involuntarily down to her belly. My mouth goes instantly dry as I try and fail to swallow, causing a painful gulp. I look back up at her face and see the answer in her tremulous smile and glistening eyes. She bites her lip. "Now, if you like," she says simply, giving me everything she has.

A tidal wave of emotion roars through me, hitting hard, leaving me almost gasping and causing me to close my eyes. I slide off my chair, my knees hitting the floor at her feet.

It finally ebbs, and for a moment there is complete stillness inside me. I wrap my arms around her.

And peace.

There is peace.

FOREVER, JACK PLAYLIST

'The Kill' – Thirty Seconds to Mars
'Sand in my Shoes' – Dido
'Last Chance' – Honor by August
'The Shade of Poison Trees' – Dashboard Confessional
'It's Over' – Civil Twilight
'Closer to the Edge' – Thirty Seconds to Mars
'Retrograde' – James Blake
'Smoke and Ashes' – Tracy Chapman
'Bonfire Heart' – James Blunt
'Waves' – Blondfire
'Green Eyes' – Coldplay
'All of Me' – John Legend

Discover where Keri Ann and Jack's love affair began in

eversea

Read on for an extract . . .

CHAPTER ONE

You know you're in the Lowcountry when the steering wheel in your old red pickup is slippery from humidity, the news on the radio is all about the projected path of the latest Atlantic hurricane and the road kill you narrowly miss smearing further is a five foot long alligator.

I shuddered as I passed the sludgy reptile remains and held my breath. Lifting my ponytail off my neck, I hoped the hot South Carolina breeze coming through the window would at least feel cool against my damp skin.

The upside of fall was the tourists had gone home. The downside was the county stopped spraying for mosquitoes and no-see-ums, so the little fuckers got to gorge themselves in a type of 'eat local' frenzy. There was one inside the cab of the truck, and I tried very hard to ignore him as I went over the cross-island bridge. But, if he dared circle my bare ankles, I was going to have to pull over and hunt him down.

I checked the rearview mirror and started to change lanes, but a loud honking and growl of an engine made me swerve back. My insides lurched as a motorcycle emerged from my blind spot. I'd nearly side swiped it. The driver pulled up alongside and looked over as I raised my hand in a gesture of apology.

His helmet had a dark visor so I couldn't see in. After a few seconds he lifted a gloved hand in salute and took off ahead with a roar, his white shirt billowing out like a sail. California plates. Tourist. That figured.

I was late for my shift at the grill. Following the biker's example, I floored it too, assuming any police officer would pull over the out-of-towner before me, or at least only give me a friendly warning. When you live in a small town, you either went to school or church with just about everybody. Not that I'd been in either for a while.

Making it home with minutes to spare, I dropped off my truck and hotfooted it to work.

The small seaside town of Butler Cove Island had nine thousand off-season, full time residents, and some days it felt like they *all* had an opinion. I tried to paste on a smile and nod as I listened politely to yet another nugget of sage advice from Pastor McDaniel. The good pastor was pretending to drink plain iced tea, *not* laced from the little flask in his jacket pocket. *Seriously?*

His portly frame was wedged into a booth and the buttons on his dress shirt looked to be taking some serious strain.

I wondered if I would get a reprieve from him going on about my house again. The Pastor sat on the town council and seemed to think this entitled him to lay it on thick. "Now, Miss Keri Ann, yo' gran-mamma would fair turn in her grave to see the last remainin' bit o' real estate in your family turn so dog eared." *Nope.* He was on it again. "You need to keep that place up." He leaned forward conspiratorially. "Why don't I send my Jasper on up there on Sunday after church to give you a little hand?"

"That's very nice of you, Pastor." I hated to turn it down, truly. My family home was the last thing left for the Butlers of Butler Cove, and it was falling apart. I needed the help, but not at the price of the pastor doing me a good turn. And from the way his beady eyes shifted, I felt sure the idea of Jasper and me together had crossed his mind. What better way to get his hands on the house? Luckily, I was certain Jasper and I were on the same page of our platonic relationship. "I'd be glad to pay him, if he wouldn't mind some sanding and painting."

The Pastor puffed his chest out a little. "Well now, there'll be none o' that. My Jasper's a gentleman helping out a lady, is all. Did he tell you he was accepted into Charleston College of Law?"

I nodded.

"He's a smart boy that one, going places. Good with his brains and his hands. I'll send him over Sunday." He adjusted his gaze and seemed to peer down his nose at me, even though I was standing a good three heads above his sedentary frame. "I'll be seeing you at service, I hope."

How did he do that? There must be school for teaching pastors how to guilt people. I smiled slightly and set down the water I was holding right in front of him.

"How about some water, Pastor?" I asked, looking meaningfully at his spiked iced tea. I hadn't been back in church for six years. I might be struck by lightning if I went this Sunday.

It was a slow night; finally calm after the crazy tourist season. The only other people left in the dimly lit restaurant were up at the bar. One was my best friend Jazz, nicknamed for her love of the genre, and the other, a hunched-up guy with a ball cap and hoodie who'd just walked in five minutes ago and literally curled onto a bar stool in the corner. He was fishing a phone out of his jeans pocket.

It was almost closing time, I seriously hoped he wasn't going to stay long, I could really use an early night and closing the place down on time sounded like heaven.

"What can I get you?" I called over to hoodie guy as I went back around the bar. He mumbled something, not looking up from the phone he was busy texting on. I sighed and went further down the bar so I could hear him. People could be so rude. I'd had enough of them this summer, and I don't think I was the only one. Reportedly, there were a few cases of locals blowing their gaskets. Not a surprise. The county even had to post billboards reminding residents most of their funding came from tourism.

"A burger, medium, with fries. To go," Hoodie Guy repeated not looking up, the peak from his burgundy ball cap hiding his face completely. "And a Bushmills on the rocks while I wait." His accent was most definitely out of town. He went back to texting. I sighed and jabbed the order onto the touch screen. It was a good thing I had the patience of a saint. Ten seconds later Hector leaned out of the kitchen shaking his head at me.

"Sorry, Hector. Last one, then you can turn 'em off. I'll close it down out here." I smiled at his grumpy face. We both complained at times, but it was good-natured. We loved our jobs at the Snapper Grill. The salary and tips were huge all summer long, and in the off season, when most of the other seasonal employees moved on, we pretty much kept the place ticking. It was only really busy on the weekends when it became more of an islanders' bar than a restaurant. It helped that our owner, Paulie, had a subscription to the local sports games. Most residents took offense to having to buy a premium package on their cable contracts just to watch the Tigers or the Gamecocks. Hector ducked his dark head back in the kitchen muttering something in Spanish.

"Sooo, what's new in the world of entertainment?" I nodded at the magazine Jazz was devouring while I filled a glass with ice and some fine Irish whiskey.

Jazz looked up and groaned in happiness. "This is such bliss. I haven't been able to sit around and read a trashy magazine for months. You know my mom won't let me even have them at the house, says I'm liquefying my mind while she's paying my tuition. I can't wait to move out, as much as I'll miss her."

Jazz was going to college up at USC Beaufort, but living at home to save cash and working in a local boutique. I smiled in sympathy at my friend and delivered the stiff drink down the bar.

Hoodie Guy was still scrolling through his phone with his long fingers, mindless of the drink I set down with a napkin on the polished wood in front of him. I sighed and strolled back to Jazz.

"You know you can move in, Jazz. It's just me knocking around there while Joey finishes up med school." She pretended not to hear. I had made the offer a million times, but Jazz and my brother, Joey had dated briefly one summer when Joey came back from college. To say he broke Jazz's heart when he left was an understatement. I wasn't sure anyone realized how much Jazz cared for him, least of all Jazz herself. For my sake they had patched a makeshift and delicate friendship for when Joey returned for holidays. But now, between school and interning and an upcoming residency, he was home less and less.

"So McDaniel still trying to set you up with Jasper?" Jazz asked, as she flicked the pages over. "You do need to have a date now and again, you know . . . stay in practice for when the real deal comes along." She winked.

"God, Jazz!" I quickly glanced at Pastor McDaniel to make sure he hadn't heard me taking the Lord's name in vain again. Oops. "You know I have too much on my plate to date right now. And who would be the real deal around here, for God's sake?" Wow, I was on a roll tonight. Luckily the good pastor was getting ready to head on out. I returned his wave as he left. It was a good thing he was walking home, I would have had to lift his keys otherwise.

"You won't believe it," Jazz exclaimed, totally dropping our topic and staring at the magazine in her hands. "Audrey Lane had an affair with her married director! That cow. I can't believe it. She's supposed to be dating Jack Eversea." Jazz looked horrified. She idolized Jack Eversea, along with possibly every girl in America.

I laughed at her. "Jazz, you do realize most of that stuff is made up, right?" I leaned over to look at the dubious and grainy photos she was tapping a lime green fingernail at, and then stopped at the abrupt sound of a stool scraping back.

We both looked over to see Hoodie Guy stand up and angle his back to us. He fished a wad of cash out of his jeans pocket, and peeling off a bill, placed it on the bar next to his unfinished drink.

I noticed Jazz's eyes roam down to rest on his extremely nice rear-end, encased in trendy denim.

I smacked her on the hand once, hard.

"Ow!" she yelped and I grinned.

Hoodie Guy tucked his chin down and walked out of the front door.

I met Jazz's eyes as she glared at me in mock outrage. "What? He had a nice ass," she humphed and went back to her tabloid. She wasn't wrong, I was just more concerned with his weird behavior.

"Order's up," Hector barked from the kitchen pass-through, passing out a Styrofoam box. Great. Oh well, on the bright side, if he didn't return in five minutes, I was taking a burger home tonight. He better have left enough to cover his tab, I thought to myself. I walked down and grabbed the money off the bar. A hundred. Huh. I rang it up and pulled out the change from the register.

"Hector," I called back through the pass-through. "It was a good tip night." I passed eighty dollars in cash over the counter and into the kitchen. As much as I needed the money, Hector needed it more.

"*Madre*." I heard Hector chuckle.

"Shoot, I gotta scoot." Jazz hopped down from her stool and quickly came around to embrace me. "I'm opening up the shop tomorrow, I hate getting up early. See ya." And with that, my bubbly friend flew out the door.

Jazz and I had been best friends since Butler Cove Elementary when my family moved here to live in the family home and look after my grandmother. Making friends halfway through a school year in a new place was not high up on my list of skills. I wasn't sure how I lucked into Jazz, but somehow this blonde ball of energy with a round face of sunshine had turned her light on me one day in the fifth grade hallway, and I had been basking in the warm glow ever since. Even during the toughest moments of my life.

I turned the music down and followed in her wake to lock up.

It was a gorgeous night. Although the humidity still had

a way to go, the heat had finally broken, and the stars were out in full. Standing in the doorway, I looked up and breathed in the fresh air. The cicadas were busy, the sound comforting in its endless and predictable rhythm. I knew a part of this place would always be in my soul. It was hard-wired in. As much as this town annoyed me at times, there was really nothing quite like this part of the world. I wanted to leave at some point in the future, I knew, I was just waiting for Joey to get done with school and trade places with me. That was the deal. That was one reason I didn't date. I really didn't want it to be harder than it had to be to leave. Another reason was I knew almost everyone in the eligible dating pool, and I was a choosy beggar.

My feet hurt. Tonight, I would probably sleep the sleep of a well-worked day and tomorrow, since I only worked dinner, I planned to continue the painting of the porch. Since funds were tight, I had to prioritize, and with Pastor McDaniel's less than subtle comments about the house's condition, I figured I better continue work on the outside.

Stepping into the restaurant's dimly lit courtyard to straighten some of the furniture, a movement in my periphery almost gave me a heart attack.

Shit!

Standing up from one of the tables in the shadows, like he'd been waiting for me, was Hoodie Guy. I slapped my hand on my chest, expelling a rush of air.

I judged the distance from where he stood to the door. Could I make it back inside before he got to me? How could I have been so careless? Joey was always telling me to have Hector do the lock up, and here I was not even knowing if Hector was still in the restaurant.

I stood still and tried to make out the guy's face under his hat. He was tall and looked strong, his dark jeans molding to his long straight legs. If he was going to attack me, at least I should try and remember what he looked like. Or wait— maybe that was worse. If I saw him, did that mean he would have to kill me?

I was aware I was frozen like a stunned rabbit, but it dawned on me slowly that he hadn't moved either, and I wasn't sensing anything menacing from him. Not that I was psychic. Unless you counted the times I was convinced Nana showed back up at the house to poke around and check on me. If anything, his stance and the way he hesitantly raised his hands caused me to stay put. Fear eased into curiosity. I still couldn't see his face. Why did the courtyard have to be so flipping dark?

I was about to speak when his long fingers reached up to his head, pausing for just a moment, like he was having second thoughts. Then he quickly grabbed his cap and whipped it and his dark hood off.

I found myself not being able to breathe for the second time in as many minutes. Standing in front of me was the most beautiful man I had seen in all of my twenty-two years on this planet. His rich dark brown hair, mussed up from the hat, stood up in a few places and framed a hard-planed face set with eyes the color of . . .

Well, I really couldn't tell the color of his eyes in the shadows, but I knew exactly what color they were, a deep gray-green. I hadn't been hiding under a rock for the last five years. And I certainly didn't need to double check the tabloid magazine Jazz had been reading, which definitely did not do him justice, to know that standing in front of me, Keri Ann Butler, outside the Snapper Grill in Butler Cove, population nine thousand, and hundreds of miles away from his expected location in Hollywood, was none other than Jack Eversea.